THE
MARRIAGE
COUNSELOR

BOOKS BY DEA POIRIER

THE
MARRIAGE COUNSELOR

DEA POIRIER

bookouture

Published by Bookouture in 2023

An imprint of Storyfire Ltd.
Carmelite House
50 Victoria Embankment
London EC4Y 0DZ

www.bookouture.com

ISBN: 978-1-83790-170-8
eBook ISBN: 978-1-83790-169-2

For everyone who's lost themselves.
One day, you will find you again.

1

A good lie can change the world, a life, someone's fate. At least, that's what I keep telling myself. Maybe it's different when someone pays you to lie. Sometimes I see it in their eyes, the secret agreement between us. A nonverbal contract, something only exchanged in glances, admitted in the shadows. I've got my lies ready, all the ones I'll need today, and the ones I may not. No one comes to a marriage counselor for the truth—in fact, most of the time when they come to me, it's too late. By the time you realize you need a referee in your marriage, chances are, it's been over for years. The sad fact is, it takes two willing participants to save a marriage—and if both of you are *in it* together, you'd never make it to my office; you'd solve the problems on your own.

I hear it all the time, someone thinks that their marriage would never end because no one cheated, they never yelled. But it's not just the big things. Over the years, the little things build up. That time that you didn't open the car door for them, the time you didn't pick them up a coffee, when you forgot an anniversary or when they needed you to grab something on the way home. Divorce doesn't happen because of grand failures, sometimes it happens because time after time your spouse makes you feel like you don't matter, like you are an afterthought.

The light knocking at my door jolts me, even though I know I have an appointment soon—I usually sprinkle my sessions throughout the day. I shuffle to the door and look through the peephole only to be met with a blue uniform. My stomach flip-flops, and my palms slick with sweat. Though I'm well versed at taming my emotions and remaining in control in most situations, a cop is enough to make even those citizens without so much as a parking ticket sweat. A war rages in my mind, *pretend I'm not home, or open the door?* As I look through the peephole again, the officer steps back. His long dark hair is swept back, his wide build shifts back and forth, he turns—it's a face I saw every day for years for years. *Cameron.* It's been years since I've seen him.

There's no guide for what to do when your cop ex-boyfriend shows up at your door. *Cosmo* doesn't cover things like this. Sure, they might tell you whether or not you're a winter or an autumn, and how to restyle that old blouse for that hot new job —but they sure as hell don't say what to do here. Did he come here for a session? That would be awkward.

I open the door and offer him a half smile. The hand that's out of sight tightens into a fist, reminding me that my ring is too tight. As he looks at me, I'm aware that I got dressed for work this morning, not to impress an old boyfriend. I wish I'd done a bit more with my makeup, straightened my hair.

"Adele, hi," he says, as if he wasn't expecting to see me here. Did he not know he was coming to my house?

I nod. "It's been a while." Fifteen years to be exact. Cameron and I dated through college, after starting in high school, but grew apart. He was the one everyone was convinced I'd marry. But we were too young and I couldn't stand another minute in Orlando. After I left, that's when I met my husband,

Patrick. Patrick met me at a low point, just as I was fleeing Naples, still fleeing Cameron too. I've always been running from something, someone.

"Can I come in for a minute?" He glances down the street. His stance tells me he's uncomfortable, like maybe he doesn't want to be here.

My experience with TV crime shows tells me that I shouldn't let him in. But the curiosity of what exactly he wants outweighs the warnings in my mind. I step aside and lead him from the foyer to the living room. As he follows me, I play with my wedding ring to distract myself from the uncomfortable silence. My house is always immaculate. Most people think it's because I meet most of my clients in my home, so my house must always be *guest ready*. But the reality is, this is what Patrick wants. He has a vision for how our life must look from the outside, and I help preserve it—because that preserves the peace.

"Is everything all right?" I ask as I sit on the couch.

Cameron takes a seat on the chair across from me. We may have been apart fifteen years, but he doesn't look like he's aged a day. He wears his hair differently now, and a dusting of stubble hugs his jaw. I'm too conscious, too curious of what he thinks of me—of how I've changed. Whatever he's thinking, it isn't playing out on his face.

"Patrick Johansen lives here, correct?"

I nod, but confusion toils inside me. Why is he asking about Patrick?

"Are you two..." he starts.

"Married," I clarify.

For a moment he's silent, a silence so thick that a bad feeling blooms inside me. Why is Cameron here? Why is he asking if I'm married to Patrick? Was he in some kind of accident? The questions swarm in my mind like a hive of bees.

"Adele, have you seen your husband today?" he asks as he opens a small notepad.

His posture, the way he looks at me—I can tell this isn't good news. There's something wrong. But what I don't understand is why he isn't just coming out and saying it. I swallow hard and cross my legs. So, he isn't here to catch up. Then again, why would he? It was stupid to even think that.

I shake my head. "No, I haven't seen him. Why?" I keep my voice casual. Cops have always made me nervous, but it's easy to talk to Cameron, to look past his badge. I just imagine that he hasn't changed, that he's still the same guy.

"Is that unusual?" he asks as he scribbles on the paper.

My hands slick with sweat, and I scratch my neck, though it doesn't itch. This feels like something I'd ask a couple, a question that seems innocuous, but really, it's incredibly loaded. The feeling of just talking to Cameron slithers away and I'm left with the hollow sickness I always get when I talk to cops. "No, some mornings I just see him as he's getting ready for work. Some mornings I don't see him at all." Patrick has always been an early riser, while I tend to sleep in. Usually I sleep through him getting dressed and leaving—I know he doesn't want to disturb me when he's leaving for work.

"Patrick didn't show up for work. And when all the calls to his cell went unanswered, they asked if someone from the station could come check on him. So, I'm here doing a wellness check," he says as he looks at me expectantly, like he thinks I might have known this.

I didn't.

"Why didn't they just call me?" I ask. It seems strange that they'd call the police, and not his wife. Why jump straight from phone calls to involving law enforcement? I glance at my cell phone, and there's not so much as a single notification.

He looks down at his notepad, and his lips twist. The silence stretches between us for a few beats as I try to decipher his expression. As skilled as I am at reading people, I have no idea what he's going to say next. "Apparently they didn't have it on record that Patrick has a wife."

My brows furrow, and my mouth goes dry. I try to swallow as my mind churns over that information. Confusion muddies my thoughts. It has to be a mistake. They have him confused with someone else, or maybe they lost his information. "That can't—" I start to say. He didn't tell them about me? No one at his work knew that he had a wife? My stomach bottoms out. It can't be true. It must be some kind of mistake. Though my first thought should be, *Why, how could he could this to me?*— instead, I'm consumed with questions about what happens if my clients find out. The fact that my husband betrayed me like this—not only is it a blow to my heart, it's a blow to my career.

Cameron holds his hand up. "Believe me, I made sure I heard them correctly."

"He hasn't even told them he has a wife? He's worked there three years." I clench my fists as my words cut the air. We've been married nearly seven years now. How could he have gone all that time without ever mentioning me? Did he erase me? Was this some kind of misunderstanding? My stomach twists as I roll the words over in my mind again.

He glares at his phone for a moment, his jaw and brow tense. "Do you have any idea where Patrick might be?" he asks as he finally looks back up.

I shake my head as I try to get my mind to work, to think of somewhere he could be holed up. "No. He didn't tell me that he wasn't planning on going to work today." Where has he been for the last six hours if not at work? I pick up my phone and glance at the notifications—there's nothing from him.

"They said that Patrick was supposed to return from vacation today. They thought he might have gotten the days mixed up—"

I sit up straighter. "Vacation?" I don't even care that I cut him off, though I know it's one of Cameron's biggest pet peeves. Patrick has made it abundantly clear, many times, that he can't take *any* vacation time. That his boss is too much of a prick about taking even a single day off. "We didn't take a vacation." Confusion needles the back of my mind. What's going on? Patrick wasn't gone. For the past week, he got up every morning and left just like he was leaving for work. If he wasn't going to work, where did he go?

Cameron flips through a few pages of his notebook. "He's been on vacation for two weeks."

Two weeks? I try to process the information, but my mind rejects it over and over again—because it can't be true. "What has he been doing for *two weeks*?" Appearances are so important in my line of work. To not know where my husband has been during the day for two entire weeks, that's absolutely embarrassing. He's been coming and going as if nothing had changed. He's told me about his day during dinner when he's got home... He's laid out his clothes for the next day as if nothing out of the ordinary were happening at all. Bile climbs up my throat and I have to force myself not to be sick.

Cameron shakes his head and looks at me like he's sorry for me. That look, the pity in his eyes, it only strokes the flames of anger roaring inside me. I clench my fists to keep my hands from trembling. I don't want his pity, I want answers. What the hell has my husband been up to? How have I missed this? How could I be so easily fooled by someone I loved? I can see through *everyone* else, but I didn't realize my own husband was lying to me for three years?

"Maybe I should call them," I say, as I wrack my mind for ideas.

"I don't think that's a good idea. I'm not sure they'd tell you anything, since they didn't even know you existed," Cameron warns. "They'd likely require proof that you were married, and even then, they may decide that since Patrick failed to mention you, that he didn't want information shared with you."

He can't be serious. I'd have to prove that I'm married to Patrick? I still can't believe that this is all real. My phone chimes. I glance at the notification on the screen. I have to get ready to meet with my clients.

"Can you come back later? I have clients coming over for a session," I ask, though it's not really a question. Whether he agrees or not, this conversation is over. For now. I need to think. To breathe. The session will do that and give me the illusion of control over something. After this, I can try to sort out all this nonsense with Patrick. Work has always given me the reprieve I need.

Cameron looks torn. He clearly doesn't want to agree, but he can't stay in my house.

"I'll be back tomorrow morning. I'm going to make a few calls. Would you mind if I take a look around tomorrow?"

"That's fine," I say as I usher him out.

I grab my phone and text my best friend Tara, letting her know that the police just showed up asking about Patrick. I know I'm in for a barrage of texts, but she needs to know what's going on. My phone vibrates in my hand as I weave back through the house. I call his work, and just as Cameron said, they refuse to talk to me.

What happened to us? What could I have done to make my husband erase me? And how do I find him?

2

"Yes, that's right, she doesn't have any appointments for the rest of this week," Emma, my assistant, says in a tone so chipper it makes my ears throb. It's the type of tone that should be reserved for travel agents booking families on vacations to Disney World, not on the phone with a marriage counselor. It's a wonder anyone takes her seriously. The phone is cradled between her shoulder and ear. She tosses her hair when she takes calls. She makes hand motions too. Though she does a good job, sometimes I miss my old assistant—David.

After Cameron's visit, I should have canceled the rest of my day, closed up shop, not taken any of my clients. But I can't do that. I feel like I'd be letting these people down. They need me, they need my help—and maybe the distraction will stop my mind from going over and over the conversation with Cameron again. So, an hour after Cameron's departure, Emma came over to help get me ready for my appointments.

There's no wait to see me. Technically, I could take a new appointment this afternoon—maybe I should, it'd keep my mind off of things. But that's not the way things work. Today I'll have an appointment that was set up months ago. In marketing, the illusion of exclusivity and scarcity works wonders. Controlled urgency. If you're hard to come by, if your time is limited, your stock automatically goes up. In a town that's known to be the *happiest place on earth*, Orlando, I could go through a lot of clients. I could bring in the tourists and not worry about my quality of care. But that's not how you get notoriety. Granted, I came into this life with notoriety, thanks to my parents. I'm the princess of marriage counseling, thanks to them. In the nineties, they were daytime television royalty. They worked the circuit for a while—*Jenny Jones, Sally Jessy, Ricki Lake, Oprah*—until finally they landed their own show. Every day couples would schlep to the east side and spill all their secrets on screen. My parents made a killing—literally, until they died in a car crash. Now, I'm all that's left of the dynasty, but some of these people are still voracious, desperate for someone to help them hold their lives together. And I want to help them, and more importantly, I want them to see that I really care.

I have to protect myself. Too many clients, and my time won't be scarce enough. Too few clients, then I won't be able to pay my bills. My goal was never to be famous, a household name; but with parents like mine, you don't get a say in the matter. When they died, my face was splashed all over the news.

Emma slides a stack of papers toward me and taps her long acrylic nails on top. The pink polish sparkles in the light. "Your two o'clock."

"Lovely," I say as I start to skim the details. My clients today have been married for eight years, they have two kids, and they desperately need counseling. I'm surprised to find that it's the husband who reached out for the session—typically it's the wife. In the initial email, the man mentioned that his wife has become aggressive, difficult to deal with, and sometimes outright hostile. Which will make the session interesting.

People don't come to me just to find a solution for their

problems—a cure for their fractured relationship—they come to me because they think somehow the ghosts of my parents will shine through and save them. Our society thrives on misery, it's prepackaged and sold to us through pop culture. Hate your job, hate your spouse, hate your family—and most importantly, hate yourself. We were not designed to be miserable, but this world created an assembly line that's impossible to get off. I help people get off that carousel, or at least I try to.

I lean back against the wooden chair; its sharp edges bite into my shoulder blades, but instead of shifting to avoid it, I lean into the pain. A bruise that's been budding on my spine aches, the throbbing so intense I nearly grit my teeth. Nearly. The blinding glow and the buzzing of the florescent bulbs above make my head pound, drawing me out from the discomfort. It's strange how in this light, with squinted eyes, all the flaws of this kitchen blur. I can't see the cracks in the tile, the smudges on the stainless-steel fridge, my husband's handprints on the cabinets; there are imprints of him everywhere, even on me. My flesh and soul alike. I hate this house, looking at it. His fingerprints, his taste, his choices are everywhere, while all that's here of mine is my DNA. Did I give up too much of me for him, for his choices —is that why he erased me?

The table moves beneath my elbows, just an inch, but it's enough to snap my attention back, to make my breath catch.

Don't be so jumpy.

My mind reorients and I focus on the present, the script I need to formulate in my mind. I'll tell this couple what they want to hear. Need to hear.

"Adele," Emma says as she snaps her fingers in front of my face.

I blink. She must have said my name a few times and I missed it. There's a crease in her forehead when she looks at me, and even with that dimple of frustration, she looks like she should be on a runway. Pursed lips, big blue eyes, nipples poking through her sheer blouse. She could do so much better than this job. Even she could do so much better than me.

"Sorry, what?" I ask as I try to push away the rising tide of frustration, the film of booze still gauzy over my mind. The staccato of her voice, tap, tap, tapping in the back of my mind. I just want her to go away. The room feels too small with her in it.

"I'm going to go do research for our upcoming appointments. Do you need anything else?"

I shake my head, and wave my hand. "No, go."

3

My clients arrive on time. They stand side by side on my porch. They're both tall, lanky, like taffy that's been stretched. From the cheat sheet I got from Emma earlier, I know they're Brenda and Malcom Parish. She's got a bob, sharp bangs that cut across her forehead, thick arched brows, and creases on either side of her frown—I'd call them dimples, but I get the impression this woman doesn't smile much. Malcom is generic, light brown hair, brown eyes, features I see over and over again every day of the week—he looks like he fades into the background often.

"Doctor," Malcom says, and I bow my head before ushering them inside.

Once I've shut the front door, I lead them through the living room, back to my office. The office is large, I think it was meant to be a den. In the sprawling space I've got an oversized couch, a few chairs in the middle, and my desk is shoved along the back wall. The silver chevron wallpaper shimmers in the afternoon light. It used to feel strange inviting people here, doing sessions out of my home, but it's felt less and less like mine. Now, even though I live here, it feels more like an office than anything else.

"Please, take a seat," I say as I wave them into the room like a flight attendant. Put your tray tables up, buckle your seatbelts, and prepare yourselves for imminent divorce.

"This is a very nice office," Malcom says as he sits on the couch. His wife sneers and lowers herself onto the opposite end, leaving as much space between the two as possible. Though I don't have my notepad yet, I make a mental note of this.

I grab my leatherbound journal that I keep all of my session notes in and perch on the sofa across from the couple. The cover is smooth, silky against my fingertips—the touch of it unwinds a bit of the anxiety tangled inside me. Somehow, when I'm holding it, I feel I can breathe a bit easier.

"So, Malcom, Brenda, why don't you both tell me a little bit about why you're here?" I start. "I know the preliminaries; I have your intake forms, but I'd like to hear in your words why you're here."

Brenda sits up a little too straight, then crosses one leg over the other. She looks down her nose at me, then glances at her husband out of the corner of her eye. The way she purses her lips, it's like she's trying to fuse them together—to guarantee her silence.

Malcom glances at her, then back to me. "Brenda and I have been encountering some problems recently. I started a new job, and it's been really tough. When I tried to tell Brenda about it, she's been very frustrated with me. She tells me to man up, that I shouldn't complain, that I need to stop being so emotional about my work." Though he gets the point across to me, he starts and stops a few times while he's speaking, as if this is difficult to recount in front of his wife. Part of me wishes that we had an individual session first to go over these issues.

"So, when you say that you've been getting emotional about work, could you tell me a little more about that?" I press. Emotional can mean different things to different people. For some, emotional means crying, while for others it can mean anger, frustration, or a number of other things.

"My new boss has been making my life a living hell." He looks down at his lap. "A couple times, I've broken down and cried when I got home—because I'm not sure I made the right choice. I feel like I'm letting our family down. I'm not sure that this job will pan out and that I'll be able to support Brenda and our daughters," he explains. "Anytime I've gotten emotional, Brenda has told me that if I need to cry, I need to leave the room. She said that it's ridiculous and unacceptable for a wife to see her husband cry." He doesn't look at me once as he recounts this.

"Brenda, are you upset when your husband shows emotions?" I ask.

She throws her hands up in the air, then slams her hand on the sofa on the space that's carved between them.

"Of course! It's absolutely ridiculous. A good husband doesn't cry. A good husband doesn't show emotion or complain. He goes to work, he comes home, and he provides for his family. That's it. It's not like I'm asking so much of him. This isn't what a man looks like, and this sure as hell isn't what a man acts like," she says in a tone that borders on mocking.

It's incredibly difficult for me to keep my composure. Her statements needle me. "Brenda," I say, trying desperately to be patient, but I know my frustration chips away at my tone. "There is nothing wrong with crying. There is nothing wrong with your husband showing emotion, or telling you that he's frustrated." Typically in marriage counseling, most often I see women who are desperate for their husbands to show some type of emotion, to open up, to tell them even a hint of how they're feeling. The fact that she's berating him for expressing himself —good God, I don't know why he's bothering with counseling at all.

"Yes, there is," she says, punctuating her words with more hard slashes in the air with her hands.

"What you're asking for, is for your husband to be a robot.

You want him to provide for your family with no emotion, no feelings, no words of comfort. You're not looking for a partner, you're looking for someone to act as a servant," I explain. It's an absolute struggle to rein in my frustration, but somehow I manage to keep my tone even.

"Exactly, that's what husbands are. That's what I told him I wanted when we got married and he agreed to it." She uncrosses her legs and recrosses them with the opposite leg on top. "I didn't marry him so that I could have a spouse be an emotional drain on me. Bringing his baggage from work home is unacceptable."

"And I have! For years. But I can't do it anymore. I have shoved my feelings down, and done everything you asked. And all I ask is that you be a partner to me in the way I've been a partner to you," Malcom says, and he's on the verge of tears again. "I listen to you, I help you, I kill myself at work every day so that you and the girls can have a good life. I'm scared that I won't be able to keep doing this. I'm scared that I'm going to fail you."

Brenda looks at him and wrinkles her nose in disgust. She shoves up from the sofa. "I'm not going to sit here while you embarrass yourself. If you want to learn to be a man, then I'll see you at home tonight. If not, then don't bother coming back," she says before storming out.

I stand up and grab a box of tissues from my desk, then hand them to Malcom. He blots at his eyes, still looking at the floor. With his shoulders slumped and his head down, he looks absolutely defeated. And I don't blame him.

"Look, I don't say things like this often, but I really don't see how to salvage a marriage like this. How she reacted, how she just treated you, that's emotional abuse. If you want, I can connect you with some resources that can help you get out," I explain.

He shakes his head. "I can't leave. Real men don't leave."

I try not to grit my teeth. "Malcom, this isn't a safe relation-ship. I'm telling you now, most of the time emotional abuse escalates."

He holds his hand up to stop me, the tissue balled between his fingers. "I know. It's fine, I shouldn't have bothered coming here, it was a mistake. I'm sorry that we wasted your time." He stands and starts to walk toward the door.

"Please, don't go. We can finish the session. Maybe I can help you work through some of—"

He shakes his head. "No, there's nothing else to talk about." He disappears down the hall, and before I can stop him, he's already out the front door. At the front door, I sigh as I watch him walk toward the street. I lock the door behind them. In the silence after the session my mind drifts to my own marriage, to my husband. I check my phone again, but there's nothing. No text messages. No calls.

I wait with bated breath as I ask myself over and over again —*Patrick, where are you?*

4

I stand in the kitchen reviewing clients for tomorrow's sessions, trying desperately to distract myself from my questions about Patrick. My mind keeps churning over the details and I imagine what the news will be saying soon. *Police are asking for any help finding Patrick Johansen, husband of local counselor, Adele Sutton-Johansen, the daughter of famed TV counselors Marcia and Calum Sutton.* Why did they need to bring my family into this, my history?

My stomach clenches as anxiety nags at me. Emma's texted me twice already to check in on how the session went, and I can't bring myself to tell her about Patrick yet. The silence of the house feels like it's closing in on me. The ceiling feels lower, the walls are too close. What if last night was the last time I'll ever see him? What if these lies are the only things I have to remember him by? My emotions seesaw, anger and sadness ebbing and flowing inside me like the tides.

My life would be so much easier if my husband were a hermit, a shut-in, the type of guy that everyone hated. Don't marry a social butterfly, because if they disappear, you've got a lot of phone calls to make. I shift in the office chair, trying for the three hundredth time to get comfortable, but it's a waste of time, energy. There's nothing, no position that could soothe this raw bundle of nerves under my skin. I need to call these people, to find out if anyone knows anything, if he said anything, if someone might have been after Patrick—but the idea that I may uncover more lies, more betrayals, I hate to admit how much it scares me.

Most of Patrick's contacts are already in my phone, mutual acquaintances I see from time to time, but if he was keeping things from me, there could be many others that he's never mentioned. And now that he's missing, I have to dig into that deep unknown. I pull up our mobile account, and filter through the numbers, cross-referencing them with the ones I already know.

The info was here all along if I wanted it, but I trusted him —I had no reason to dig through our accounts to see who he was talking to. Patrick was always my refuge in this world, and I was his—or at least, that's what I thought. But if he wasn't telling anyone I existed, what was I to him, really?

There are message logs, back and forth with his business partner Lucas, and countless others, including with Emma. It looks like he spent most of his day texting. Why was he texting Emma? I have questioned their relationship a few times, but there's no way that Emma would ever bother with someone like Patrick. She could do so much better. Though I'm not surprised, the outgoing texts all stopped last night.

It takes me a few hours to sort through everything. The whole time I feel sick. I don't want to see just how much someone I loved could betray me. I don't want to dig through his messages to find *dirt* or *evidence*. I want Patrick to show up and to tell me the truth. At this point, I'm not sure anything I find could be worse than him lying about going to work for two weeks and never bothering to tell them that I exist at all.

I have to make these calls, to see what any of his acquaintances or his family might know, if he said anything. Though the police are looking into his disappearance, I'm not sure I trust them to look at all the angles... or to keep me up to date on what they find.

I make a long call to Ella, a friend that's mostly mine, but has tolerated Patrick. Ella and I have been friends for years, we met before college, and she's one of the few people that I've kept in touch with over the years from those days. My first and only year of college, I met Jenene at a party. Ella and I had already been friends for a while, and Ella was having the hardest time finding girls she liked. Enter Jenene, the perfect match for her, and I knew it. I didn't believe in love at first sight until I saw the two of them together. Then they became one of those nauseatingly perfect couples. Finishing each other's sentences, sitting on the same side of a booth at a restaurant. They still celebrate anniversaries like they just got together. I can't deny that it gives me a sick thrill to see them together. Though it's good to catch up with her for a bit, she hasn't heard from Patrick—and has nothing to add to my search.

Again and again, I hear the same shocked tones, the apologies, the promises to spread the word on social media—though the last thing I want is for his disappearance to end up all over social media. Facebook is the digital herpes of our generation. It should be exterminated, burned out of existence, but that will never happen. Mindless posts aren't going to help anything, but it'll make them all feel like they're doing something *good*.

The calls to Patrick's family go to voicemail and I can't help but wonder what I did for such a merciful break. I feel wrung out, defeated before I'm even halfway through the list. No one knows anything, I'm wasting my time.

I reach two other voicemails for numbers I don't recognize, but Patrick contacted frequently. These ones, I'm the most suspicious of, and I doubt they'll be returning my calls.

The call I'm dreading the most, the one I've saved for last, is the call to Lucas. Things didn't end well for them when their business fell apart, a new type of walking tour aimed at millennials, which never took off. It seemed to me that Patrick gave up on their dream three years ago when he took a day job. But they kept it going longer than I expected. They were barely making anything. If it weren't for my sessions, we wouldn't have been able to pay any of the bills. I haven't spoken to him since they both went their separate ways. It takes longer than it should for me to call Lucas.

On the other end the phone rings and with each silence between them, my whole body tenses. I have to force myself to breathe as I wait.

Go to voicemail, go to voicemail is a mantra replaying in my mind over and over again. I don't want to talk to any of these people, to pour out my heart to these people for help—and admit that maybe I'm a failure. I hate that I need their help, that someone might know more about my husband than I do.

"Adele," Lucas says, his deep voice cutting across the line. The words are cold, like he can't bother with pleasantries anymore.

"Hi, Lucas, do you have a few minutes to talk?" I ask, finding my voice.

There's a long pause, the kind that tells me he's weighing saying no, but curiosity is getting the best of him.

"Look, it's about Patrick, he's missing," I add, when the silence has stretched for so long, I think he'll really say no.

"Missing?" he finally asks, his voice inching upward.

"Yes, Patrick never showed up for work. The police are involved, but I'm calling anyone who might have seen him, or he might have reached out to. I know it's still early, but they asked that I take this step," I explain for what feels like the hundredth time.

A low chuckle cuts through the line. "You think that Patrick just tried to call me up for a nice chat? He wouldn't have called me if he needed a kidney and I was the only match on the planet. But if he could have tricked me out of it, that's a whole other story."

It's hard for me to process his bitterness, since I wasn't privy to all the breakdowns in their relationship. I heard a bit second-hand from Patrick, but so many pieces of his puzzle are missing. "Jesus, Lucas, what happened between the two of you?" I ask, as I pace my living room.

"That's a long story, and frankly, not one I think you're ready to hear. Good luck with Patrick, but to be honest, if he's gone, you should count your blessings and never look back."

My mouth drops open and though I want to say something, anything, words escape me as Lucas ends the call.

5

My mind is threaded with worry, my heart racing every time my phone dings with a notification. I'm desperate for news, for answers, for someone to tell me that this has all been a mistake. Because it can't be real. I keep waiting to wake up. It's been over twenty-four hours now. The first forty-eight are the most important, and with every beat of my heart, I hear the clock ticking down, mocking me.

This morning I counseled a couple I've been seeing for months. For the moment, they seem like they've reconciled, moved to a better place; though I tried to feign happiness for them, I'm not sure I came off genuine enough. It was a young couple that reminded me so much of Patrick and me when we got together. My heart ached as a I watched them, their giddiness, the love radiating between them. Afterward, I cried in my bedroom for twenty minutes. It was so hard to keep my walls up, to lean into my training. But I tried to remember how my parents did it, even when I know they were having a hard day, they cleared their mind for their patients—they made space for them. And that's what I try to do every day.

I sit at the kitchen table as questions burn in the back of my mind, my eyes still swollen from tears. The front door opens, and I crane my neck, looking for Patrick's slender frame. My mind floods with all the questions I have for him, all the lies he'll have for me. It's funny, all the lies we've exchanged over the years. I wonder if you weighed them, what would win—lies or love.

"Hey," Emma calls as she slams the door.

"I'm in here," I call as I take a sip of my tea. My mind is heavy, laden with all the questions, and the guilt I can't let go of. Disappointment settles in my stomach like a stone. It could have been him. Patrick could have walked through that door, but he didn't. And what if he never does again? What then?

Emma's hips sway exaggeratedly as she glides into the room, a pencil skirt clinging to her slender thighs, a tight blouse hugging her chest. She drops a stack of mail on the table. She's got a box of chocolates tucked under her arm and I eye her. Emma doesn't eat candy. She subsists off green juice and cleanses—and loves to remind me that she's either vegan or doing paleo depending on the month.

She slides the chocolates in front of me, all while sweeping her blonde locks off her shoulder. I glance at the box. All I can think of as I look at it is how she'll lecture me about the hormones in milkfat as the chocolate melts between my teeth. This candy, it's a Trojan horse.

"Someone sent them to you. There was no name on it," she explains as she waves her hand toward the box. Even so, I'm surprised she didn't just toss them in the trash. "They were in the mail this morning when I grabbed it." Though her words are even, as smooth as silk, I don't believe them. Everyone in psychology lies after all—and even though she's still working on her degree, it's something that starts early. It's an easy thing to do. Once you learn your tells, those small ticks we all have when we lie, all you have to do is iron them out.

I flip the box over and over, as if it might have clues on it.

But there's nothing. Patrick used to bring me little gifts like this. Looking at the box reminds me of all the times he'd surprise me. Back when I was the only woman in the world to him.

"Do you have a boyfriend I don't know about?" she asks, bemused. Her head tilts to the side and I half expect her to twirl her hair.

I roll my eyes at her. "If I did, I'm pretty sure you'd know about it." The chocolate tempts my empty stomach, but I'm too stressed to eat.

"Maybe you should consider it," she offers as she sits across from me and leans her elbows on the table. "Maybe it'd motivate you to look after yourself." I'm not sure if it's for my benefit or hers.

I shrug. "Maybe I should," I say without an ounce of conviction. The last thing I need is another man in my life. I'd rather keep my money all to myself and not clean up after a man. I grab the stack of mail, because I have no desire to continue the conversation. But all I find is a stack of bills.

"Are you doing okay?" she asks, appraising me a little too carefully. This makes me feel like everyone must see it, that I'm a vase balancing on an edge, so close to slipping, to cracking. But I press my lips together instead of responding. I have to tell her. I can't put it off any longer.

"Did I see a cop car pull up when I was leaving earlier?" Emma asks.

I nod, but don't bother to look up at her. The stress must be painted all over her face, but I don't need to see it.

"Why were they here?" There's a thread of concern in her voice, something I rarely hear.

I finally glance at her and it's not the anxiety I expect to see marring her features. Her eyes are hungry.

"They aren't sure where Patrick is. He didn't show up for work yesterday." The words don't hold the impact they should. I sound as haggard as I feel. The concern that's clenched inside me like a fist, it doesn't punch up my words. If I were anyone else, I'd pretend, I'd act. But with Emma, there's no point. She'll hear the truth, how he erased me. Hell, I'm sure the betrayal is written all over my face. There's only so long I can keep this from her.

For a beat her mouth hangs open. "Why didn't you say something sooner?" she asks, her voice pitching up an octave. She shoves off the table, standing to her full height as if there's something she can do about this herself, as if *she* might go find him.

I shrug. "Maybe I'm still thrown for a loop. Apparently, he didn't bother to tell anyone at work that he had a wife. And he didn't tell me that he'd taken the last two weeks off work," I say as I cross my arms and lean back in the chair. Saying it aloud reopens the wound. Pulling away is one thing, but erasing me? That's something so much worse. Tell me you hate me every day, but don't you dare pretend I don't exist. My heart aches and I hate that I've given him this kind of power over me. Why did I give myself over to this—to him? I knew better, and yet, here we are.

Her brow furrows and her face flushes. All at once, Emma shifts from runway model to barely restrained beast. Anger swims behind her eyes as she clenches her fists on top of the table. Why is she so mad about this? Why would she even care? "Two weeks off? But he kept going to work."

I eye her carefully. "That's what I said," I say, my words deadpan.

Emma might be good at helping me in the office, but she's always been weak when her emotions are involved. Unless she's got a talent she's been hiding for years, my guess is, she didn't know about the vacation either. She's as blindsided as I am.

"Where the fuck has he been?" Emma growls. She paces the kitchen, her heels clicking on the tile. "Have you tried calling him?" Her anxious energy is palpable, filling the kitchen like static before a lightning storm.

I want to roll my eyes. Of course I've called him. "Seven times."

"And?" she asks pointedly.

"It goes to voicemail every time, like his phone is off or dead," I say as I glance at my cell phone again, as if there might be something there. But I only find a picture of the beach that I made my wallpaper, I took it months ago when Patrick and I celebrated our anniversary with a little trip. Looking at it now is like I'm being stabbed in the heart.

She doesn't say anything and I'm thankful. I have to cut the silence though, otherwise we'll each continue to stew in our respective suffering.

"Do I have any appointments tomorrow?" I ask. Usually she puts them on the calendar, but if something pops up last minute, it tends to slip her mind.

"No. Nothing until Wednesday. But then you've got three appointments," she says. For a moment she glances at her phone and taps on the screen a few times. "There are two others that inquired about Friday, but they haven't confirmed yet. They'll book at some point. So, I went ahead and asked for them to fill out the intake forms."

"Please make sure they fill them out." My words come out harsher than I mean for them to be.

"I always do," she says as she pops her hands on her hips.

"Thank you," I say, a little too stiffly.

"I'll send you their info as soon as I get it," she says as she slings her purse over her shoulder. "I'm heading out. If you hear anything about Patrick, will you call me, please?"

"Sure," I say, though I'm not sure I have the mental space to keep my promises. If I hear from Patrick, the last thing on my mind will be updating everyone. There are so many questions I have for him—so much that we need to discuss.

Once Emma is gone, I pace the living room while calling Patrick a few more times, because at some point he'll have to pick up, right? When the calls all go to voicemail, I send a few texts that are increasingly anxious. I don't want to be too crazy in writing, that wouldn't serve me well. I have an image to protect after all. I want to throw the phone across the room, to scream into the void—where the hell is he!

My phone has slowly filled with voicemails throughout the day, Patrick's friends, acquaintances, and family calling me back—but no one has any news, any updates that make me feel any better. There's one thing I notice, the two mystery numbers—there isn't a single call or text from either of them. Emma's words nag in the back of my mind. Was he cheating? Are those women he was seeing? I don't want it to be true.

I tap the edge of my phone case with my nails as I stare at the screen. The not knowing, that's the worst part in all this. Unanswered questions are something I just can't live with, and allowing Patrick to have more secrets, that's not an option. I stroll through my house, back to my office. It's got two doors, one that leads into it from the hallway, and there's a back door that goes into my bedroom. My guess is the builder of this house envisioned it being a nursery.

On the top of one of the bookshelves, my laptop is stashed. I grab it and walk to the living room, nestling myself into the plush blue couch, and open the computer. It takes a minute for it to whir to life. Once it does, I turn on my VPN, open up my incognito browser, and navigate to a site where I've researched numbers in the past for clients. There's a lot you can gather from a phone number, addresses, family members, and from there, if you know the things to search for, you can find out pretty much anything.

I type in the first number. Ashlee Madison. Age: twenty-four. Location: Orlando, Florida. My temple throbs as I look the information over. A headache awakens in the back of my skull. I click away from the site and onto social media.

Ashlee Madison is a thin blonde with big blue eyes and a body I'd have to pay for at my age. A little more googling shows me that she's passionate about bottomless mimosas at brunch, puppies wearing sweaters, and purses that cost more than my mortgage. She looks like a *real* winner. I hate to jump to conclusions, but I can't help but wonder what he had to discuss with this woman. Was he cheating on me? Her Facebook account doesn't show much, because it's private, and the same for her Instagram.

I text Tara about Ashlee before moving on. The next number belongs to Brynlee Travis. A nineteen-year-old that moved here from Miami. She looks like a jailbait version of Emma, and my stomach roils. Brynlee's passions are pretty close to Ashlee's in vapidity. *The Bachelor*, dollar flip-flops (she has over thirty pairs), and bar trivia. She must have a great fake ID if she's making it into bars. I send her info to Tara too so she can commiserate with me.

What I can't understand is how a guy like Patrick even has numbers for girls like this. How is he roping them in and, more importantly, how is he keeping them interested? It's not his personality or his charm. That's for sure. Is this what he spent the two weeks doing? Did he spend his vacation time with strange women instead of with me? The idea of that slices straight through me.

I pull up the accounts we shared—bank account, credit cards, all of it. To be honest, I haven't watched the accounts as closely as I should have—they're all nearly empty. Seeing the balances so low, it guts me. What have I worked so hard for? For Patrick to take it all? With the trust fund I got when my parents died squirreled away and my income from sessions, money has been the last thing on my mind. My phone vibrates in my hand, and I glance at the screen, hoping that maybe one of Patrick's friends is calling me back. Tara's—my best friend's—name lights up on the screen. I slide my thumb across to accept the call.

"Hey, you," I say as I wedge the phone between my shoulder and ear.

"Girl, you are not going to believe this," she says without even waiting for the words to leave my mouth.

"What?" I ask, though I know I don't need to. The way Tara's talking, I know she's about to dive into a one-sided conversation that means she barely even needs me to grunt an acknowledgement.

"I found the bitch on Facebook." Her voice is muffled, like she's whispering and cupping her hand around the phone. It makes me imagine her skulking on the phone in a dark alley somewhere, though I know she's probably just in her bedroom.

"You didn't," I say, trying not to laugh. I wonder which mistress she looked up, Brynlee or Ashlee. Hell, knowing Tara, she's already looked them both up.

"Oh, I did. I know it's her. And there's a picture of them together."

My stomach bottoms out, and my heart seizes. He was cheating. On top of everything else, I wasn't enough. He lied to me, he erased me, and he found someone else—because even though I bared my soul to Patrick, he didn't like what he saw, so he looked elsewhere.

"Which one? How? Their accounts were private," I say, the words rushing out of me. There's a war raging in my mind. Do I want the proof? Do I really want to see it? The question makes me sick, and I just wish I could escape from this. Like I could wake back up and none of this ever would have happened. I've dealt with this so many times with my clients, but I never imagined that I would be on the receiving end of this. I took care of my marriage, I checked on my husband, I made sure that I catered to his needs—sometimes at the expense of my own.

How, after all that I gave, could he have done this to me? How was it not enough?

"Ashlee. I sent her a friend request with a fake account I have. She and Patrick have been in a relationship for a year, according to her account." Her words are sharp, but careful, as if she knows the impact each one could have on me.

A year. Jesus Christ, I'm the stupidest woman alive. My palms slick with sweat and my heart pounds. I can't believe that he did this to me. Who is this man and what happened to the Patrick I married? Was it always a façade? Did he ever really love me? "Were they Facebook official on his account?" I ask before I can help myself. I want to shove my fist in my mouth for even asking it. What. Is. Wrong. With. Me?

"With one of his alternate accounts, yes," she says, her voice low. "I can't believe I never saw this account before. How did this get past me?"

"Don't beat yourself up over a stupid account," I say, though I know she'll do it anyway. It's not like I saw it either. I pace my living room, my phone wedged between my ear and my shoulder as I pick at my fingernails. "Send me the pictures."

"Adele, no."

I stop in the middle of the room, anger rising inside me. I have to know. She'd want to see it too.

"Tara, I need this." The words cut their way out of me.

"Don't say I didn't warn you," she says her voice further away, like she put me on speaker.

My phone vibrates several times as messages containing screenshots from Tara hit my phone. Anger flares inside me, and I feel that sickening rage from the first time I suspected what he was up to. In the pictures, they're huddled up together, looking very much like the couple Patrick and I never were. He never wanted to take pictures with me. He didn't want to be seen with me. My heart splinters.

"That asshole," I growl.

"Exactly! Hold on to that rage, girl. You're going to need it," she says.

And I know she's trying to be supportive. But that rage, it isn't going to do me any favors right now. There's a knock at my door, and I grind my teeth together.

"Let me call you back," I say before ending the call.

I walk to my door, exhaustion dragging me down. I look through the peephole and find a woman, probably in her late twenties, standing on my porch. The sun is slowly sinking toward the horizon, casting the palm and oak trees lining the street in gold. I debate opening the door. I don't even like to answer my phone if I don't know who's calling—but with my husband missing, this could be a lead.

I open the door just as she starts to knock again. She freezes, her hand in midair, her eyes wide.

"Oh, hi. Are you Adele Johansen?" she asks.

I nod.

"The Adele Johansen that used to be Adele Sutton?" she continues as she sweeps a lock of her curly brown hair behind her ear. The light on my porch is a little too bright, making her pale skin glow.

"Yes," I say, trying not to sound as annoyed as I feel. Is she about to serve me legal papers or something? "What is it that you need?"

"I was hoping to talk to you about your parents," she says.

"You should call my assistant, Emma, and set up an appointment. I don't take walk-in sessions," I say, ready to shut the door.

She raises an eyebrow at that. "No, I'm not here for a session."

"Why do you want to talk to me about my parents then if you're not here for a session?" Over the years, I've had plenty of my parents' fans book sessions, not to get any help psychologically, but instead they wanted details of my life, my childhood, what they were like as parents.

"I'm Denise McCaffery, a journalist, and I did a story recently, a 'where are they now?' on all the old talk show hosts from the nineties, and I found some inconsistencies when I was looking up your parents," she explains a little too quickly, stumbling over her words.

"Inconsistencies?" I parrot back at her. The ghosts of my parents have been following me since they died in 1997, so this is nothing new. But no one has ever mentioned inconsistencies. I'm actually not certain that anyone has really looked very far into their deaths. It was just a car accident, after all. All the conversations I've had have been around how it was a tragedy, how awful it was, how I'm continuing their legacy.

"Yeah, based on what I've seen, before their deaths, there were several coverups related to the show. I think they paid people off after they appeared on the show," she explains.

I want to scoff at that, at the entire idea. But I was thirteen when they died. Then I was shipped off to live with my grandmother in Naples. They could have done lots of things that I never knew about—but if there were really coverups, I'm sure someone would have found them by now.

"Good luck with your story," I say before I shut the door and lock it.

She may think that she'll find something, but I have a feeling my parents' secrets died when they did.

6

Before I've fully shed the tethers of sleep, I'm already squinting, staring at my cell phone. He's been missing almost seventy-two hours now. I've been so sick with worry; I've barely eaten in days. There's a hollowness inside me, and I'm unsure if it's hunger, or something else. I call Patrick again, without a single hope that he'll answer. But I still hold my breath when each ring ends, as if I might hear his voice.

Several notifications on my phone inform me that the news has started circulating a story about Patrick. The police are still asking for tips regarding his whereabouts. I knew it would come eventually, but it's still like a punch to the gut. But there's something new buried among the fluff. Denise has published a story about my parents.

> *Questions are rising regarding allegations that former famed TV hosts Marcia and Calum Sutton were involved in shady dealings on their show before their deaths. The story is evolving as more previous patients that were on the show come forward. The most striking of which, so far, is that DNA results may have been faked or altered for the sake of television drama.*

The time mocks me, and I close out of the article—it's trash reporting. Eight a.m., but not a single missed call or text from Cameron, Emma, or Tara. It's not like I expected there would be. But somehow, the loneliness is so palpable I feel like my heart must echo in the void inside of me. I roll over as I debate whether to get out of bed at all. There are no appointments today. I could sleep the whole day if I wanted. But my mind is too awake for that, so I drag myself from bed.

As I walk through my house, I scroll through the local news, and an article catches my eye. *Local Counselor's Husband Missing.* My stomach clenches, like it's being squeezed in a fist. I hate this. Not only because I have no idea where he is, but because everyone is now going to speculate about my husband, where he is, what's happened to him—did he leave me? Who did he leave me for? The idea that people are talking about my life, what's happened in my marriage—it cuts to my core. They may not know he was cheating... but it's only a matter of time. In my line of work, your life has to be perfect—the reason my parents had such notoriety is because their marriage was the kind of relationship everyone dreams of having. If people find out my husband erased me, that he cheated on me, no one will see that as his fault; it'll be my fault for not keeping him interested, for not being *enough*.

I was hoping—though I know it was stupid—that the little impromptu interview would lead to nothing. But no. Things like this never go away. It's just getting started. And now with the journalist sniffing around about my parents—what if this gets so much worse?

How did I miss this? In a situation like this, I'd tell a client that it's only natural to feel as lost as I am right now. But this doesn't feel natural. This feels like the earth is sliding out from beneath me. It's my job to anticipate people's needs, to know what they'll do next. Hell, most of the time I feel like I can read minds.

I put the kettle on the stove, grab a coffee cup, hoping to settle my nerves, but before I can even set it on the counter the doorbell rings through the house. I tense up as I look toward the door. *Not again.* I can't face the media right now. What would I even say? Dread coils inside me as I stalk toward the front door. Anxiety spiders beneath my skin. When I look through the peephole, Cameron waits on the other side. Long wavy brown hair hangs loose around his ears.

I open the door and offer him a slight nod. "Morning." My words come out without an ounce of the stress that's plaguing me. Working in psychology has trained me for this. Every morning, when I start a session, I leave my problems behind, compartmentalizing them before I even see a single client. That's exactly what I have to do now, because otherwise, the weight of all of this could drag me down into a place that I'm not sure I can pull myself out of.

"Morning. Can I come in?" he asks as he steps toward me. I wonder if he's seen the news covering Patrick's disappearance. But there isn't a hint of it at all on his face.

I step back and wave him in. But I can't help asking myself if I should be letting a cop into this house, if I should be letting anyone into my house when there's a shitstorm brewing. It'll just be too suspicious if I say *no.* "Sure. I'm making some tea. Do you want some?"

"Sure, that'd be great," he says, but it feels wrong. I can sense all the things we should say hanging in the air between us. The awkwardness this situation brings.

He follows me through the house as the whistling of the kettle echoes down the hall. After walking through the sparse hallway, we emerge into the kitchen and I pour myself a cup, then one for him. Cameron sits at the small table in the kitchen and I slide into a seat across from him. A lump forms in my throat as he watches me. Is he here about Patrick? Did they find him?

"There's no nice way to ask this—" I hesitate as I wrestle over the words. In my line of work, the value of every word that leaves my lips is paramount. The weight of those words, it's not lost on me. "So, why are you here?" I ask, knowing the questions are going to be much harsher than I mean for them to be.

"We haven't found anything yet. And my captain is getting antsy. There are some things I need from you that will assist in our investigation," he says as he draws a small notepad from his pocket. His words sound rehearsed, stiff.

I glance to the notepad clutched in his hands. I've been trying to puzzle it out, where Patrick could be. None of his friends have offered any leads, no one has seen him as far as I know. "Okay, what do you need?"

"A list of friends or family he might have reached out to or be staying with."

"I can email you a list. I already reached out to them, so no one will be surprised to hear from you," I offer, because it'll take me a little while to gather all the contact information that he'll need. "But, I'm not sure how accurate it'll be. It's not like Patrick was honest with me about who he was in touch with." Bitterness hangs on every syllable as I speak, though I don't mean for it to. I'm not sure if I should add in my suspicions about him cheating. Maybe I should tell him, but I won't, because it's too embarrassing to admit aloud.

He nods. "That'll be great. We also need you to sign off on a few forms so we can track his phone and credit cards."

"So, you've officially opened a missing person investigation then?" I ask. To me it seems like they should have done it on day one. I'm not sure what took them so long.

"We have."

"I'll sign whatever you need," I say, because I just want them to find him, so I can confront him and ask him all the questions that have been piling up in my mind. "What are the next steps?"

"We're going to look at his movements for the past few weeks along with his contacts. That might give us an idea." For a moment he pauses and glances at his phone. "Look, I'm not supposed to tell you this, but Patrick's employer is very interested in his whereabouts."

"Why?" I ask. My heart pounds. What was my husband up to? The fact that he didn't tell them of my existence still needles the back of my mind. It's a stab to the gut. I'm not sure I'll ever be able to get over that.

"Quite a bit of money went missing right before Patrick went on his vacation. They did some looking around and they believe he's the culprit."

What the hell? I nearly spit the words out but instead I grit my teeth. What was he planning? My skin prickles. Is this how he's gotten by without touching the credit cards? I've looked into the bank account, and he'd been withdrawing more than usual. If I'd paid attention, I might have seen this coming.

"If you don't mind, can I take a look around to see if I can find anything for Patrick's employer?"

I shrug. "I have nothing to hide. Knock yourself out," I say and sweat slicks my palms. Anxiety prickles the bottom of my stomach and my chest tightens in response. I just want this to be over. When they find him, I'm going to divorce his ass so quickly it'll make his head spin. But then what? I'll be alone in my late thirties, having to start over, *again*. What would a divorce do to my career?

Cameron smiles and takes another sip of his tea. "Do you mind if I finish this first?"

"No, not at all," I say, wishing I could excuse myself to clean the house before he starts searching. It's not like I live in filth, but if I knew my ex-boyfriend was going to search for evidence of my missing husband, I would have done some tidying up. I look down at my cup and the amber liquid swirling inside. In the back of my mind, I know the part I have to play here, and the information that I need out of him. But I can't just come right out and ask for it. Instead, I need to beat around the bush. Being too direct shuts people down. You never get the real information you're after that way.

"Did Patrick have an office?" he asks.

"Straight down the hall on the right," I say as I point. "Across from mine."

We walk down the hall together, past my office to get to Patrick's. He flips on the light and stands in the middle of the room, looking for a place to start. The walls of the office are a deep navy blue with white wainscoting. Patrick's desk sits in the middle, so that the backs of the monitors face the door. I shouldn't hover here. I should give Cameron some space, but I'm desperate to know what else Patrick was up to, what I might have missed. How did he hide it? How did he keep this from *me* of all people? I've always been able to read people, that's what made me so good in sales.

He turns on the monitors and clicks around for a few seconds. "Ah, no password. That makes my life so much easier."

The only sound in the room is the frequent clicking, which somehow manages to be faster than my racing heart. For a long time, he's silent. My stomach is in knots as I watch him, waiting for the truth to come tumbling from his lips. As time ticks on with Cameron not speaking, my mind fills with all the terrible possibilities.

"Adele, were you two having problems?" he asks after one of the longest silences of my life.

I know what's coming. Before he says anything, I see the words forming on his tongue. It's enough to make the life in his eyes dim.

I weigh my answer, what I could say, what I *should* say. It's not as easy as answering a cop's questions. This is a cop I have a very complicated history with. I'm not sure how much I'd want him to know in normal circumstances. I'm embarrassed by how long I let it go on, by how long I kept silent. "Not that I knew of, not until he disappeared," I say as I hug myself. This isn't a role I have to play, there's no disguise to pull on. I know the sadness is etched on my face. Though I'm not sure I should be giving the cops information about the suspected cheating that I've found—it'll look worse if Cameron figures out that I knew about the cheating and didn't say anything to him about it. So I come clean. I unload everything that I've found.

Cameron stands and walks over to me. "It's not your fault he's a dirt bag. You know that, right?"

"Yeah, I know. I wish I'd never met him. Almost ten years wasted. Time I'll never get back." One third of my life has gone down the drain with this. How do you reconcile that almost a third of your life is gone? That you gave it to the wrong person. That you wasted the years you could have had children. He fooled me, and that's what makes all of this worse. I'm trained to see through bullshit, and he still deceived me. There have been so many times I've looked down on clients who I assumed didn't see warning signs. I figured they just had their heads in the sand. Is this my karma?

All I want is to escape this. For the pain splintering me to go away. I can't believe I ever let Patrick worm his way into my heart like this. I should have hardened myself and never let anyone in, focused on my work, never bothered with love. To know that I tried so hard and failed, I think that's the worst part. I couldn't see through him, I couldn't see those lies.

"Do you want me to stay so we can talk? Do you need me here right now?" He stands with his hands in his pockets, like he is desperate to hang his head, but he's keeping it up —for now.

I shake my head.

"What's happened, Adele? I can see the shift in you. There used to be a light in your eyes, and now it's like you've dimmed." His hand reaches for mine, but I pull away.

Maybe he sees the sadness in my eyes. Or maybe it's that I'm a shell of who I once was. I let the walls fall away and the truth rise to my lips.

"Most people say they've grown apart. I guess he grew apart, and I just didn't see it." I shared my soul with him, and I guess he didn't like what he saw. Whose fault is that?

"You deserve so much better than that."

I look down and lace my fingers together because I have no idea what to say. Maybe I don't deserve better, maybe I deserved this for not noticing the lies, how he pulled away. Cameron reaches out and takes my hand. But he doesn't speak until I look at him.

"Look, I know that all of this has knocked your feet out from under you. But you need to put in more effort to look like you're concerned about him," he says as he squeezes my hand.

My stomach churns, and I force myself to nod. Though I search his face, it hasn't changed the way he looks at me. And that's my real concern. I'd never want to do anything to change the way he sees me. I thought once he knew about who my parents were it'd change his perception. But he always told me that I didn't choose my parents, and that their fame didn't matter to him.

"So, what should I do then?" I ask, because I have no idea how to make people believe I'm more concerned than I am. I internalize everything, I always have—but that's been when I've dealt with the feelings of clients, not something like this. Right now, I don't care if I never see him again. How do I act like I want my cheating husband back?

"Post online that he's missing. Reach out to the media about it. Call friends," he says.

"Patrick had a ton of acquaintances, but no one he was really close to, no one he confided in," I say. My anger rises inside me and reaches my words. It still burns in the back of my mind that he didn't even tell his work that he was married. How many more secrets did he carry around? How many lies did he tell me? What else will I have to uncover?

Cameron shakes his head. His lips are a thin line. It's the face he makes when he's frustrated. I should be surprised that I remember it. But I think I remember everything about him, as if it were imprinted on me. It's strange that Cameron has existed in the back of my mind all this time. Does that mean something? Or is the history of everyone we've loved written inside of us somewhere?

"I'll need you to find a recent picture of him. We'll need it at the station so we can make flyers, distribute it. We will contact the media, but it will look better for you if you did it too."

I nod.

"Did he change his routine recently?"

Rage builds in the back of my mind, piercing my thoughts. "You mean other than him taking a vacation from work that he never told me about?" My words are far harsher than I mean for them to be. I sound bitter, scorned.

Cameron is quiet for a moment. "Yeah, other than that."

"No, I don't think so. Sometimes he'd been leaving earlier than usual, but I figured he was busy at work. He had seemed a little stressed, I guess. He was biting his nails again—he hadn't done that in years. But every time I brought it up, he denied it."

He makes a note of it, though I feel like there's nothing to note.

"They're talking about your parents on the news again, not sure if you've seen," Cameron says, not meeting my eyes as he makes a big show of writing on his notepad.

I cross my arms. "What exactly are they saying?" I ask as a knot in my gut tightens.

"There's a lot of speculation about their show... some of the people who were on it... and how much you might have known."

"I was thirteen when they died, the show started when I was like five. Do they think I was a business partner or something?" My words edge up with frustration.

"I know, I know. I just thought I should tell you," he says.

And I appreciate it, but I plan to avoid this for as long as possible. Maybe it'll all just blow over. Maybe it won't become some *big thing*.

"For the rest of the world, you need to be a concerned wife —not the daughter of talk show hosts. If they try to interview you again, hold your head high. No one else knows how he treated you, that he cheated," he says as he pulls me into a hug.

"Thank you," I say as I pull away. Hugging a cop investigating my husband's disappearance feels *wrong*. Hugging Cameron—well, right now, that feels even worse. Somehow, even after Patrick's betrayal, someone else's touch feels like I've crossed a line, as if my toe is clunking against an invisible forcefield.

"If you're all right, I need to head out." He digs in his pocket and pulls out a card. He writes his cell on the back and hands it over. "Email or text me that picture of Patrick later. If you hear from him, call me right away, okay?"

I nod.

Cameron leaves and the house is quiet, stone cold around me. This isn't a home anymore, it's a museum of what Patrick and I once were, a monument to the lies he told me, a still life of betrayal. I send the list he asked for over to him, if only to distract myself.

My phone vibrates on the counter and I flinch. No good news has been coming from it lately. Calls have still been flowing in from Patrick's friends and family. None of them have seen him—of course—but they all want to help. Every time I've made the mistake of answering one of the calls, I get an eager tone asking if there's anything they can do to help. As if I have a list waiting. But I don't have the mental space to tell someone else how to help me right now. I feel like I'm drowning, like this is all going to sweep my feet out from under me.

I stalk across the kitchen to the phone, knowing from the single vibration that a text waits for me. The moment the plastic case hits my palm, it vibrates again. My body tightens as I read the name on the screen. Emma. A window with her name on it hangs in a shadow, obscuring my beach background. The settings don't give me a hint of what she's said, but I doubt it will be pleasant. I have to know though; I can't let this sit forever. Swiping the screen, I bring up the message.

Emma: Clients are canceling left and right.

What the hell is going on?

They mentioned Patrick??? How do they know about Patrick?

For a long time, I stare at the texts, unsure what to say. I have to tell her sometime about what's on the news. It's not like anyone in her generation ever watches anything outside of Netflix, so unless I go viral, she's never going to happen across it. I text her back. She clearly hasn't seen the news, the speculation about my parents, their show, my missing husband—and what that means for me.

Me: It's a long story. I'll tell you the next time I see you. Do we have any bookings left this week?

Emma: Two. That's it. Tell me what's going on.

How do they know about Patrick?

My chest tightens as I consider what to say and how to say it. Emma isn't in charge here. I don't have to explain myself to her, but at the end of the day, she could be the nail in my coffin with everything that's going on. She could say I wasn't the doting wife, that I didn't give Patrick what he needed—that I was the one to blame in all of this. That's why, despite everything, I've done what I can to stay on her good side.

Me: We'll talk later. Now isn't a good time.

The moment I send the text, my phone buzzes with a call from Emma. She's never been one to take a hint. I click the button on the side of my phone, silencing her, and I wish that I could do the same when she's in front of me.

I'll face Emma eventually, but for now, I've got to plan what I'll say to her and when.

7

The whole night, instead of enjoying my day off, I wallowed and cursed Patrick's name. Maybe I should have made more calls, texts, or social media posts. But I couldn't bring myself to do any more than hate him—than question what else I might have missed. After I drink my coffee, I finally have the nerve to look for Patrick's old phone to get pictures of him. If I was a better wife, I'd have more recent pictures of him on my phone, but I don't like hoarding images like he does. And he always complains when I take pictures of him. In the past, I thought that he didn't like being photographed, maybe because of some childhood trauma, but now that I know he was taking pictures with his mistresses, I wonder if he just didn't want many records of our time together.

I search all of his drawers in the bedroom but find nothing—I know he had an old iPhone lying around somewhere, he made a fuss about not wanting to trade it in. Next, I head down the hall to his office and start to search through the rest of his drawers. Beneath old files, hidden away at the bottom of the last drawer, I find a stack of papers held together with an alligator clip. I flip through the papers, trying to discern what they are.

Halfway through the stack, I realize they're documents for the failed business Patrick shared with Lucas. All of it's here, the itemized statements, tax information, the blueprints of his failure. Beneath the stack, I find more sheets that are bound together. They're similar, but this is for a different business, one I've never heard of. My chest tightens as I look through them. Stacks upon stacks of lies. Patrick had more failed businesses, ones he never told me about.

Maybe I should talk to Lucas to get his take on what happened. Patrick lied about everything else. I can't believe him about the businesses.

At the bottom, I find the most recent business, another that he had with Lucas. Patrick is thousands of dollars in debt. I know I should hope that my husband is alive. But honestly, with all this piled up in his name, it's probably kinder to him if he's dead. I glance back into the drawer and find another bundle. This one is different from the others, lighter.

All I have to do is glance at them to know what they are. Divorce papers, and a sticky note warns me they're supposed to be delivered to me in a week. I imagine Patrick smirking as he planned to have me blindsided.

Can you divorce a missing man? If so, I'll sign the papers now.

It takes me twenty minutes to recover enough to find a picture of Patrick on Facebook to send to Cameron. I've given up on finding the old phone. After I send the picture, I ask him to come over after my sessions. Somehow, with everything going on, I manage to make it through the sessions without so much as a stutter. Maybe I can weasel my way through these meetings but putting on the mask of a concerned wife is the most unnatural thing in the world. There's so much hurt and rage simmering beneath the surface, I know I can't face the media. I can't pretend that everything is okay. Patrick isn't just missing, he destroyed everything, but that's a truth I can't spell out for everyone else. I can't admit that I was a failure, that I couldn't keep him happy.

My phone buzzes on the table next to me, and I glance at it. An email notification waits for me on the screen. *INTERVIEW REQUEST*, reads the subject line. As I scan the small snippet of a preview, I see that the email is from Denise, requesting an interview with me to discuss the scandal that's growing around my parents—she's used the email address from my website that I list for my clients. My anxiety kicks up a notch and a sour feeling blooms in my stomach. Can't they understand that I don't know much about my parents' life, the show they had? Sure, I was aware of it, but it's not like I was their business manager.

That thought sparks something inside me, and I realize that I should call Jansen, my parents' manager. Maybe he has some clues as to what this journalist might find. I dig through the contacts in my phone to find his number, then click on it. He answers on the second ring.

"Adele, how you doing, kid?" he asks, just like he did when I was seven—as if in his mind I haven't aged at all. He's got to be pushing sixty now, does he think that I stayed a child? Then again, he hasn't seen me since the funeral.

I guess the news hasn't reached him about Patrick, so I decide to skip that update. That will detract from the real reason I'm calling. "I was hoping to talk about my parents. Do you have a few minutes?"

The pause that thickens on the other end of the line tells me that he doesn't have a few minutes, but he also doesn't have the heart to tell me so. Instead of brushing me off, he clears his throat.

"Sure, of course," he says, but there's still hesitation in his tone. "What's this about?"

"A journalist approached me. They were telling me that they'd discovered some things about my parents—some things I should be concerned about when it comes to the show." I pause for a moment, giving him the opportunity to jump in—when he doesn't, I continue. "I was hoping that maybe you could fill in the blanks for me. Did I miss something? Is there something I should know?"

"No, of course not," he says a little too quickly. At least with him, my instincts are still sharp. "Look, I've got to run, but stay in touch," he says, and he ends the call.

I'm left reeling, trying to digest what was said—and more importantly, what wasn't. I weave back through the house, past the living room, the kitchen, and down the hall to the bedrooms. As I go back downstairs and pass Patrick's office, a flicker of something catches my eye. I stop and turn to inspect the room from the doorway. The movement draws my attention and in the split second my brain has to process it, sweat prickles on my neck. Was someone watching me? I rush to the window. But by the time I get there, there's no one outside. If someone was there at all.

———

Cameron knocks on my door at six, exactly when I asked him to. He's dressed in plain clothes, not his uniform, and thank God. The last thing I need is the news seeing a cop show up on my doorstep again. I open the door and I don't bother with pleasantries. Instead, I pass him the divorce papers and wait for him to follow me into the living room. For a long moment, he stands on the stoop reading them before following. The couch swallows me and Cameron sits across from me, as if he's keeping a careful distance. His eyes are still on the papers.

"He must have been planning this for a while," I say. He obviously planned to have the papers show up after he disappeared. "Damn coward," I mutter.

"I think we should go somewhere and talk about this. And I

have a feeling you need to get out of this house. Have you eaten today?"

I must look like a wreck if he can tell that I haven't eaten or left the house. Every minute that passes, I swear I get an inch shorter. I cave in on myself a little bit more. The weight of all this, Patrick, my life crumbling, it's going to do me in. I can feel it. I've never failed quite so entirely before—it makes me wish I hadn't built my life on this dynasty. If I wasn't the descendant of psychology royalty, none of this would matter—I could grieve properly, but instead of being able to process this, I know this could get so much worse. I could lose my career, the life I've worked so hard to build.

"No. Are you sure we should grab food?" The warnings of yesterday echo in the back of my mind. I need to keep up appearances, to look like a concerned wife.

"We'll go somewhere low-key. We need to go over the papers and some other stuff that we've found." His expression is grim, and my mind goes over his words again and again.

My stomach churns with unease. I'd rather know what the *other stuff* is now. But I can tell by his stance, the crossed arms, his feet set as wide as his shoulders, that he's not budging on this.

"Yeah. Let's go," I say, though I don't want to leave this house. The more I'm out in public, the higher the chance that I'll slip up. But can I really stay trapped in here forever?

I throw on some clothes, run a brush through my hair, and meet Cameron outside in his car. As Cameron starts the engine, I buckle my seat belt and lace my hands together in my lap. My body feels stiff, and I stare straight ahead. It's awkward being next to him now, after all this time.

"You okay?" Cameron asks as he glances at me. "You seem really tense."

I roll my shoulders as if it will do me any good—it doesn't. Stress curves my shoulders inward, as if there's a weight sitting on the top of my spine. "Just didn't sleep well," I say, because I know it's the answer least likely to lead to any follow-up questions. Right now, I have to guard every single word that leaves my mouth. Lies usually come so easily, but now I'm off-kilter.

"You mind if we go to Mack's?" he asks.

I shrug. It's as good a place as any. For most of the locals it's the best hot dog place in Orlando. It's a small stand, a hut really, in the middle of the parking lot, right off a busy road. It's outdoor dining only. But it's worth it. With the crowd that always lingers, we'll blend in, and I doubt anyone will notice me.

"You know I can always go for Mack's," I say as I look out the window.

"So, not much has changed then?" he asks, and though I don't look back at him, I can tell from his voice that he's smiling.

"I guess not."

It takes us about ten minutes to weave through the streets while my stomach growls. We pull up to the hut and thankfully find it nearly empty. Only two of the twenty tables are occupied.

"You wanna take a seat and I'll grab the food?" he offers.

"Sure," I say as I start to scope out the tables. I aim for one near the edge of the parking lot, huddled beneath a Southern live oak tree. Spanish moss hangs low, nearly dangling to the top of the table.

"What do you want?" Cameron calls as I walk away.

"Two hot dogs with mustard."

"Haven't changed a bit," he fires back.

I roll my eyes at him and walk toward the table I chose. If only Cameron knew how much I've really changed, how hollow I've become. As I walk, I feel Cameron's eyes on me. But I don't turn. I don't acknowledge his stare or his presence. I occupy myself with my cell phone and finally tuck it away when Cameron slides a tray onto the table.

Just like the old days, Cameron got extra food. Several orders of French fries are piled high on the tray.

"You know you don't have to worry about me not having dinner anymore," I say as I look up at him. Though, lately I haven't been great about keeping myself fed. It feels like there's a ball of stress taking up too much room in my stomach to eat.

He shrugs. "What can I say? Old habits die hard."

After my parents died, things were tough. Though my grandma took me in, she barely took care of herself—so I was very much an afterthought. A lot of days, I scrounged for food for both of us, some days, we both starved. Though I had a trust fund set up, the way my parents arranged it, I wouldn't get access until I'd graduated college. And despite being on TV, they barely had any money when they passed, so it made the years difficult.

Cameron got used to how hungry I always was when we started dating in high school. It was his goal in life, to feed me. To save me. And that's where trouble always brewed between us, because I was never the kind of person that wanted saving. The memories of those fights are still fresh in my mind. They're etched in the deepest recesses of my memories. Looking back, knowing what I know now, I was so stupid to push him away. His fault was caring too much. Mine was being the wrong kind of person for him.

"So," he says as he slides onto the bench in front of me. "We need to talk about Patrick."

I pull the divorce papers from my purse and slap them onto the table a bit harder than I mean to. Deep down, I know I'm not so much angry about the papers, as I am that he lied, hid *more* from me. The rage bottled inside me is bitter. I shift in my seat as if it will help settle me. It doesn't. It's funny how restless this all makes me.

Cameron is silent as he looks over the papers and I eat a hot dog while I watch him read. After he flips through the sheets, he looks up at me. His face is drawn, his lips tight.

"It takes four to six weeks to get divorce papers like this in the state of Florida. Could be longer though, depending on the lawyer. They have to go back and forth about settlements, alimony, financial documents, and they outlined it all here. He wanted you to get nothing. He's even going after your trust fund."

He says the words as if there's anything I could have gotten out of the divorce. Now that I've seen our finances—minus my separate accounts—I know how deep of a hole Patrick dug for us. The bank is going to take the house, unless I pay it off—Patrick had been paying the mortgage but apparently gave up and hid the statements. Our shared accounts are empty or overdrawn. What could I have taken?

The idea that he's been planning this for months, that stings. My fingers twitch and I clench my fists in response. I want to kick myself. How did I not know? How did I miss this? Every day I told him I loved him, while he was secretly planning to take everything from me. Was I really such a bad wife? Did I make him *this* unhappy? Cameron reaches across the table and squeezes my hand, as if it'll help me calm down. It doesn't, but I offer him a slight smile, as if he's appeased me. It's what he needs me to do. So, I do it and I hope I can camouflage my rage. If I don't, he'll keep trying to talk to me, to make it all better. That's the last thing that I need right now.

"Can I ask you a few questions?" he asks.

I pull my hand from his, my fingers slicking with sweat from the midday heat, and wave him on. "Yeah, go ahead," I say, though I have no desire to answer a single question. But I know I have to toe the line here, just helpful enough to not end up a suspect—that's the goal. There's also a soft spot I have for Cameron and that's difficult to balance, to ignore.

"Did Patrick have a family out of the state?"

"His mom lives in New Hampshire. And his sister just moved to New Mexico. She lived in Tennessee before that though. Why?"

"We need to make sure he didn't reach out to them and tell them where he was going," he says as he types something on his phone. "Or he could be staying with them."

I unlock my phone and bring up the info for his mother and sister, even though I already called them and included their info in the first list I gave him, then let Cameron take them down. Maybe he overlooked it. After my last conversation with them, I have no desire to ask them any more questions about Patrick. They called back and left me voicemails that showed they weren't worried about Patrick, he'd done this before. *Good, then*, I told myself. They've never seen me as family. And thankfully, now they'll never have to.

"Thank you," he says. "What was his relationship with them like?"

I look at the table as I try to find the right words. "They weren't close at all. He actually made a point to keep them out of our lives as much as possible." He's always kept them at such an arm's length. Knowing that familial issues are a major stressor for most people, I never pressed the issue. Everyone has their own reasons for why they distance themselves. I never even met them. "I'm sure if you call them, they can fill you in. Patrick never told me much about them." Maybe I should have pressed, done my own research. I guess when you lose your own family, you never think twice about it when someone else has lost theirs—whether from death or by choice.

"It's going to take me a while to dig through all of the contacts you gave me." He looks up and there's a spark behind his blue eyes, like he just remembered something.

"Do you have any leads at all? Any idea where Patrick is?"

He shakes his head. "We're no further along than when we

started." He presses his lips together and glances toward the parking lot. "You want to get out of here?"

I nod. Though the sun is starting to sink toward the horizon, it's still hot against my back and I'd like nothing more than to be in the air conditioning again. As we walk back to the car, I catch Cameron looking at me. But I ignore it. We hop in his car and he turns to me.

"It's for the best, you know? Everything happens for a reason," he says, his voice rising in pitch over the blasting air conditioner.

And I appreciate the gesture. But is that what a cop should be saying to the wife of a missing man? Cameron is good at generic pep talks.

We get back in the car and he starts the ten-minute drive back to my house. As he drives, I ask, "Where are you living now?"

"Over on Bumby, in my uncle's old house."

"That sea foam-green atrocity?" I ask and can't help but laugh. The house always looked completely out of place. Cameron's uncle lived on a busy street lined with small wood-frame houses, built in the fifties. They're all painted pastel colors, like a bag of Easter M&M's. But for whatever reason, his uncle decided to paint his house bright green. It looks like a bungalow on the beach. Though Orlando is close to the water, it's not really a beach town like Cocoa, Key West, or Miami. No one *comes here* for the beach, the drive is at least an hour.

"That's the one," he says with a smile. "I can't believe you remember that."

"If you're living there, where is he?" I ask, but after the words are out, I regret them. I hope nothing bad happened to him.

He smiles and shakes his head. "He met this free-spirited woman on a casino cruise a couple years ago. They live in Nevada in one of those underground dome houses now."

"He would," I say as I laugh. Frank, Cameron's uncle, was always an *I'll go wherever the wind takes me* kind of guy. Of course he'd do something like that.

It feels good to laugh again. As sad as it is, I can't remember the last time I laughed. Time slips through my fingers that way. It's hard to believe that Cameron and I have been apart for nearly fifteen years. With him at my side, it seems like no time has passed at all. With Patrick, I was always fighting to be more interesting than everyone else he surrounded himself with—I had to fight to be interesting, to not fade into the background. No matter what I do, Cameron sees me. I don't have to fight or try. Maybe I shouldn't have tried to fight so much to be the center of Patrick's universe when I was always everything to Cameron.

He nods and looks away, his gaze lingering on traffic. "Do you miss him?"

"Are you asking me as a cop or as a friend?" I ask, my question a bit more pointed than I mean for it to be.

"As a friend."

"No," I say as I cross my arms. And I'm surprised by the truth of it. The truth that has never come easy for me. I prefer to get the truth from my patients not from myself. I wish I could make myself miss him, to feel something more than what I do. But most of the time, I'm just numb. It feels like I've been hollowed out.

"Are you glad he's gone?"

I stiffen, looking out the window as we pass a park filled with ancient twisted oak trees. This isn't something I should say to a cop *or* a friend. "I..." I start to say, but my words fall short. Am I happy he's gone? Yes and no. Yes, because in a way, it makes things easier. No, because I wish I could scream at him, throw the papers in his face, call him a cheating douchebag— and he robbed me of that. If he never comes back, if they never find him, I'll never get the chance to do it.

We turn onto my street, the row of cookie-cutter builder houses greeting us. I've always hated how these houses look together. Nothing about them is unique. The houses look like they were built on an assembly line. I never wanted to live here, but Patrick talked me into it. He loved the location; he loved the price. I wanted to live anywhere else, but in the end, he won. Because he always won.

"I don't know," I finally say, because it's easier than the truth. Lies are always easier.

He pulls into my driveway and I reach for the door.

"If you need anything, call me, okay?" he says as I pop the door open.

I nod. "I will, thanks."

I walk to my house, my chest still tight, my mind buzzing. As I reach for the door and slide the key in, the door pushes in before I even turn the key. There's no way I left it unlocked. I'm super paranoid about leaving my house unsecured. I creep inside. My stomach knots, as I question whether or not I should call Cameron. Silence pools inside the house, thickening the further I walk. It doesn't feel like anyone is here, but the imprint of them lingers. It's times like this I wish I were actually the psychic I claim to be.

Though I search each room, it isn't until I reach my bedroom that I find that something has been disturbed. Several items of clothing lie on the floor in my closet. Someone was here, going through my things.

8

A nagging feeling stirs in the pit of my stomach, like someone is still here, watching me. I've felt unsettled since yesterday, when I realized someone was in the house. I tried watching the news, but a story about an unnamed man killing himself in his home didn't do much to put me at ease. Following that story, the news turned to new revelations about my parents—a woman whose life was ruined when she found out while on my parents' show that her husband was cheating on her. She blamed my parents for her losing everything. She was institutionalized, and later paid off by the producers. Though the story is sad, my parents didn't make the man cheat, all they did was give him a platform to come clean—but it still doesn't look good for me. Now the media has turned on them, saying they were in the business of *ruining lives*. They're hinting that I did the same to Patrick too. The idea that I ruined his life instead of the other way around—it's ridiculous.

The stack of divorce papers looms in front of me. I've stared at it so long, even when I look away, I can see its sharp edges burned into my mind. There's something about knowing in your heart that your marriage is over that is so different from actually seeing the papers that will take *us* to *him* and *me*. Everything we were has dissolved over the past few days, but this is the nail in the coffin. I've tried to decide if this is worse than being erased at his work. Being erased is more of a gut punch.

At the top of the papers, the lawyer that Patrick used is listed. It's staring back at me, tempting me. This lawyer, or someone in his office, can answer questions that I have. And I can't keep ruminating on unknowns. No, I've got to do something here, and to get the information I need. I've got to dig deep into my skill set.

I grab my laptop and fire it up. It takes me thirty minutes to find licensing paperwork for a private investigator in the state of Florida, and to Photoshop it. Then the new me, Adrienne Walters, looks like a real, licensed private investigator in the state. A quick call to the office tells me that Jarred Harris—the lawyer—is out of the office for the rest of the day.

To pull this off, I have to be careful. Not only do I have to put on heavy makeup to obscure my true features, I'll be wearing a wig to change my hair. I'm too recognizable otherwise. When your face has been on the news recently, you've got to be careful. I also have to consider, what kind of outfit does a private investigator wear? I peruse my closet as I turn the question over in my mind again and again. Dress pants and a blouse … jeans and a T-shirt? The goal would be to blend in, but I do a little cursory googling of PIs to see how they dress. Button-up and jeans it is.

I climb in my car and drive toward downtown, where the lawyer's office is nestled in a craftsman bungalow house off a main drag. The house is dark green with yellow shutters and bright white trim. Gold and burgundy mums dot the flowerbeds in front of the house. The afternoon sun makes them shine brilliantly.

When I called earlier, I didn't give the secretary any hint that I was showing up today, but she was a chatty thing, telling me how lonely she was, being in the office all by herself for the day. Bingo. That's like an invitation. The only other thing I need to worry about are security cameras, but considering that this is a small office, chances are, cameras aren't something that Jarred wanted to pay for.

I pull into the parking lot next to a beat-up Ford Focus and head inside. A small porch frames the house, and I step up toward the yellow front door. In downtown Orlando, it's very common for lawyers to set up shop in old houses. Through the glass front door, I can see a young woman sitting at a desk, playing on her phone. I open the door and step in tentatively, looking for cameras. Nothing. The woman looks up and offers me a smile.

"Hello, can I help you?" she asks as she brushes bright red hair away from her dark eyes. Even behind the desk, I can tell she's tiny, probably barely five feet tall.

"I sure hope so. What's your name?" I ask as I grab my papers from my bag. It was carefully chosen for this occasion, a fake Louis Vuitton that I found online years ago for a Halloween costume. It looks real enough to the outside world, which is all it needs to do. It's a subtle statement that I'm successful. Good enough at what I do to afford luxuries, not just necessities.

"Cassie." She says her name like a question, as she flips her phone facedown on the desk. Her attention is back on me in an instant. She's much younger, probably Generation Z, so I'm surprised by her manners.

"Well, Cassie, I hope you're having a better day than I am," I say, offering her a sheepish smile.

She returns the smile. "Oh, it's not so bad."

This little exchange, it puts me on good footing. One, Cassie is in a good mood. This she's already revealed to me. Two, I let it slip that my day isn't going so well. Most people will try to fix this—especially woman to woman. By design, women are fixers, people pleasers. It's nothing we can help; we're trained to do this from a young age. It's something I try to help women work through frequently in my office, but here, I need to lean on that natural inclination.

"Look, I'm hoping you can help me out. We have a mutual client—Patrick Johansen," I explain.

"Client?" she asks as she straightens in her seat.

"Yes, I'm a private investigator. I'm helping Patrick gather information about his ex-wife for the divorce, and he doesn't want to relay the information twice. So, he recommended I just grab a copy of your files. That way we can keep him happy," I say as I hand her the papers, along with a document I forged of Patrick signing off on the release of information to me.

She takes the stack, looking them over slowly. My heart pounds. She's analyzing it much more than I expected.

"Do you mind if I make copies of this?" she asks, as she holds the papers up.

"Not at all," I chirp, though I wish she wouldn't. The less proof I was here, the better, but none of this should be traceable back to me. And with what I've done to change my appearance, it should be even more difficult.

"I'll make copies and get those files for you right away. If you want to take a seat," she says as she walks down the hall with the papers in her hands.

I take a seat in the small lobby in the front of the old house. They've kept the old charm of the house. Small built-in book-shelves hold legal tomes bound in leather. In the corner, a sad plant stands. My leg bounces as I sit back in the chair, trying to be patient. It takes every bit of restraint I have not to pace the room.

Finally, Cassie re-emerges with a folder tucked beneath her arm. A wide smile cuts across her heart-shaped face. "Got it here for you," she says as she walks across the room. I stand and meet her halfway. She hands over the folder and my heart rate immediately slows.

"Thanks again, Cassie. You've been a great help," I say.

"Anytime. Just give me a call if you need anything else. Also, please tell Mr. Johansen I said hello," she offers with a thin smile, like she doesn't mean the words at all. Ah, so she really has met Patrick then. I bet the creep tried to hit on her.

I stroll out of the office, the folder tucked beneath my arm. The information inside digs at me, begging me to take a look. I can't yet though, I need to wait until I get home. As I pull out of the parking lot, I practically feel the folder pulsing on the seat beside me. The drive home seems to take ages, and at every stoplight I have to force my fingers to remain on the wheel.

As I turn onto my street, I'm thankful that today no news vans are hovering around. I pull into the driveway, and dash into my home to shed my disguise. My phone is where I left it, on the counter in the kitchen. The tracking on these things is the worst, and I don't want there to be any digital evidence that I've been looking into the divorce papers—none of this will look good for me if I become a suspect in Patrick's disappearance. I've got several notifications of missed calls waiting for me.

I listen to the voicemails, angry clients canceling their appointments mostly. Then one call from Emma, angrier than the clients. But right now, what I have to focus on is in this folder. I crack it open and hold my breath.

Six months ago, apparently that's when this all started. When Patrick decided it was time to chuck me to the side once and for all. There are notes back and forth between him and the lawyer trying to decide what I *deserve*. Nothing—obviously. Emails are strewn throughout detailing how Patrick felt I squandered all the money, I ruined his businesses, I cost him everything. *I* got us into debt. *I* destroyed the life we were supposed to be building together. Oh, the lies. All of them. Patrick is detailing what he did to me, as if I were the villain. It doesn't take long for me to see the accusations that *I* drove him into the arms of another woman.

I feel sick seeing it all like this. My fist clenches at my side. It's unfair that I couldn't defend myself. Patrick deserves whatever he gets for this. I wish I could find him and kill him. Maybe then I'd feel better. Right now, I'm not sure he'll ever get what he deserves.

———

From my kitchen, I hear the sound of someone stomping their way up my porch. My palms slick with sweat. Is it another reporter coming to drag me through the mud? Cameron? Emma? There are too many unpleasant options that could await me on the other side of the door. My whole body is tense as I await the inevitable knock. I creep forward, hoping to get to the peephole before my visitor can make their presence known.

I look out and catch Emma holding her phone to her ear, pacing back and forth. She's practically growling into the phone, but through the door I can't make out what she's saying. I crack the door open and stand with my arms crossed as I wait for her to finish her call.

"Instead of canceling, it would be much smarter to reschedule. Right now, we're booking Adele's appointments at least three mon—" she says, frustration dripping on every word. "No, I'm not calling you stupid. That's not what I said—I just..." She goes silent and stops in her tracks. Her gaze cuts to me, as if she could feel me watching. There's a wild look in her eyes, and I know I'm in for a piece of her mind. "I understand," she finally says, after I expect she lets the other person speak. It looks like she's finally learned some customer service. She ends the call and stalks toward me.

"What the hell is going on, Adele?" she snaps, her words practically stabbing the air between us.

"Did you finally make the calls stop forwarding to me?" I ask. "I was getting cancellation requests all day yesterday."

"I know, I needed a break. Every single person that had an appointment within the next two weeks has canceled," she says as she crosses her arms and narrows her eyes. When she looks at me like this, I know she thinks intimidation will get her what she wants. That's why I don't think she's ready to see patients yet on her own—not that she's finished her degree. She can't read the room; she has no patience. Again and again, her temper is her downfall.

"Emma, have you seen the news?" I ask, knowing what she'll say, but I've got to set the stage for what I'm going to tell her.

A humorless laugh slips out of her and she looks rather feral, too much teeth exposed, eyes wide. "Of course I don't watch the news. What would be the point of that?" Her final words are almost a question. Almost.

Before all this started, admittedly I didn't watch it often either. Once your husband disappears, your parents' legacy is called into question, and the police start sniffing around, a news-pulse check on how demolished your life actually is becomes necessary.

"You might want to. A few things have happened," I explain.

Emma's temper doesn't scare me. Not physically anyway. I know that there's nothing she can do to me. This though, the intimate details she knows about my life, that changes things. There's a reason I've never kicked her to the curb. She could sink me with a few words. She's seen Patrick and me fight a few times. She knows we've had some issues in the past. She heard about Patrick's business failing, the fallout. So, I have to play this carefully. I'm worried that maybe she could paint a picture that I was never a loving wife, that Patrick's disappearance is my fault. I have to stage-manage her. I have to protect my image, the legacy that I'm carrying.

"Like what? Are the reporters sniffing around because Patrick went missing? Are people canceling because you could have had something to do with that?" she asks as she straightens. In the shade of the porch, backlit by the sun glowing on my half-dead lawn, her eyes look almost black.

"Not exactly. I'm sure people are saying that, but that's not the main issue here. The day that Patrick disappeared, someone informed the news that my parents may have covered up things that happened because of their show. That they may have done some bad things." The timing is still so interesting to me. How the hell did both of those things happen so closely together? Would it still have happened if Patrick didn't disappear? Are they somehow connected?

She steps forward, her cheeks painted red. "And you're just now telling me this? What the fuck, Adele?" she snaps. Her words practically cut the air as she hurls them at me.

"There was a high chance that it'd all blow over after five minutes of coverage. It's local news, they normally get distracted by a hurricane or a tourist losing their wallet. I didn't think my story would be part of the news cycle for this long. How they have this much to talk about is completely beyond me," I say, but I know they're still covering it. There's literally nothing else for them to talk about right now. "Now that they've got my parents' story and Patrick, I'm sure they're going to track down every damn person that's spoken to me for more than five minutes in the past ten years."

"What's your plan then? What are we going to do?" she asks, some of her anger fading as her arms fall to her sides. Maybe the reality of what this could do to both of us might be sinking in for her. It's not just my ass on the line here.

"I want to lie low; I'll do whatever sessions I can for now. Stop telling anyone that bookings are months out. We will take whatever we can get," I explain. Even if we can keep half of our normal income rolling in, we'll both be fine. I just have to be very careful about who I see and where I go. "If we keep doing this though, we have to make sure there are no slip-ups. I can't be doing any sessions with someone that's a reporter."

She nods and takes out her phone, like she's making some notes.

"See if anyone that has an appointment booked next month wants to move theirs up," I say. I've thought through our options here, and I think this is the best we can do. It's either this or shut down for God knows how long.

"Are you sure this is going to work?" Emma asks. Most of the wind has been knocked out of her sails. That's all I needed to do. For now, I've won.

"It better. Let's get to work."

9

A rare drizzle shrouds Florida, making it feel more like New England than the tropical climate I'm used to. Most of our storms roll through fast, but this rain is lingering. The air is thick with moisture, cloaking the street, so I can barely see the end. The palm tree standing sentinel at the end of the driveway is heavy with rain, making the fronds droop. I need to grab the mail, but the weather is making me second-guess it.

A man clearing his throat startles me. I cross my arms reflexively over my chest and stumble back. How long has he been watching me? Lucas steps toward me from my driveway. He's got about a foot on me, and it's always surprised me that, though he has a very muscular build, he never played football. Seeing him here like this is startling. He's pretty much the last person I expected to see here.

"Lucas," I say, my voice more unsteady than I'd like.

He walks closer, his sharklike stare centered on me. His thick brow shadows his already dark eyes. "Where's Patrick?"

"I called you the other day. He's missing. We still haven't heard from him." I raise a brow as I rehash our conversation. Has he started drinking again? Did it slip his mind?

He shakes his head. "So, that wasn't all some kind of stunt then?"

"A stunt?" I echo. He's confusing me. Why would this be a stunt?

"Missing, huh?" he asks with his hands in his pockets, and rocks back and forth from his heels to his toes. "That sounds just like him. Or did he tell you to say that?"

I shake my head. "No, we didn't have the kind of relationship that would make me lie to you for him. I never did that before, so I'm not sure why you'd think I'd start now," I say, surprising myself with my honesty. Does he really think that I'd play some kind of game with Patrick where we tried to convince him that Patrick was missing? Why would I even go along with that?

He looks down at the driveway, then back up to me, his gaze sharper than ever. "You should think real hard about what side you want to be on here, Adele. You know what Patrick was up to, what he was capable of. If you don't tell me where he is, I'll assume that you're picking his side, that you want into this as deep as he did."

My mind reels. I have no idea what he's talking about. Did Patrick lie to Lucas about the kind of relationship he had with me? I thought that he confided in him, that Lucas was the one person he actually opened up to. That's the view I was given anyway. "I have no idea what you're talking about," I say, frustration clipping my words. Desperation claws at me. I need answers. There are too many missing pieces of this puzzle, and all I want is for someone to fill in the blanks for me.

He shakes his head, like he's disappointed in me. "When you speak to Patrick next, tell him that it's caught up to him, that he can't escape it this time. I won't let him."

"What the hell are you talking about, Lucas?" I ask as my heart pounds. The anger edging on his words, his stance, it makes me uneasy. I move back automatically, though I don't mean to.

Lucas doesn't say another word, he just glances up at the house, like he expects Patrick is watching from one of the windows, before he turns and stalks back to his car.

I pull my phone out of my pocket and text Tara about the interaction. It was so strange; I have to tell her about it. Once I'm sure that Lucas is gone, I cross my driveway, drizzle clinging to my hair with every step. A pile of mail awaits me inside the mailbox. I grab it before dashing back toward the front door. Inside, the chill of the rain still clinging to me, I sort through the damp envelopes. Bills, probably all of them telling me that Patrick didn't pay—again. My blood pressure shoots up just from looking at them, making my head pound.

In the middle of the stack I find an envelope without a return address or a stamp. Someone must have shoved this into my mailbox. I deposit the bills on the dining table, then slide my finger beneath the flap of the mystery envelope and open it. Inside, I find a folded slip of paper.

Karma is going to get you bitch. And if it doesn't, I will.

10

I tap my phone on my leg as I try to calm myself, but being in this house alone makes me antsy. After the letter yesterday, the sneaking suspicion that someone has been in my house, it's hard to be here by myself. Patrick has been gone over a week, and I thought by now we would know something. But I find myself constantly on edge. Like I'm waiting for something to drop. I know I should get out of the house, but I've been lingering here for fear of encountering an angry customer or the media. This morning, I did a session, it was short, and my client is thinking about divorce and wanted to talk it through with someone. It went as well as it could, but I still feel unsettled.

My phone dings with a text from Emma.

We NEED to talk.

Call me NOW.

Though I hate for Emma to scream *jump* and I ask *how high*, in this case, I know I have to call her. I select her contact info in my phone. She answers on the first ring.

"It's about time you called," she says, anger hanging on her every word.

I want to snap that she texted me seconds ago, but instead, I grind my teeth together. "What do you need, Emma?" I ask, as I pick at a rough edge on one of my fingernails.

"You sent the police after me?" Her words tiptoe a line between a question and an accusation, kicking up a notch at the end.

A laugh almost bubbles out of me. Almost. Confusion hits me. "You can't be serious."

"The police showed up at my house asking me all kinds of questions about Patrick," she says, venom still thick on her words.

"Of course they did. I gave them access to his phone records to see if they could trace him. I'm sure if you two were in contact"—I say carefully, because I saw that he called her on the phone logs I already pulled—"then they'd reach out to you. I'm sure they've called everyone he spoke to in the past six months. You were here daily. You saw him *daily.*"

"If I find out that you pointed them in my direction, I'll spread so many lies about you to the media you'll never be able to work in this country again."

Her threat hangs in the air long after she's hung up. This is a side of Emma I haven't seen before. She's always been supportive, helpful as an assistant. But threatening me? That's not something I ever would have expected.

Scrolling through my contacts on my phone as my head throbs from the conversation with Emma, I tap on Tara's number. Tara is my oldest friend. We actually met before I dated Cameron. Tara and I met the first day of high school and ran from the school security guard while we tried to sneak a cigarette. We've been friends ever since.

The phone rings three times before she says, "Oh, so your

bitch ass didn't up and fall off the earth." I realize I haven't spoken to her in days, not since we spoke about Ashlee.

I know why she's annoyed: I haven't been the most responsive to her texts. After all, I have a lot going on. Though I've texted her when I could, I haven't been the best about responding. "I missed you too," I coo as I walk to the bedroom and look for an outfit. "How have you been?"

She lets out a sigh. "Oh, you know. Wonderful. Everything is fantastic." Her words are dripping with sarcasm. "Please tell me you called to get me out of this house," she pleads. Two years ago, Tara's mother-in-law moved in with her and her husband, Peter. Though they get along—mostly—Tara doesn't want to live anywhere within a thousand miles of her mother-in-law. Right now though, she's got a short reprieve, since her mother-in-law is visiting her other kids in Maryland.

"It just so happens, I did," I say as I thumb through my closet, and I can't help but smile.

"Thank God," she says so loudly in my ear I have to pull the phone away for a moment.

"It needs to be a bit low-key though. Just wine or something," I say as I grab a black sleeveless shirt with a deep V-neck. And a tight pencil skirt to match. I look a bit bloated for the skirt, but to hell with it. I usually wear bright colors on my billboards, so I'm hoping a black outfit will help me blend in.

"Why?" she asks, dragging the question out like she's suspicious of me.

"I'd rather tell you in person."

"Oh God, you're pregnant," she says, and I can hear the horror beneath her words.

"Ugh, no. I'm not pregnant. You know that's never going to happen," I say as I bristle, as if her words might curse me. "Just get over here as soon as you can." I hang up the phone so I can avoid any more awkward questions from her. Tara doesn't do well with surprises. If I didn't end the call, there'd have been follow-up questions and scenarios.

Tara makes it to my house in half an hour and when she knocks on the door, she holds her side like she jogged the entire way. Her car sits outside, so I know that's not the case. She's got on yoga pants and a shirt that looks like she's had it on for the better part of a week. Her brown hair is yanked back into a greasy ponytail.

"Did you just run a marathon or something?"

She laughs. "I came as quickly as I could. What's up?" She eyes me up and down. "Okay, so I'm underdressed. I'm going to need to borrow something from your closet."

Everything I have will swallow her, she knows that. But if she needs clothes, she can borrow them. I wave her into the house, lock the door behind her, then lead her through the house. I cross my arms and lean against the doorway between the kitchen and the living room, trying to find the words I need for her.

"The police were here." This part shouldn't be a surprise to her, I told her this much. But there was a big piece I left out. I didn't tell her that Cameron was here. "They've been asking questions about Patrick. Sniffing around. The media is up my ass." I sigh, trying to rid myself of stress that's been weighing me down. I've called and given Tara a few updates, but for the most part, I've tried to keep the burden of this on myself. I can't do it anymore though.

"Are you okay?" She blinks and furrows her brow. "What happened?"

I tell her everything that I've already told the cops word for word. Though I've gone over the words a thousand times, they don't come out that way. My voice hitches just enough that it sounds like I've got real emotions lingering beneath the surface. But what do I really feel about this? Nothing. Where my anguish should be, there's a void. Maybe it's fitting. Patrick hollowed me out, and what he left, this shell of a person, she just doesn't know how to care anymore. After I've got all that out, I go on to my parents, what the news is dragging out about them. Though it feels good to get it out, I hate dumping it on her.

Her eyes go wide. "Wait, Cameron, as in your old Cameron?"

I nod sharply. I should have texted her that detail. "That's the one."

"Holy shit, he's back?" she asks as she chews on her thumbnail. She paces the room like a caged animal, and I can't help but wonder why she's reacting like this. It's not like she gave two shits about Patrick. She commiserated with me about what an asshole he was on a regular basis.

"Apparently he's been back for a few months. I had no idea until he showed up here." I wave her down the hall and back to my bedroom. While we talk, I need her to get dressed so we can get out of this house.

I let out a shuddering breath, and I go over everything else that's happened, the papers, the cheating, the stuff with his job, business partner, debt, foreclosure. Tara dives into my closet, and I chew my bottom lip.

"Seriously? We knew Patrick was up to something, but this?" She pokes her head out of the closet, three shirts folded over her arm. She clenches her fist, which peeks out from the pile of clothes, and her lips press into a thin line. "So, it wasn't with Emma then, like you suspected?"

"Apparently not." I grind my teeth together. How did I not see it all? I'm the queen of recognizing double lives. How did he pull the wool over my eyes for so long? Love makes us do such stupid things.

"So, wine?" she asks, and I nod eagerly. It takes about three seconds for her to shed her yoga pants and T-shirt before putting on a new outfit.

We walk side by side to her small Mazda. Her husband has been hounding her to get a large car for years. But I know she won't give it up. It serves as a good excuse to not invite her mother-in-law out. I think she's also solidifying her stance on not having children with her vehicle of choice.

We carve through the city making small talk, to a small bar that will allow us to avoid the media, and I fill her in on my conversation with Emma. Tara tells me for the five-hundredth time to fire her, but I can't do that. I need someone to help me handle the calls, my appointments—it won't look good if I'm doing it all myself. It takes a few minutes for us to leave my neighborhood and pull through the historic section of Orlando.

When we pull up in the parking lot, I let out a sigh of relief when I see that it's nearly empty. The last remnants of the afternoon heat linger in the air as we walk to the door. The rustic interior greets me as soon as we enter, the warm hues of the oranges and wood putting me at ease. Brick arches frame the bar in the back of the restaurant. To the right of it, a full wall of wine bottles is nestled into wooden shelves. Small tables are scattered throughout the open space. Thankfully, it's nearly empty, so we won't have to sit at the bar and watch what we say. We get a table, order our wine and tapas. I catch her up on the investigation and the situation with Cameron.

The door opens, drawing my attention from the conversation. A slim woman slips in through the door and walks toward the front of the restaurant. She's got shoulder-length blonde hair that's stick-straight. Her blue eyes are a little too big for her head, framing her thin nose. Tara taps me on the arm.

"That bitch," she hisses.

The words make it click in my mind. Brynlee, *that bitch*. I know it's stupid that I'm angry with her. Chances are she didn't even know he was married—if he didn't tell his coworkers about me, why would he tell this woman? I feel like every time Patrick left the house he started living a brand-new life, one where I never existed. Rage bubbles inside me, but my training tells me that it's misplaced; I want to take it out on Patrick—he deserves this anger.

"Wait, is she—" Tara starts, but the words die on her lips.

"Is she what?" I ask finally, once my mind catches up.

"Pregnant."

I suck air in through my teeth like I've been punched, though I don't mean to. I shouldn't stare. A normal person would look away, play it cool, but I can't. My eyes sharpen as I survey her every curve. Though I don't mean to, I compare them to my own. She's got the kind of body men dream about, that mid-twenties frame, pinched in all the right places. I hate that I wish I looked like her, that I had whatever it is that she has that's lured him in. I lash myself again for not being enough, for not holding his interest. Even though I scour every inch, I see no evidence that she's pregnant.

"No, she's not," I say a little too defensively.

Tara clucks her tongue and I glance at her to see that *oh honey* look on her face that she reserves for people she pities. The look stings.

"Anyway, let's get back to Cameron," she says, pulling her attention away from Brynlee.

It takes me a minute to shift gears, to tear my gaze away from the girl. "You know as well as I do that Cameron deserves better than me. Better than this goddamn town." The words come out with a venom I don't expect. But it's the truth. Cameron has never deserved the baggage my life comes with, the media attention, the scrutiny. I knew that Patrick could handle it, the social butterfly that he was, but Cameron was different—I wanted to protect him from it all.

"Yeah, well, he doesn't want better. He's always wanted you. That should count for something."

I sip my wine as I let her words ruminate. I should call her a bitch, but I don't. "You talk like you've spoken to him recently," I say, a bit more suspiciously than I mean to.

"I talked to him about six months ago. We catch up every now and then," she says as she pops a piece of a chip in her mouth, her thin lips disappearing as she chews.

"Oh?" I ask as I straighten in my chair. She's never mentioned this to me.

"Mmhmm. And I will tell you, there's only one thing he ever wants to talk about," she says as she takes a sip of wine. "And I bet you can guess what that is."

I say nothing and wait for her to confirm my suspicions.

"You. All he ever talks about, asks about, is *you*," she says, her eyebrows peaking as she speaks.

I cock my head. If he's been thinking about me that long, I could use that to my advantage. "So, what did you say the last time you two talked?"

She looks away and for a fleeting moment, I think she's going to keep me in the dark about it. The words I might say to pry the information from her roll around in my mind, flit across my tongue as silence brews between us. "I told him that you were sad."

"That I'm sad?" I ask, my voice suddenly seeming too loud for the quiet room. I scan the tables nearest us to make sure no one heard me. But if anyone heard, they make no indication they did.

She nods slowly. "That's the only way I can really describe it. You're always sad now, distant. You're a shadow of who you were before you married Patrick. I know the old you is in there somewhere, buried beneath the layers of protection. I want you to be able to shake this off, to be you again," she says as she squeezes my hand. I want to pull away, to distance myself from her, from her words. But it won't make them any less true. It won't change anything. The reason we've always gotten along is because we don't lie to each other. And I don't want it to start now. "I don't want you to become the sum of everything that Patrick did to you. I don't want his betrayals to cut you so deep that you never heal. You gave him so many years already, don't give him more."

The weight of her words crushes me. I hate that she's right again. That she knows me so well. It kills me though that Patrick—the man who was supposed to love me—didn't see this change. I can't say that I haven't felt the pieces of me drifting away all these years like icebergs. I knew it was happening, but sometimes, it's so easy to rationalize, little sacrifices, giving up who we are bit by bit—that's what you're supposed to do in a relationship after all, isn't it? When every day you give up a piece of yourself for the person you love, you have to ask yourself at some point, who it is they love? Does he even see me? "I'm sorry," is all I can manage to say.

"You have nothing to be sorry for. This isn't your fault. This is his fault, and don't you forget it," she says as she offers me a smile. And though I don't really have it in me, I manage to smile back, if only for her.

I sip my wine until warmth spreads from my stomach and I'm able to dull the anxiety coiling inside me. It would be such a mercy if I could shuck off my life with Patrick like old skin and pretend that none of it happened.

"Can we talk about something else?" I ask, desperate to shed this dread circling me.

She fills me in on the struggle of fighting with her mother-in-law over a kitchen remodel. I want to smile at the banality of her problems, everything. As much as she hates her mother-in-law, she loves her husband fiercely, in a way that makes me wonder if I've ever really loved anyone at all.

As we're finishing up our wine and getting ready to leave the bar, my phone rings and I glance at the screen. An unfamiliar number flashes across it for a moment. I reject the call, suspecting it's spam. But once the voicemail notification dings, I press the phone to my ear and a woman's voice crackles through the static—I can't make out much. The words and her anger are sharp. But the one thing I can hear, the one thing I'm sure of, is Patrick's name.

———

The scant moonlight hides me and my car as I roll down the backroads of Orlando. My phone is at home, giving me an alibi. Should I ever need it. The layout of the route I need to take is burned into my mind, as if I don't already know the city like the back of my hand. On both sides of the car, shadows of old wood-frame houses paint the street. Seeing the city like this, it's like all the beauty has been muted.

My destination is two streets away. Somehow, Brynlee has been able to afford renting a four-bedroom old colonial downtown that I'm sure will make a beautiful Airbnb one day. I have a feeling that many of the Venmo payments on our credit cards went to her so she could pay her rent.

Three minutes, two turns, and I make it onto Brynlee's empty street. Her neighbors are all in bed, their lights off, not even a flicker of a TV in a window. It's odd for a neighborhood downtown to be this quiet, but I take that as a positive omen.

I roll my car to the end of the street and pull into the driveway of a house that's for sale, but currently unoccupied, according to the online listing. The night air is balmy when I slip out. This time of the year in Florida is fickle. Some nights are cool, some are so humid it's hard to breathe. I don't mind the heat, I've lived my whole life with it, but the humidity makes me wonder what it'd be like to live up north.

The walk down the street is short, the tree branches popping above me as a slow wind whispers through the night. When I make it to Brynlee's house, my heart is pounding, and I'm unsure if it's my nerves or a testament to how out of shape I am. Maybe it's both. I stroll under the large oak tree that shades Brynlee's lawn.

Inside, she's sleeping in the same spot where I'm sure he slept. I let the night and my rage swallow me as I step toward the house.

A breath of wind rustles the trees around me, their branches casting long spidering shadows on the siding. Hairs rise on the back of my neck, like someone is watching me. Swallowed by the night as I am, there's no way anyone can see me, but yet, a question still blooms in the back of my mind. *Am I really alone out here?*

Behind me, a branch snaps and my heart creeps into my throat. The letter, the signs someone's been in my house, the dead woman on the news, it all flashes through my mind at once. I shouldn't be out here.

The unmistakable thud of a boot on earth sounds to my left, where the snapping came from. My breaths threaten to come out too loud, but I force my lips closed as I press my back to a nearby tree. The faint light of the moon outlines a figure shifting in the night. I try step back, the bark of the tree biting into my flesh. I'll take blood, bruises, whatever I have to, to not be seen.

A man slinks through the darkness like a cat, looking between the two houses. I slide to the right, keeping my back to the tree. I need to get out of here. My heart pounds, threatening to crack through my rib cage. As I step back, the figure stops, and turns, as if scouring the darkness for me. I freeze, certain that from where I stand, half-hidden by a tree, I must be visible.

The figure turns away again and continues toward the house. The moment he rounds the corner, I bolt toward the street and back to my car.

11

I sit outside Lucas's house with a thousand questions piling up in my mind. The morning sun makes the dew wink on all the blades of grass that dot the lawns on this street. I've already asked myself several times if I should be here, if I really want to do this. I try to stare out the windshield to the street that's littered with new-build houses that are so similar they look copy-pasted. Orlando proper is filled with older wood-frame homes that are beautiful and haunting, then a little farther there are midcentury modern houses. But the longer you drive, the new builds pop up like anthills. They're devoid of any character, and they make my soul long to be back in the city.

I loathe these houses and the people that live in them—though I guess I'm one of them. For a few more beats, I watch drizzle freckle the windshield, then finally force myself out of the car. A large SUV sits in the driveway, the black paint, dark windows and rims mirroring the ominous skies above. The walk to the door of the large house makes my stomach shift with unease. This is the worst part, staring down the truth. I'm not sure that I want to. It could change everything. It could change nothing. But there are truths you can never forget.

I knock on the door, then cross my arms. Before Lucas showed up at my house yesterday, I hadn't seen him in months. For a while, when he and Patrick started working together, I saw him often. But that trickled away as their friendship dried up. I can't believe that I didn't pressure Patrick for more information, I just let it all go. Why did I do that? I can't even remember anymore. What did it matter anyway? He would have likely fed me more lies. I spent so much time avoiding conflict because I didn't want to end up like the people in my sessions—and yet, I still ended up here anyway.

My stomach knots as I wait. Behind me, the rain kicks up, hissing as it falls against the large oak tree that stretches above the house. The door opens slowly and Lucas peers out at me. He's a handsome man, in his late forties. Gray hair is folded in along his temples, mingling with his dark hair. His bone structure is well defined, the kind you'd see on a Greek statue, not in a middle-class neighborhood in Florida. He hasn't got the rounded belly that you expect from a man of his age; no, you can tell that Lucas spends plenty of time working out

"Adele," he says, and his words shift, like he's not quite sure of my name.

I'm still uneasy about the conversation we had yesterday, but I need to keep my wits about me, to play it cool. "Hey, sorry to just show up like this, but I was hoping I could talk to you about what you said yesterday."

He glances back into the house as he stiffens. He doesn't want to invite me inside. After a beat, he waves me inside. "Sure, yeah. Come in."

"Thanks," I say awkwardly as his veiled threat still replays in my mind.

Lucas leads me through the foyer, lined with large beige tiles, toward a living room that's overly filled with furniture. I can only describe the style as secondhand chic. Everything is mismatched and not in the cute, "this is rustic and adorable"

HGTV way. We end up in the kitchen in the back of the house. The cabinets pine, with a granite countertop that's almost yellow. With the red walls, the kitchen looks like a sunset.

"I really need more context on what happened with Patrick," I say again as he waves for me to take a seat at a small table nestled into a bay window. "I know you don't believe that he's missing. I've got no right to ask, but I need your help with this." Though I don't want to sit—I prefer to pace as I talk—especially with all the nerves wound up inside me, I assuage him and sit.

"I saw on the news that he's really missing. Sorry I blew up on you like that, but pretending to take off, that's something that I could see Patrick do," he says carefully. I'm unsure if his tone is because he's sorry for what he said or because he wants answers from me too. Either way, I can sympathize.

"As I already told you, he's been missing for over a week now. Both me and the police are looking for answers. He's left quite a mess behind."

Though I expect something to shift in his gaze or demeanor as I say those words, he doesn't so much as flinch. He grabs a couple bottles of water from the fridge, tipping one toward me, a silent gesture to ask if I want a bottle. I incline my head slightly. He sits across from me a few seconds later, passing the water over as he does.

"I can't say I'm surprised," he says, the words and his features not holding an ounce of feeling or empathy—not that I expected them to. "Are you here because you think I had something to do with his disappearance?" His eyes glimmer, a silent challenge lingering in them that seems to say, *Breathe the words that I did this, I dare you.*

"No," I say, a little too quickly, because that's really not the reason I want to speak to him. Patrick had so many secrets, a world that I knew nothing about. Lucas can clearly offer me an insight that no one else can. That's information I can't discount or take for granted. "I was just hoping that you could give me those answers."

"What questions do you have, then?" he asks before taking a sip of his water.

"Patrick didn't tell me about what really happened with the business. Why it all fell apart. I want to know what happened. The more time goes on, I find out more and more about him that I didn't know. And I'm starting to wonder if I really knew him at all." The words aren't an accidental admission. If I can tug at Lucas's heartstrings, make him realize that Patrick screwed us both over, he's more likely to give me information. I need him to think that we're on the same side.

"And why are you suddenly interested in that particular bit of information?"

Patrick gave me such vague answers about the business failing. At the time, I didn't think much of it, honestly. So many new businesses fail, I suppose I had expected it from the moment he brought up the idea. Patrick was great with ideas—he was always coming up with them—but anything that required his own hand, that's where trouble would rise. So, when he told me his business folded, I shrugged it off. Especially since he already had a job on the side. Patrick wasn't great at anything, but that was fine. Greatness wasn't what I wanted or needed from him.

"Because I've encountered a lot of inconsistencies since he's gone missing," I say, trying to keep my words even and my face blank. There's only so much information I should give him. But I know if I'm honest about the lies, he'll likely trust me enough to tell me more.

A grin, the kind more at home on the face of a predator, creeps across his thin lips. "I wondered if you'd ever see him for what he was."

I've always hated when people withhold information from me. Sure, maybe I didn't know Lucas well enough for him to tell me what he really thought about Patrick. These people always love to slink out of the woodwork when a boyfriend or friend betrays you, spewing crap about how they saw it coming.

"Obviously, I didn't until now, but I'm hoping you can help me understand him better," I say, making an effort not to grind my teeth with annoyance after every word. Though I have to keep a level head in my line of work, boy oh boy, sometimes I don't want to. The grin slips from his face for just a moment, a blink of an eye really. I feel like he's just toying with me, like he wants to see me squirm.

"The first thing you need to understand about Patrick is that he's a liar. Goddamn good one too. Took me the better part of five years to figure that out myself," he says as he takes a sip of his water.

Lucas and Patrick were friends the past five years, which was a rare thing in and of itself. Patrick seemed to have no close friends before we met, no confidants. He always had people around, but none of them saw beneath the surface. Normally, that'd be a red flag for me, but Patrick had shed his old life in New York and fled for Florida for a fresh start. It made sense that he'd cut ties with everyone. It did always stick out to me, though, that in the years that passed, no new bonds formed that were strong. Sure, he had many acquaintances, but no one really seemed to stick out until he met Lucas. It's odd for someone who's such a social butterfly to form no solid friendships.

"What did he lie about?" I ask, feeling completely blind to this portion of their relationship. Patrick spoke of Lucas often, but never mentioned lies to me. As far as I know, their relationship broke down because of the business.

"At first, little things. Stuff I didn't notice until later. Why he was late, why he didn't show for something, that he was low on cash. He told me often that you were barely pulling in any money. I felt bad for him, so I'd usually pay for drinks, lunch, whatever it happened to be," he says as he shakes his head. The look on his face tells me that he's kicking himself.

Anger flares inside me that Patrick made it sound like I wasn't pulling my weight. I made most of the money. Patrick was a liability to our accounts, not me.

"We were doing fine," I say, the sting of my rage adding a barb to my words.

His brows raise as he nods. "I'm sure you were."

"What else?" I ask, wanting to move away from the lies about me, though I'm sure there were more.

"For a while, the business was doing pretty well. I'm not sure if he told you about any of that. We had plenty of tourists wanting to come on the tours. But slowly, the money wasn't matching the amount of business that we were getting. I'm embarrassed now about how long it took me to catch it. We were coasting. I didn't think about it until the numbers really started to slide. Patrick had hired someone to manage the tours. He was changing the books so that it looked like we were getting less people on tours than we were. He was skimming a lot off the top."

Patrick was stealing money from him, from his job, from our accounts—where the hell was it all going? What was he doing with it if he wasn't paying our bills? Was he funneling it into something else or giving it to his mistress? It had to go somewhere. And it sure as hell never ended up in our accounts.

"That business failing cost me a lot, Adele," Lucas says, his eyes meeting mine.

I nod. "I know, believe me. Patrick cost me plenty too."

"No, I don't think you quite understand," he says, his voice growing grave. "I lost *everything*. I need that money back."

"I wish I could help you."

"You need to find out what he did with that money." There's an urgency to his words that's unsettling and not something I expected from him. Lucas has always been so even-tempered, but right now, he seems slightly unhinged. Like he's on the edge. Behind his eyes, something wild lingers.

"If there was money to be found, I would have found it," I say, a bit more defensive than I need to be. But I can't help it. What the hell does he really expect me to do? I'm not giving him money from my trust fund to pay for Patrick's sins. Patrick already did enough damage to my life that the trust fund is the only way that I'll recover from the damage he's done to me.

"I'm not sure I believe that. I've heard about the business you were running. Well on your way to being a TV psychologist, conning vulnerable people out of their money, just like your parents did. You weren't any better than Patrick; in fact, you might be worse."

I push my chair out and stand up. I won't sit around here and defend myself to him. I owe him nothing. I didn't take his money. No one made him start a business with Patrick. That was his own choice.

"I have to go."

"Got a pressing meeting with a widow or a divorcee that you need to pry some money out of?" he asks, his eyes darkened by the shadow of his brow. "I'm sure you can listen to their problems and *fix their whole lives for them.*"

"That's enough," I say before rushing from the room. A hand tightens around my bicep, stopping me. Lucas yanks hard, dragging me backward into the kitchen. My mind reels. He can't actually be doing this. I whip around, facing him.

His eyes are wild as they narrow on me. "You don't understand how badly I need that money back, Adele," he says as I push back, forcing him to release me.

"I'm completely broke, Lucas. He took everything I had." I growl the words at him. If he takes one more step toward me, I'll defend myself if I have to. My shoulders are tight, my arms straight at my sides as I fight with my mind. I need to get out of here, away from him. I was stupid to come here by myself and not tell anyone where I was going.

He stalks toward me, grating his jaw so hard I can practically hear his teeth grinding together. My hands raise automatically, and I shove him back, hard. It's only because I caught him off guard that he stumbles. Time seems to slow as he falls backward, and it doesn't snap back into place until I hear the hollow thud of his head hitting the floor.

I don't hesitate, or check to see if he's okay, I just run.

I'm anxious as I emerge from the house. That's not what I expected to happen. I can't believe that Lucas thinks that I have his money or that I would keep it for Patrick. He can't be hurt too bad, he probably just hit his head. In the car, I lock the door and text Tara about what happened, skipping over the parts I can't document electronically. I'm going to need her help with this.

When I pull back into my driveway, I'm still on edge. Tara's said what she can to help make me feel better, but being blindsided like this, it's not something I ever expected. How did Patrick lie to me for so long? How was I so blind to it?

I walk into my house, still uneasy, like it's not mine anymore. Though there's no real obvious sign that anyone else has been here, the air feels wrong in a way that I can't quite put my finger on. I shuck my purse onto the table in the kitchen, turn on far more lights than I need on, as if it will make me feel better—it doesn't—then head into the living room to collapse onto the couch.

A glance at my watch tells me that it's almost time for the news, and though I should stop watching it, stop exposing myself over and over when I know it won't make me feel any better, I turn it on anyway. The pit in my stomach opens up. I'm desperately hoping that there's literally anything else for them to talk about during the broadcast. Can't a dog save a baby from a fire or something? How can I really be this interesting?

The program opens with a woman sitting behind a desk, as usual. My entire body is tense as I watch, praying for the best. For the first fifteen minutes, she rattles on about traffic, the weather, local politics. Maybe I'm in the clear.

The feed cuts to a reporter I recognize, and I suck in a sharp breath. This can't be good. This is the woman who has it out for me.

"We have an update on local psychologist Adele Sutton-Johansen, whose husband, Patrick, has been missing for over a week now," the young woman says with her chin held high and a smug smile on her face. "A few days ago, news broke that a man who has now been identified as Malcom Parish killed himself the same evening that he had a session with Adele. According to Brenda Parish, Malcom's wife, she believes that Adele urged Malcom to take his own life."

"What!" I rage at the TV. "They cannot be serious. I would never have urged someone to kill themselves. This is defamation." They're tarnishing my reputation, my life.

"Adele's husband is still very much missing, his whereabouts and safety very much a concern for the general public. I reached out to local law enforcement for any updates but as of this moment they're still telling us that they cannot comment on an ongoing investigation." The woman sweeps her short hair over her ear before they cut away from her feed and show the main anchor again. With that, I shut the TV off. As annoyed as I am that they're still covering my story, it's clear they have nothing.

12

My heart pounds as a wet warmth spreads around my feet, between my toes. Though I can't stomach looking, the copper tang in the air tells me that it's blood. I wish I were brave enough, strong enough to verify it. But I've seen enough already. Nausea climbs my throat and I swallow hard to try and push it down. My hand raises automatically to my chest and a streak of red ensnares my attention. Blood. My hands are completely covered in blood.

I run for the bathroom, the hall blurring around me. I throw on the hot water, plunging my fingers into the stream. I gasp, trying to steady my breathing, and when I look down, the blood is completely gone. Both on my hands and feet. Did I imagine it? Was it a remnant of a dream, a memory? I blink away my confusion, desperate to rub my eyes, but the blood—I can't.

In my dreams, I've lost control. My whole life is spinning out of control. Everything I've worked so hard for is slipping through my fingers like water, no, like blood. My heart pounds as my mind reels. Patrick has been missing for over a week, and in that time *everything* has changed. Not in the ways I imagined it would. Not for the better. I've found so many charges on my

credit cards over the last year but none from after his disappearance. At first, he claimed the charges were all fraudulent. We
got new cards, made claims. But they became such a regular
occurrence, it was clear he was the culprit. We fought about it a
few times, but he always was so convincing that it wasn't him, I
always dropped it—too exhausted to bother. Maybe it wasn't the
best coping technique. I probably should have asked for more
proof. I should have pushed harder. I just didn't have it in me.

I flip on the news and plop down on the couch. Though
anxiety still has me firmly in its grip, I hope that the blathering
of the anchors will ease my mind. The ticker on the bottom of
the screen scrolls past as an aerial shot of a field plays on the
screen: *Cell Phone of Missing Orlando Resident Found in
Wooded Area. Unidentified Woman Found Dead on North Side
of Town.*

"Jesus Christ," I breathe. They found the cell phone and
Cameron didn't call me? Does he not know? I thought that
Cameron was still bound to me enough that he would have told
me if they found out anything new. I want to be angry, hurt that
he didn't bother to even text. But can I really be mad at that? He
was doing his job. But that just means I need to do mine better.

A headache blooms in the back of my mind as a hangover
grips me. My stomach churns. How much did I drink last night?
Everything after 8 p.m. is blurry. Hours are missing. I glance at
my phone to see if I called Tara or Cameron, but I didn't so
much as text them. As the news rambles on about the new
evidence, I walk through the house back to my bedroom and
into the bathroom. I reach for the mirror, opening it to reveal the
space behind. I grab a couple of aspirin from a bottle, then reach
for the faucet for a drink. But as I glance down, something
catches my eye. A single drop of blood waits on the edge of the
sink. I stare at it as though it will tell me all its secrets as I work
through how it would have gotten there. I reach toward it, finger
extended.

The doorbell chimes, and I nearly jump out of my skin. I glance toward the door, as if I can see through all the walls separating me from it. An electric feeling prickles in the pit of my stomach as I throw the pills to the back of my throat and walk toward the front of the house. The doorbell rings three more times.

"Jesus, something better be on fire," I grumble. I throw the door open and find Cameron pacing on my porch.

"Why didn't you answer your phone?" he asks, wide-eyed. His face is flush, sweaty.

"You didn't call me," I say as I cross my arms. I just checked my phone. There's not a single missed call on it. It's been two days since I've seen Cameron. And he hasn't called or texted. Though I've heard nothing from other officers of Orlando PD about Patrick's whereabouts, they've updated me that there are no new charges on his credit cards, as if I wasn't going over them myself. And though they've asked the media for tips, so far, all of them have led nowhere. It's not like I expected him to show up and assault my doorbell, especially not after his disappearing act and his failure to mention the cell phone to me.

"Yes, I did," he says as he glances at his phone. His tone reminds me of a scolding parent and puts me on edge. I don't need his permission to sleep in.

"No, you didn't." I throw the words at him like daggers before showing him my call log. But there it is. How did I miss it? Is time slipping through my fingers? Anger hits me hard, making me rise to the challenge. Shedding the layers of depression I've collected seems to be impossible at this point, but him arguing with me, I swear it brings the old me out for just a moment.

Cameron pushes past me to get into the house.

"Sure, come on in," I say sarcastically, after moving out of the way. I'm not normally the most welcoming in the morning anyway. But so far, in the few minutes he's been here, Cameron has pressed every button I've got. If he keeps it up, I may just deck him.

"Sorry," he says as he turns to face me. He's standing too straight, and his eyes are wild. Cameron is usually centered, well put together. It's throwing me off. If he's acting this way, then what's wrong?

I try to shrug it off. But I can't help asking. "What's wrong?"

"I need you to pack," he says as he edges farther into the living room.

"I'm sorry, what?" I ask, because I'm sure I heard him wrong. It's not like he's going to whisk me away for a weekend in Vegas or something.

"I need you to pack a suitcase." His eyes are wide, almost feral, like something is seriously wrong. He walks further into the house, and I follow him into the living room.

"Cameron, I need more to go on here. What am I packing a suitcase for exactly?" I ask, my heart kicking up to a gallop. Everything about him is off. It's making me nervous. My chest is tight with the weight of the anxiety blooming in the room.

He pinches the bridge of his nose. "I think you should sit down," he says as he waves toward the sofa.

I want to refuse. Sitting before a conversation is never good news, I should know from experience. Nothing good in my office happens when anyone is sitting down. A hundred conversations of patients being told about tragedies crosses my mind, followed by my own: the moments before I found out my parents were gone—that life would never be the same again. My throat goes dry, and all my best efforts to swallow do nothing. I perch on the edge of the couch, as if almost sitting might do something to change the news he's about to give me. I'm on edge figuratively and literally. I'm not sure what I want him to say, what I want the news to be.

Did they find him? Do they know what happened? Would it be easier if he were dead? Would I feel good about that?

Cameron sits across from me and leans his arms on his knees. He stares at the floor for a moment. The look on his face isn't one I've seen before. It's never this hard for me to read anyone, not even someone I know. I shift uncomfortably where I perch.

"We need you to pack and stay at a hotel, because we have reason to believe it's not safe for you to stay here." His voice is low, careful.

I search my mind for the right words, and it takes me too long to find them. What is he talking about? Why would it not be safe for me to stay here? I play back what I've been seeing on the news, how it's been looking for me, the threatening letter I received. I was honestly scared that they were going to think I had something to do with Patrick's disappearance—but now they think I'm in danger? From who? "What reasons?"

"We found several locations on your husband's phone that seem to be frequent stops for him." He pauses and sighs. "All I can say is that we have reason to believe that he may be a danger to you."

My brows furrow. Patrick may be a royal cheating douche, but he doesn't have a violent bone in his body. The only things he's a danger to are my heart and my sanity. But why the hell do they think he's dangerous? Where could he have gone that they'd jump to these conclusions?

"Cameron, you've got to give me more than that," I plead, and I know I'm verging on begging.

"I'm not telling you this as a cop; I'm telling you this as a friend, okay?" he asks, his voice serious. He doesn't continue until I nod. "Patrick may have killed a woman we believe was his mistress. If that's the case, he could be a danger to you as well."

"How did you know about the mistress? From his phone records?" The mistress I saw two nights ago, she's dead? Or did he have another one that he killed? I swallow hard. Did she die close enough to when I saw her for me to be a suspect? I wrack my mind for the alibi I might need. If I have to, I know I can call on Tara. If you can't count on your best friend for an alibi, then what good are they?

Cameron nods.

"How did you find the body? What happened? I need more to go on here, Cameron," I say as my mind scrambles for footing. How guilty will this make me look? I need a story and I need to piece it together fast.

"Her mom lives in Virginia and hadn't heard from her in a couple days, which was unusual. She asked us to do a wellness check, and well, that's when an officer found her." Cameron looks down. "There's more. Some news broke this morning."

I swallow hard before croaking, "News?"

"A journalist reported this morning that your parents' deaths were not what they seemed. I know you were told that they died in a car crash, that it was all just an accident."

I nod. Because that's true, they did die in a car accident. All of it was in the news. There were pictures of their car engulfed in flames. Sometimes when I close my eyes I can still see it burned on the back of my eyelids.

"Apparently, it's come out that it wasn't an accident at all, their car was tampered with. The TV station covered it all up. They didn't want anyone knowing that there was a possibility that the show led to the deaths of your parents. You could have sued them for millions," he explains.

It's hard for me to digest everything that he's saying.

"I don't know what all of this has to do with anything," I say.

"Whoever killed your parents is still out there. Patrick isn't the only danger. You're in the media now too."

His meaning all clicks into place in my mind. There could be two murderers after me right now. I bolt up from the couch and Cameron reaches out, gripping my shoulder, as if he thinks I'll fall over. I swallow down the arguments inside me, the ones that beg me to say that Patrick isn't a killer. That he'd never do anything like that. But I can't say anything, because suddenly, I'm not sure who the hell I married. Did I know this man at all? The fact that I even still feel the need to defend this man makes me sick.

Automatically, I turn toward the bedroom and walk down the hall. Cameron follows close behind.

"How long am I packing for?" I ask. I have to go along with this, so he doesn't think I killed Brynlee. It looks bad enough as it is.

"Just plan for it to be while, just in case."

I drag my largest suitcase from the closet and throw it on the bed. Without bothering to filter through options, I grab anything I touch and heave armfuls of clothes into the luggage.

Cameron mercifully waits outside while I pack. He's so tense I know his anxiety will fill the room like fog and put me on edge. As I make what feels like my twentieth trip back and forth to the bed, my toe hits something hard under the bed. Though it didn't really hurt, just startled me, I curse anyway. What the hell would there even be for me to kick? Maybe the remote fell under there last night.

I lean down, peering under the bed. It's not a remote I find. No, in the darkness I can make out something sleek and smooth, a handle maybe? As confusion muddles my thoughts, I grasp it, holding it up to the light. I suck in a sharp breath as I see red for the second time this morning. Blood and metal gleams in the buttery light of my bedroom. A knife. There is a bloody knife under my bed.

My mouth goes painfully dry as I try to swallow the bile climbing my throat. How the hell did this knife get here? After thinking I'd seen blood on my hands this morning, I'd searched the house for any signs I hadn't imagined it. And there were none. I blink, hoping that the knife will disappear like the blood did this morning. But it doesn't. The weight of it alone threatens to drag me down. What the hell am I supposed to do with this knife? Cameron's just outside, I can't get rid of it. If he sees it, I'll look so guilty. What if it's Patrick's blood or one of his mistresses?

Hide it. My subconscious screams. I could do that for now. As far as I can see, the police aren't seriously investigating me. Thankfully Patrick has cast enough doubt on himself that they don't think he's dead. Not yet. I could hide the knife in the house, and they'd never find it. Even if they searched. I run into my office through the door it shares with my bedroom, feeling like gasoline is pumping through my veins instead of blood. In the corner of my office, there's a loose bit of carpet that I've been meaning to fix but haven't. My hand shakes as I pull it back and place the knife on the floor. I step back and survey my handiwork. In the shade of the bookshelf, it doesn't look like anything is out of place.

I sneak back to the bedroom, hoping that Cameron didn't notice my absence. As I resume my rummaging in the closet once more, my bedroom door creaks open. Silence thickens in the room behind me. My heart is still pounding so loud I'm sure that he can hear it.

"Adele." Cameron says my name in almost a questioning way, like he's not sure he'll find me in here.

"Yeah?" I call back.

"Can you come out here for a sec?" he asks. When I walk out of the closet, Cameron hovers with his back to me, beside the bed. He's facing the nightstand by my side of the bed.

"What's up?" I ask.

He holds up a small slip of paper and hands it to me. I unfold the paper to find *Love you* with a heart scribbled inside. My brows furrow as I look up at him.

"It was on your nightstand, with this," he says as he points to a tiny vase with a single red rose in it. "Are you seeing someone?" The words slip out of him, and I swear I see pain linger in his eyes. If I weren't hollowed out, if I were a better person, seeing that agony on his face would do something to splinter me, but it doesn't. All I can think about are the implications of my seeing someone with a missing husband. How bad would that look? But more than that, all I can think of is the implications of that flower. How it got there. Who was in my house?

"No," I manage to choke out as the fear crowds my throat.

My face goes cold and I clutch the footboard to steady myself. The beat of my heart is thunder in my ears. How did I miss that flower? Did I walk past it and not see? Or was someone else in here with me? The thought makes my head swim as terror climbs my throat.

"Where did that come from?" I ask, as I throw the paper down so quickly, it may as well have burned me.

"I was going to ask you. The note was on top of your phone."

"It wasn't there when I woke up. My phone was on the nightstand and I grabbed it from there when I woke up." A shiver crawls down my spine. In the space of waking and now, someone was in my house. Why would someone leave that for me? Now of all times? My skin prickles and I rush back to the closet to pack the rest of my things. I'm not spending another minute in this house.

"I'm going to take this to dust for fingerprints," he calls as I scramble in the closet.

"Do whatever you need," I snap back. Someone was in my house. The knife already told me that much. I didn't think that was me. But this letter, the flower? That tells me for sure that someone was here. Someone is messing with me.

13

After I've got everything packed, Cameron drives me to the hotel that's conveniently a two-minute walk to his house and about ten minutes from the police station. I try not to think of the knife, the flower, a killer who could be after me, whoever was in my house. Knowing that Cameron will be right there, so close, makes me feel immensely better.

"You'll have an officer in an adjoining room. So, if you need anything at all, you can just ask," he says as he rolls the car to a stop in front of the hotel.

The building is huge, modern, and must be at least six stories tall. It's not the largest building in downtown by a long shot, but it's in a great part of the city. Beside the hotel, on the other side, is Lake Eola, and I hope I get a room that overlooks it so I can see the fountain and swans. In my ventures downtown, I've passed the small hotel probably a thousand times, but I've never been inside.

Cameron grabs my bags from the back and an attendant rushes from the front door with a trolley to grab them. We follow my bags as the man wheels them inside, and the lobby gives me my first taste of what to expect in the hotel. Beige tile lines the lobby with diamond patterns inlaid in much darker stone. The pattern forms a path guiding us to a deep mahogany desk. Fabric shrouds large pendant lights that hang above the front desk. It's one of the few light sources in the dark lobby. It's not the nicest hotel I've ever been in—Patrick had a penchant for the finer things—but it will do just fine. I've never been a fancy hotel kind of woman anyway.

As we walk up to the counter, I grind my teeth, and lag behind Cameron. It takes a few minutes for him to get me checked in and once we're in the elevator my heart still pounds. My chest is heavy from the lingering adrenaline. No matter how many deep breaths I take, it doesn't seem to unwind the anxiety a bit. If anything, my chest only gets tighter. Out of the corner of my eye, I see Cameron glancing at me, but I keep my eyes straight ahead, on the attendant with my luggage. Cameron reaches out and laces his fingers into mine. His touch unwinds the chains around me slowly. And it takes all my strength to not lean into him. But I know I shouldn't. That would just make this entire situation more complicated.

After my luggage is dropped in the room, I check out the space provided for me. It's much bigger than I expected. It has a separate bedroom and living room with a tiny kitchen along the side of the living room. It's bigger and nicer than the shitty studio apartment that I lived in in college.

"Damn, this is a pretty nice setup," I say as I plop down on the floral couch.

"Glad you like it," he says with a nod. "The door across from the bathroom leads to the room the officer will be staying in. Please leave the door unlocked so she can come in if you need anything. Do not answer the front door. If you order room service, you need to send it next door."

"So, you're not staying next door then?" I'd feel a million times better if I knew he was on the other side of that door. Right now, my relationship with law enforcement is as tenuous as the wife of a missing man and being an outed scam artist, but Cameron can give me insider information. Especially now that I know there's a knife hidden in my house. Any hint that they might search my house, and I need the warning. Even if all I can do is burn the place to the ground. I know that when it all comes down to it, he'll look out for my best interests first and put his career prospects second. Or at least I hope so.

"No, I've got cases I have to work on, but I'll come by to check on you as often as I can," he says with a smile as he leans against the wall next to the couch. He's too calm, collected, for all this, and I can't decide if it's because he wants to be sure he doesn't frighten me, or if he has orders to keep the severity of the situation under wraps.

I stand and walk to the kitchen to check the small fridge. They've stocked it with some basics, water, stuff for sandwiches, fruit. It's more than I thought they'd do. I guess they *really* don't want me leaving. The thought of being trapped inside this hotel for God knows how long makes my skin crawl. As I stare around at the four walls that didn't seem so bad before, I swear I can see them pulsing, begging to close in on me. I've never been good with small spaces.

"Is it going to cost you guys eleven dollars a bottle if I have some of this water?"

He laughs. "No, I stocked it for you. Not the hotel."

"You didn't have to do that," I say, the surprise lifting my voice. It almost makes me feel bad, stringing him along so I have an ear on the inside. Almost.

"Well, you're not supposed to leave and you kind of need to eat."

"Thank you," I say and find him hovering a few feet behind me. Too close. Much too close. Though I left the part of me that loved Cameron behind long ago, my body still reacts to the sight of him. As if he left some kind of imprint on me.

He steps closer, so close it makes my head buzz and my

breath catch. I start to retreat automatically, but he reaches for me. I freeze. I don't want him right now, not even a little. But doing this, it could sway him in a way my words can't. He brushes my long dark hair behind my shoulder and rests his head there. The feel of his flesh against mine makes goosebumps tickle across my skin.

"It's very important that you don't do any sessions in the hotel. Don't tell anyone you're here unless completely necessary, okay?"

"So, I just have to sit in this room by myself and do nothing?"

"Unfortunately. You brought your laptop, right?" he asks.

"Yeah, but that's only going to keep me entertained for so long."

"I'm sure you'll figure something out," he says. I walk him out and lock the door behind him. I lean against the door and take a deep shuddering breath. Already I'm in over my head, but for the first time in a long time, I don't care. Most of the time, it feels like I spend every single minute overthinking everything. For once, I'm doing what I feel, and hopefully, at least for a little while, my brain will stay the hell out of it.

I grab my phone and scroll through the contacts before my thumb hovers over Emma's number. I press the contact and it rings three times before it clicks.

"Yes," Emma says, her voice stiff, stilted, like she doesn't know it's me calling her. But of course she does.

"It's me," I say, annoyance flicking through me. I shouldn't have to tell her. My number is saved in her phone.

"Oh, hello, Adele," she says, her voice cold, lilted with fake saccharin.

"Could you please cancel all my appointments for this week and next that aren't willing to do a phone session or a virtual appointment?" I ask, though it's not a question. It hurts for me to say it, the words taking effort to get out. It'll be a blow to my ego and to my wallet. Though I may recover from both, I'm not sure how long this'll be. Weeks, months. My savings won't go far. Two months, *maybe*. If I'm lucky. After that, I'll have no choice but to dip into the trust fund I've worked so hard to avoid touching. While some might see that money as a safety net, I see it as a sure sign that I've failed, that I couldn't cut it on my own.

"What? You just made me move these appointments up, and now you want me to cancel them?" she snaps. Somehow, she manages to get so much venom and rage into her few words that it's surprising. I expected anger. She's paid a cut of each session, but I still flinch at it. I'm not sure why.

"With everything happening, I can't see patients in person right now." Not that there are many people knocking down my door for appointments anyway. With the news that Malcom killed himself shortly after his session with me, I seriously doubt anyone is going to want me to help with their problems.

"So, let me get this straight," she seethes, then pauses, but not long enough for me to cut in. "You mess everything up, and I'm made to suffer for it? We have hardly any clients left. They don't want phone sessions. You need to take the clients that will see you."

"This isn't all my fault. Your research is part of what got us into this position," I fire back before I can think any better of it. "We need to take what we can get, or nothing."

"You are such a bitch, Adele," she says before hanging up the phone.

I pull the phone from my ear, staring down at the screen. *That went well.*

14

A soft knock at my door raises me from sleep. Morning light filters through the burgundy curtains and bathes the room in red. I curse the light. Last night was one of the worst nights for sleep I can ever remember. Over and over again I woke, a shadow standing over me, a flower on the nightstand. Every time, I'd wake up with my heart pounding, finding both my room and the nightstand empty. Though I'm on the third floor, I got up every time to check the window, to make sure no one was watching me. I know it's trauma, that I'm well on my way to PTSD, but my training—knowing this will pass eventually—doesn't help. Not even a little.

I slide from the bed and stalk across the room, shedding sleep with every step. When I crack open the door, expecting to find Cameron or another officer on the other side, I nearly stagger back when I find Emma. I open the door slowly, as if part of me expects her to force her way inside.

"What are you doing here? What time is it?" I ask, blinking against the bright light in the hallway. How did she even know that I was here?

She shoves her way into the room and I back away, knowing

the look on her face well. Based on her expression, I'm lucky she didn't already bulldoze me.

"What the fuck do you think I'm doing here? You think you can just cancel all of your appointments and get my face splashed all over the news and I'm just going to fall over? Like I'll slink away as if nothing ever happened?"

My heart skitters as I process her words, the weight of them slamming into me. "Your picture is on the news?" I ask. I haven't been able to force myself to watch any of it for fear that it'll all spread like wildfire. If they're still carrying the story and now dragging others into it, that's bad news for me. Seriously bad. My stomach churns. Maybe I should just burn it all down and start over.

"They're saying that I'm somehow involved with that guy who killed himself after his appointment with you," she says, as she crosses her arms over her ample chest. "They think that I was somehow aware that you knew this guy was a danger to himself and that both of us did nothing. This is ridiculous. This is going to ruin me. How am I ever going to make a name for myself now? All anyone will ever think of when they hear my name is *Malcom Parish*," she seethes as she stalks around the room.

"I didn't want it to end this way for us, you know that," I say. Maybe if I try to reason with her, that will calm her down. But knowing Emma, there really won't be much I can do to diffuse this. This is a wildfire that I have to let burn itself out. "I had no idea that Malcom would hurt himself. Nothing during our session indicated as much. You know I would have had him go into inpatient treatment if I thought he was a danger to himself or anyone else."

"Oh, bullshit, Adele. You know if you'd played this right, we could have kept going. But you had to be selfish, keep bringing in more and more clients, so it was impossible for you to even give them the real attention that they needed. This is your fault.

And you're going to pay if this costs me my career, the plans that I have for myself," she says, stalking toward me, her finger punctuating her point in the air.

The door swings open, and Cameron storms in, his hand hovering over the gun at his waist. He's in full uniform. The hand not hovering over his gun has a carrier with coffee balanced on his left hand.

Emma turns the second that he busts in, her eyes wide.

"What is going on here? Can I help you?" he snaps to Emma as he looks from her to me. I have the high ground here; I could make him haul Emma out of here.

"Emma was just leaving," I say, motioning toward the door.

She grinds her teeth together and swivels to face me again. "We're not done. We will finish this." Her words are a grim promise, and so is the look on her face. Fury paints her features crimson. Though Emma has always had a temper, I can't say I've seen her so on the edge like this. Maybe it's Patrick. Maybe it's the veiled implications that we're both involved in a man's death. Maybe it's the media. Hell, it might be a toxic mix of all three. All I know is we are both in way over our heads here.

Emma disappears, stomping down the hall in a way that makes it absolutely clear that she's leaving a warpath. Heaven save anyone that gets in her way.

He whips around, his eyes tight, his arms stiff at his sides.

"I made it very clear that you weren't supposed to have anyone here. We put you here for your protection. It's not going to do any good if everyone in Orlando knows that you're here," he says, his voice too high in the small room.

I tense and my pulse pounds in my ears. Who the hell does he think he is? Accusing me like this is ridiculous. He has no idea what even happened. I want to rage at him, but instead, I tamp down my frustration so I don't scream—the last thing that I need is for people in the hotel to say I've lost it. "Excuse me? I didn't tell her that I was here. Maybe you all should have done your jobs better, so she didn't find me. Did you ever think of that?" I snap.

"You didn't tell her where you were?"

I cross my arms. "Are you kidding me? No. I know how to follow directions. I already told you I don't know how she knew I was here. You figure it out, you're the cop."

He deflates, his shoulders falling. He nudges the bag and coffee cup toward me.

"You brought me coffee and breakfast? Do you really think that's going to fix this? You can't come in here and accuse me of inviting people to the hotel and then try to fix it with breakfast. That's not how this works." My words are razor sharp as I hurl them at him. The last thing I need is to be yelled at first thing in the morning by both Emma and Cameron.

"Look, I'm sorry. I'm under a lot of pressure at work. This case is taking a toll on everyone. My boss is up my ass and the rest of the squad's asses because we don't have much to go on yet. After Brynlee turned up dead, that really changed things," he says, looking at the floor as he talks.

His words diffuse my anger. My pulse slows and I walk across the room to slump on the bed.

"Where's Linda?" I ask. I'm surprised the cop that's in the room next to me didn't come over when Emma was yelling.

"She called me a couple minutes before I pulled in. She needed to run home to help her wife out with the baby. Since I was so close, I told her I'd pop in to relieve her for a few hours." Cameron walks over to the coffee, grabs a cup and hands it to me. This time, I accept his peace-offering.

I nod as I test a sip of the cup.

"What the hell was all of that about with your assistant?" he asks. "Do you need me to take care of her for you?"

"Don't ask," I say, waving toward the hallway, as if the gesture might remove the memory of Emma. "And I don't think I can properly describe how badly I slept." I dump creamer in my coffee and take a sip. "And thank you for the offer and the coffee, but I can handle Emma myself." I tip the cup toward him.

He nods. "Why couldn't you sleep?" he asks with a crease between his brows.

I shrug. "Nightmares."

"The old ones or new ones?" he asks.

I sigh. It's actually been so long; I'd forgotten about the nightmares I had when we were together—the ones about my parents, their accident. For a long time I dreamt that I was in the car, burning alive with them. "New ones. I kept waking up thinking someone was in here leaving more flowers." When I say it out loud, I realize how stupid it sounds. "What's happening, Cameron? Being kept here, not knowing what's happening with Patrick, having to leave my home, it's getting to be too much." Vulnerability makes my voice hitch. I hate this. Being *me*. Being honest. It's so much easier being someone else, letting the lies speak for me.

His eyes bulge a little, obviously surprised by my rare show of emotion. "Everything we know, you know. I swear. We have the phone, but we haven't been able to locate his car or any other hits on his whereabouts. No tips have come in. Nothing. If it weren't for his cellphone, I might think he vanished."

"So, what exactly do they think happened?" I ask carefully as I arrange my features. My use of *they* and not *you* is purposeful. The more I remind Cameron that he's not one of them, the more he'll think of him and me as an *us*. That's exactly what I need him to think right now. At some point, I may need his help with some of the decisions I've made.

"Since his vehicle is missing and he moved money before the disappearance, we're still treating it as a missing person investigation. With the missing money and some of the other questions his employer has, they're putting some major heat on the investigation. They're a pretty major player around here, as you know, so if we don't get them the answers soon, some asses will be on the line." He shakes his head as he digs in the bag, pulling out two muffins.

"That's it? That's all we know?"

He nods. He takes my coffee, sets it down on the desk, and pulls me into a hug. This close to him, with my head buried in his chest, I could drown in his scent and be fine with it. All I want is to feel him against me, his arms around me. He hugs tighter and the anxiety melts away into his embrace.

"It's going to be okay," he says into my hair, and I believe him. Or maybe I just want to believe him. This is a long road we have to walk together, and we haven't even hit the first curve.

I nod against his chest and when I step back, he hands me my coffee.

"I should never have let you go," he says, his face darkening.

"Then how would I drink this amazing coffee?" I joke.

"You know that's not what I meant." There's an edge to his voice.

A sad smile curves my lips. "Yeah, I know." Sometimes I wonder what would have happened if I didn't push him away—if I had stayed. I open the paper bag on the table and find four apple Danishes inside. They're my favorite. Cameron hates them. It's striking how much he remembers, how easily it's falling into place. And everything inside me wants to fight it. Because it shouldn't be easy. I can't let myself be vulnerable again, my wounds are still too fresh. The reminders of why we failed the first time, why I let him go, it's so hard to grasp them when things are good. "So, is there a chance I can leave the hotel, or do I have to stay here?" I ask, feeling cooped up. I don't want to spend the entire day here.

His face tightens and his brows pull together. "We really shouldn't."

"But I'll be safe if I'm with you, right?"

He shakes his head and rubs the back of his neck. "You know that's a bad idea."

"Fine," I say as I try not to pout.

He steps closer, his hands resting on my hips. "I've got the day off. We can spend the whole day watching movies, doing anything else you want."

I smile. As impossible as it feels, for a moment, things feel like they might be okay, as if all this uncertainty won't come crashing down on me any moment.

15

After Cameron leaves, I can't sit still. There's no way I'll be able to spend the rest of the night in the hotel room. At the very least, I should be able to invite Tara over for drinks. There's no way that Cameron will yell at me twice in one day. I gather my courage and knock on the adjoining door. Though I hate that there's a cop assigned to watch me, I hate the idea of being a bother even more. But it's either I be honest about wanting to leave the room or I sneak out and risk running into whoever left that flower in my house. I've got to stick to the safe path here.

"Hey, Linda," I say in the calmest voice I can manage, because I don't want her to panic. I don't know her well enough to know how jumpy she is. Some people are skittish by nature, especially cops.

She answers the door and I offer her a smile. Her long blonde hair is braided and draped over her left shoulder. She's not in uniform, instead she's got on a pair of jeans and a button-up black shirt. There isn't a single bit of makeup on her face, but her skin is flawless, like she doesn't have a single pore.

"Everything all right?" she asks, and her eyes sweep over the room behind me.

"Would it be all right if I invited a friend to have drinks with me at the hotel bar?"

Her brows furrow and she presses her lips together. "Technically, I don't think I'm supposed to. But then again, they said you weren't supposed to leave the hotel. The restaurant is still in the hotel." For a long moment, I think she's going to say no. But when she finally nods, my heart quickens with relief. "I'll sit down there too though, just in case you need anything."

I wish Cameron were this accommodating. But he's always been as high-strung as a guard dog. After I have permission, I text Tara and she says she'll meet me in an hour. I take a quick shower, throw on some makeup. Linda rides the elevator with me down to the restaurant, and I feel a bit odd having a bodyguard. As creepy as the note and the flower were, I think this is a bit of overkill. There's no way whoever did that would think to come here. Putting me in a hotel should be enough. At least this will also keep the media away. The last thing I need is more reporters hanging around outside my house. My stomach clenches as I think about it, my chest tight.

As the elevator edges toward the lobby, I glance at Linda. "So, how long have you been a cop?"

"About three years. I absolutely love it though. I know it's what I was meant to do," she says with a genuine smile. The kind that lights up her eyes. "I started out as a beat cop, and I'm trying to work my way up to detective at some point."

"Oh yeah?" The elevator dings as we woosh past the floors.

"Yeah, I just got back from leave. My wife gave birth to our daughter six weeks ago, so I'm happy to be back." She pauses for a moment. "Not that I want to be away from them, but I missed the job. I mean, I miss them too." She fumbles with her words, like she's not used to talking about her family. Maybe she doesn't talk about them at the station.

"I understand," I say. I don't want her to feel like she has to explain herself to me. She doesn't. "They're just different kinds of challenges and you need both."

She grins and nods. "Yes, exactly."

"Your wife doesn't mind being stuck with the baby by herself?" I ask, though I know it's none of my business. It's something I've seen couples fight about a lot in the past. Resentment about childrearing is very common, especially in the first year.

"Nah, her dad is here helping us for a couple months." The elevator finally dings, and we exit into the lobby.

The restaurant is tucked away into a cubby off the lobby. It's larger than I imagined it would be. Right now it's half-full of patrons. Navy blue walls frame the restaurant with mosaics on several walls. Black tablecloths swaddle each table. They're each illuminated by small lights that barely cast a glow. The lighting is way too dark, giving it an ominous feel. At the back of the restaurant sits the bar.

I see Tara at the empty bar. She's wearing sleek black pants and a silk blouse and looks like she dressed for a job interview. Her long dark hair falls in waves to her shoulders. Under this light, her olive skin looks a few shades darker. And though I know she's making an effort to look casual, her face is pinched, tense. She's got two distinct lines between her thin eyebrows.

"I'll be sitting over there," Linda says as she points to a table in the corner of the room. It's got a great view of the bar and both doors. I nod and walk over to the bar where Tara's waiting weaving my way through the restaurant.

"Thanks again," I say as Linda walks toward her table.

I slide onto the stool next to Tara. "Hey there, pretty lady, waiting for someone?" I say as I nudge her arm. She laughs and looks toward the bartender.

"He's taking forever with my wine, and there's no one here. That's not a good sign."

The bartender is hunched over a bottle and has it held between his legs as he struggles with the cork. I can't help but wonder if it's his first time opening a bottle. He's toned, but not in an overly muscled way that really hints at narcissism. His black hair is coiled tightly atop his head.

"Oh, don't be hard on him. It's obviously his first day," I say as I laugh. Poor thing doesn't even look like he's out of high school.

Tara's posture is too straight and her fingers twitch on top of the bar, like she's desperate for a drink. Her stress level must be high. I'd think, with her mother-in-law gone, she'd have relaxed a bit.

"What's wrong?" I ask, leaning in, my voice low.

She shakes her head and waves her well-manicured hand. "It's nothing." Though her words are light, the look on her face says it all. There's something going on.

"Oh, come on, tell me." We have an agreement that I won't psychoanalyze her, I'll only give advice as a friend, not unless she asks anyway.

"Peter has been up my ass about trying to have kids. And you know how I feel about that." She sighs and her shoulders slump as she says it, as if the weight literally falls away with the words.

It's not that Tara doesn't want to have kids, unlike me. She wants to wait until her forties, when she thinks she'll magically feel more maternal. But he's been at her since they got married and it's only gotten worse since his mother moved in. He always harps on about how they should start while they have the help. But in my mind, if she's not ready, he shouldn't pressure her. And I know that if he does keep pressuring her, he'll risk driving her away.

"Anyway, the last month he's been insufferable about it. I was actually starting to consider it. But he's already traveling.

Then he tells me today that he's going to Europe for six weeks for work immediately after this trip. So, that means once his mother is back, I'll be alone with that miserable woman for six fucking weeks." She spits the words out with flair, like it's a death sentence. But with how much she loathes this woman, it may as well be. Being stuck with someone you hate for six weeks can feel like the end of the world. My mind flashes to Patrick, though I don't will it to.

"Did you call a divorce lawyer yet?" I joke.

She sips her wine. "If I didn't love the bastard, I would." She clenches her teeth and her cheeks blaze. "This whole damn world would be so much easier to navigate if it wasn't for love. No one ever tells you that you're marrying a whole family."

I shake my head, but I don't say anything, because she knew exactly what she was getting into with her mother-in-law well before she even got engaged. But I don't need to remind her of that. "So, what are you going to do?" I ask.

"Grin and bear it like I always do? Isn't that what good wives do? We bend and bend and bend, so God forbid, we aren't bitches." She shakes her head. This is how we lose ourselves to men. It starts with one compromise. Then years later, we don't even recognize ourselves anymore. How much will we let get whittled away? "Anyway, why did you want to have drinks all the way down here?"

"I'm staying here," I admit, waving my hand upward, signaling the floors above.

Her eyes go wide, and she nearly chokes on her wine. "Why on earth are you staying here?" she asks, her voice too loud in the quiet room.

I look around the restaurant and notice a few people staring daggers at her. Since I sat down, at least ten tables have filled up. The restaurant is nearly full.

"Can you please keep your voice down?" I ask as I take a drink and meet Linda's eyes across the room.

"Sorry," she whispers as she covers her mouth. When she drinks, she tends to get louder and louder.

"I have to stay here. The police wanted me here for safety reasons," I admit as quietly as I can. My eyes cut across the room, but in the space of one breath, everyone has lost interest in us.

She props her head on her hand and stares at me for a moment. I'm not sure if it's curiosity or horror, maybe it's both. "What the hell happened?"

I tell her about the cell phone, the dead mistress, and the note I found on the nightstand. It sounds so much worse than it is when I say it all like this. Disjointed, spread apart, it's easy to think that just maybe these things aren't related.

"Are you serious?" She shakes her head. "So, they think Patrick killed her and that, what, he might kill you too?" Her brows pull together. I can see her puzzling it all out on her face.

I shrug. "I guess that's what they're thinking, but there's no way," I say.

"What would even make him do something like that?"

"Maybe if she threatened to tell me?" I say, but I'm grasping at straws. It seems like he was planning to leave me for her. So, I don't see why he'd want to kill her. Wouldn't he want me out of the way?

"Maybe there were more?" she offers. The look on her face tells me she's sure of it. How long has she suspected? As long as I have?

Based on what Cameron saw on the computer, I know there were at least two. But how many mistresses could he really have? He wasn't able to balance anything else in life, he couldn't manage his business. How the hell could he balance multiple women? This second life where I didn't exist. I pinch the bridge of my nose. Even now, after everything, my instinct is still to defend him.

I sip my wine, hoping it will dull the ache. It doesn't.

Nothing seems to help. Maybe I'm beyond help. I like the sound of that, honestly. It's a malaise I could give myself to. The affliction: scorned wife, broken woman. But I don't want to be that person, I don't want to let Patrick reshape who I am because of the things that he's done to me.

"Can we talk about something else?" I ask, as my temple throbs. I'm not sure I can stand to spend another minute thinking about Patrick or all the women he was probably seeing while he erased me. What did they have that I didn't? I gave everything to this man and for what? For him to pretend I didn't exist? To lie to me? To decide that after all these years I didn't even deserve my own money if we split up?

"What are you looking at?" I ask, trying to figure out what she's looking at, but failing miserably.

She glances at something behind me. "That guy over there keeps staring at us. It's freaking me out," she says as she shivers.

I look over my shoulder, trying not to be obvious about it, but there's no one in the direction she was looking at. The table is empty except for a half-empty wineglass on the table.

"There's no one there," I say, as a bad feeling snakes in the pit of my belly, like an oiled adder.

The fragrance of tapas being delivered to tables around us wafts over and my stomach protests. I clearly have not eaten enough and what I have munched on throughout the day didn't satisfy me. The day has not been fulfilling at all, clearly.

Tara and I order more food than we'll both ever need. And I glance at every member of the waitstaff as they walk by, practically begging for food. As I glance toward the door, I recognize a face in the crowd and it sends my stomach through the floor. Lucas.

His eyes meet mine before he starts stalking across the room toward us. My skin twitches with discomfort as he eyes me. The intensity of his glare burns. My eyes cut to Tara and she looks at me with uncertainty.

"Do you want to get out of here?" she says, her voice low. Though I appreciate her offer, there's no way to back out of here without him seeing or being able to follow. In the corner, Linda sits, eyeing us carefully, and that makes me feel a little better at least.

"No, it's fine," I say, right before Lucas is within earshot.

"Adele," he says to me, offering me a smile that looks more like a sneer.

"What are you doing here?" I ask him.

"I'm having dinner with my wife and her sister," he says, waving toward the table. I glance over, taking in the women.

"How lovely," I manage to say between my teeth.

"It is, isn't it? Anyway, Adele, I wanted to ask if you knew that Patrick was in the business of stealing identities?"

The question lodges in my mind. Stealing identities? Patrick? There's no way that he's smart enough for that. Patrick couldn't even set up an account on a website or file his own taxes. Hell, I had to set up email on his cell phone because he couldn't figure it out. I shake my head and I can't help my reflex to defend this man. It's like my foot twitching when my knee is hit. I wish I could stop.

"See, the thing is, I know he did it. I have proof. I also know that a man like Patrick, if that even was his name, didn't up and disappear."

I swallow hard but refuse to let my anxiety show on my face. Tara leans in, like she's about to interject, but I hold my hand up to stop her. Of all the things I've let Tara do for me, I will *not* let her defend Patrick. Ever. I would not ask that of her.

"If you have that kind of information, I suggest that you speak to the police." Though I wonder what Cameron's take on it would be.

"You need to find that money, Adele. My patience is wearing thin."

"Is there something I can help you with?" Linda asks from

behind Lucas. Her voice startles me. I didn't even see her walk over.

Lucas whips around, facing Linda. Even if she weren't flashing her badge, which she is, she has that typical air of a cop. He glances back at me, and growls, "We aren't done here," fury shimmering beneath the surface, before he stalks off. Once he's a few feet away, he rubs the back of his head and glances back at me, making sure I see him. He's got a score to settle with me, that much is clear.

"You all right?" Linda asks.

"Yeah, thank you," I say. But his exit doesn't make me feel any better. Not in the least. "Could we have a few more minutes?" I need to let Tara in on my suspicions. And I can't do that in front of Linda.

"Of course, just let me know when you're ready to go back upstairs," Linda says before walking back to her table.

Tara raises her eyebrows. "Okay, you've got some shit to fill me in on."

"I know, I know," I say before sipping my wine. Tara stares at me, her eyes hungry for information. I fill her in on my last encounter with Lucas, the failed businesses. We spend a while talking about much lighter subjects, like TV, and thankfully Patrick doesn't come up again. Just as I push my wine away and decide to call it quits for the night, I catch Tara staring off toward the corner of the room.

"I think I'm going to go back to my room."

"Would you rather come sleep at my house?" she offers.

"Thank you, I really appreciate that. But I don't think there's a chance that Cameron will let me."

"Want me to stay here with you?" she asks with a pained smile. I wave her offer away.

As she heads toward the door, I join Linda and we walk toward the elevator. The sound of someone running snares my attention, and I turn to see a woman I recognize stalking toward us. She cuts us off, standing in front of the elevator. Linda's arm juts out, and she pushes me backward, behind her.

"You." Brenda growls the word, her hand slashing the air before she points her index finger toward my face.

"Adele." Linda says my name, and it's almost a question.

"This is Brenda, she's a patient of mine," I explain. I don't think I'll ever forget Brenda, or how she treated her husband in my office several days ago before he killed himself. The media might think that I'm to blame for what happened to him, but I know this woman is the cause.

"Are you here hiding after what you did to my husband? It's going to be on the news tonight. I told them that you are the reason my husband is dead. He told you he was going to hurt himself, and you did nothing. Now that he's gone, they're going to take my kids. They don't think I can take care of them without Malcom," she says, spitting the words at me.

"You need to leave," Linda says, pushing Brenda out of the way just as the elevator dings. She drags me into the elevator and holds Brenda at bay. Brenda stalks off, but I know it's not the last we'll see of her. And I can't shake the sneaking suspicion that Emma might have told her where I am.

As the elevator rises, she asks, "Have a good time?" Sarcasm edges her words.

I let out a dry laugh. "Yeah, thank you for letting me come down here. I don't think I'll be doing that again."

"I was going to say it had to be the last time."

I nod. Suddenly, I feel terrible that she's going to be stuck in that room for as long as I'm here. Hopefully they'll find Patrick soon, and we'll both be free to leave.

"Sorry you're stuck up there," I say.

"Don't be. It's not the worst thing in the world. At least it's a nice hotel."

"Isn't that the truth."

After we exit the elevator and walk down the hall, Linda

slides the key into my door and lets me inside. "Don't forget to lock it. Good night."

"I won't. Good night." I slip inside and lock the door.

I shed my clothes, text Cameron, and fall into the bed slowly as I close my eyes. With a warm belly that's filled with wine, I drift away as darkness envelopes me.

16

Hot water pelts my face, my shoulders. Surprisingly the water pressure in this hotel is decent enough to sting my skin. Though I wish this could wash everything away, it won't. Not even a goddamn river could wash away the mounds of bullshit in my life. I had a good time with Tara, but the wine and the conversation weren't enough to relax me. As a professional, I know the toll this stress is taking on me—but it's not so easy to shed it. There isn't a simple switch to lower my cortisol levels, try as I might.

Water rains down on me, but I swear over the noise, I hear someone knocking. I want to lose myself, to give myself over to this bliss, but if it's Cameron, I need to let him in. On the counter, my phone vibrates, and I know I'm truly done with the shower, though I haven't gotten my fill. I swear there's no peace left in this world.

I whip the curtain open, the metal hangers shrieking against the rod. I squint at the screen, but there's too much fog for me to read the name. With a swift movement downward, I swipe it away, or at least I try to. The sounds of someone on the other end shouting at me, cursing, blaming me for Malcom's death tells me I must have accidentally accepted it. It's Brenda, clearly. Instead of listening to her rant, I end the call, then block her number. I'll have to tell Cameron about it, though I'm not sure he'll be able to do anything to keep Brenda away from me.

I throw on the plush white robe provided by the hotel and secure it around my waist. As I fling the bathroom door open, a plume of mist escapes with me. I stagger backward automatically, clutching my robe tighter. A balaclava-clad man stands beside the bed, his hands tightened around the footboard like he's about to launch himself over it. He's got a mop of messy black hair sticking out from the bottom of his mask, and through the slit his blue eyes are wide, feral. Down the front of him, he's soaked through with blood. His shirt is smeared, and red is streaked on his arms. He's covered so thoroughly it looks like he's been doused in paint.

"It's about time you got out of there, Adele." He says my name low and slow, almost purring. It sends a shiver down my spine and a bad feeling slithering in my gut. The voice, the way he says my name, it's familiar, but I can't place where I've heard it before.

"What do you want?" I ask and my voice nearly cracks. I look back into the bathroom and eye my phone. I grab the edge of the door, planning to slam it and lock myself inside the bathroom. The second I move, so does he, so close, too close. His hand makes contact with the door and he holds it open.

He raises his free hand, ticking his finger back and forth like a metronome. "Don't."

I settle back and try to figure out the best way out of this. He's standing in front of the only way out of here. I hope the blood isn't Linda's. I hope he didn't hurt her. My stomach churns at the idea. All I can imagine is her wife and new baby. In the back of my mind I know the chances are high. There's no way he got all the way up to my room covered in blood. Hotel staff would have stopped him.

"What do you want?" I ask again, hoping this time he might give me some hint of why he's here.

"Maybe a little thanks? Do you have any idea what I've done for you?" he asks as he waves his arms around, pacing farther into the hotel room. The raving descends into a stream of words spoken so quickly the only thing I can make out is my name, because every time he says it, he says it slowly, emphasizing every syllable.

As he paces, distracted, I bolt out of the bathroom. My heart races and he grabs me, his fingers digging into my flesh. I wrench my arm away, but he yanks my robe, pulling me close enough to smell the iron, the sharp scent of the blood all over him.

"Let me go," I scream and kick him in the leg as hard as I can. Pain shoots through my foot with the impact, but he stumbles, giving me the opening I desperately need. He flails behind me, but I propel myself through the small hotel room and find Linda's door wide open. A large pool of blood surrounds her head. And the vacant look in her eyes is enough to turn my stomach. I run from the room, through the winding hallways, and down the stairs.

The stairs bring me to the back door, and I burst out into the cool morning air. It's still dark out, but the tendrils of morning sun have just begun to paint the horizon with streaks of purple. The streets that would normally be filled with tourists are empty. My feet move on their own, my mind a blur of panic. Adrenaline dulls everything. The pain I should feel in my bare feet, the screaming of my muscles, it all fades away. I look behind me over and over, praying that he isn't following.

I run until the adrenaline fades, my feet ache, my legs burn, and my lungs feel like they're about to burst. I can't go home. I'd lead whoever that was to my house—as if they don't already know where I live. The police station is farther than Cameron's house. I'm too out of shape to keep up this pace. My mind races as I try to grasp where to go. Cameron's. That's the only option. When I see the sea foam-green house, my heart leaps. I climb the stairs. My palm pounds against the door, and I pace the front porch as I wait for Cameron to answer. Deep inside the house, I hear a dog barking.

"What are you doing here?" he asks, groggily, as he opens the door. I must have woken him.

I shove past him and wrap my arms around my chest as I stand in the warmth of his living room. It's exactly the way I remember it, yellow shag carpet, oversized navy-blue furniture. Any other time, I'd have to fight off a wave of nostalgia, but right now, there's not a chance I'll feel anything other than panic. My heart pounds as I try to settle myself.

"Linda's dead," I stammer, and steady myself by gripping the back of an armchair. The words burn my throat as anguish grips me.

Cameron grabs me, steers me onto the couch, and I sit down automatically. "Where are your clothes? Is that blood?" he asks as he surveys me. "What happened?" he asks, an edge to his voice. He's already got his cell phone out. He grips it so tight that his knuckles are white.

"I got out of the shower and there was a strange man at the end of my bed. He was covered in blood. He was talking crazy, he knew my name." Saying it out loud makes goosebumps crawl up my arms and down my legs. Was it an old patient of mine? Did he come back to attack me for some reason? Though I try to go through the list of everyone I've seen in the past few months, my mind is a blur of faces and names—I can't pinpoint anyone it might have been.

Cameron grabs his phone, dials a number, and starts speaking quickly into it. He relays everything I've told him to the person on the other end. "We need a bus and a CSI team at the hotel. Rooms 351 and 352," he says and hangs up the phone. "It wasn't Patrick?" he asks.

I shake my head. "No." The words come automatically. But I know in my heart that wasn't his voice, his frame. He wouldn't have, couldn't have, killed Linda. Or anyone—right? God, I have to stop thinking that. I don't know what he's capable of anymore.

"Was it someone you knew?"

"He had a mask on." My voice is still as unsteady as I feel. Some part of me considers telling him that I recognized the voice, that some part of me knew that man, though I can't say who he was.

"Is there anyone you could think of that could have or would have done this? Any of your old patients?"

"It's always possible, but I don't know who it would have been. There's no one recent that comes to mind." I tell him about Brenda, but she wasn't the attacker in the room, that I know for sure. I can't think of anyone else that would do this. I can't believe they killed Linda. I also tell him about our trip to the hotel restaurant. "Lucas, Patrick's old business partner, is mad at me. He seems to think that I owe him money that Patrick took. He confronted me at the restaurant, talking about how Patrick had stolen his identity."

"Do you think he could have been responsible for this somehow?"

The question lingers in my mind for a long time before I speak. Do I really think that Lucas is capable of killing Linda? I don't know. And I know it wasn't him in the room. But could he have hired someone to try to scare me? That I don't know.

"I really wish I knew. He's mad, but I don't know if he's that mad."

Cameron sits next to me and he wraps his arm around me, pulling me into him. The scent of him envelopes me, musky and sweet at the same time. His warmth bleeds into me, and the lies all fall away. Somehow, even with everything, it still feels natural to be in his arms. He holds me until I stop shaking, until my heart slows, and I finally pull away.

"I'm going to call and see if they've found anything. Are you all right if I do that?" he asks, his voice measured, careful, like he thinks I'll shatter into a million pieces on his couch.

I wave my hand. I don't need him to babysit me, and I certainly don't want him to feel like he has to. Though my nerves are still shot, at least I know if I'm here, I'm safe.

He grabs his phone and walks into the kitchen. Though a wall stands between us, I can still hear him dial and pace the tile floor. As he drones on, the weight of it all crashes into me. The reality that Linda is dead, that someone who could have killed me too was in the hotel. My limbs turn to cement and I'm not sure I could force myself to stand even if I wanted to. Why are they doing this? Who is doing this? An angry client, Patrick, Lucas? I try not to listen in on Cameron's conversation, but the baritone of his voice is comforting.

"You all right?" Cameron asks after he's off the phone. He sits next to me and rubs my back in slow circles.

"I don't know right now. Did anyone see who did this?" I ask, my voice cracking. I don't want to come off as unhinged, but right now, I'm not sure if I can control it. I used to have such a handle on myself, my emotions, but lately I feel like I've completely unraveled.

He shakes his head. "No one in the hotel saw anyone come in around the time of the attack. And unfortunately, their entire security system was down, so they don't have footage from the cameras."

I sag beneath the weight of it. And tears spill down my cheeks, my throat goes dry as I try to swallow my grief, my frustration. Though I want to say this is an act, it's not. The emotions come swiftly, overwhelming me.

"So, what, they won't be able to figure out who did this?"

"We won't be able to figure it out right away. It will take

time to process the scene, to go through all the evidence. We'll keep you safe while they go through everything. I'm going to swab some of the blood from your feet. I'll need to take the robe too," he says, his words careful.

I nod and Cameron grabs a bag from his kitchen. With skilled hands he swabs the blood from the bottom of my feet in several places and puts the evidence into individual containers, then places each of them into a plastic bag that he labels. After that is collected, he gives me a flannel robe of his and takes the one from the hotel. Though I don't think there's any blood on it, I'm glad to be rid of it.

The layout of the room is burned in my mind. The blood all over the floor, the bed, Linda's body limp on the floor. I'm sure there will be evidence all over the room. Whoever killed her was sending a message, and was not after a clean kill.

"They must have some connection to Patrick. And if they do, we'll find it," he says as he squeezes my hand. "They want to put you up in another hotel."

I shake my head. "No way. I'd rather sleep in a holding cell then go and risk this happening again," I say and I'm surprised by the truth of it.

"You can stay here if you want," he offers, as if that's what he wanted.

"Do you really think that's a good idea? What if someone tries to break in here?" The idea of Cameron getting hurt is enough to turn my stomach. It also can't look good, all the legal trouble I'm in and sleeping at a cop's house.

He holds his hand up, signaling for me to hold on. Then he walks to the back of his house. The sound of dogs running down the hall fills the room. Two huge black creatures come barreling into the room, tails wagging. Their tongues hang out of their mouths, revealing sharp white teeth. Cameron points toward me and tells the dogs to lie down. They lie down on command.

"They'll eat anyone that tries to open the front door," he says as he waves to the two huge dogs lying at my feet.

They may be huge, and look threatening at first glance, but these dogs are obviously sweethearts. I raise an eyebrow at that.

"Don't believe me? Watch." He pushes off the sofa and walks out the front door. I wait, unsure of what he's doing. A few minutes later, the screen door at the back of the house slams shut and the dogs erupt into a vicious flurry of barks. One stands in front of me, guarding me, while the other bolts to the back door. Once Cameron comes in the back door, the barking stops, and both dogs wag their tails like they've never been happier to see him.

"Are you sure they aren't all bark?" I ask, after he gives me the *you see* look.

"They're retired police dogs. They're trained to attack on command," he says like I should have guessed it.

And that makes me feel a million times better, knowing they'll be here, and Cameron will be too. I'm way more protected than I was at the hotel.

"No one at the station is going to think it's weird I'm staying here?" I ask, glancing at the dogs, not him. One of the dogs comes over, as if sensing I need him, and lets me scratch him behind the ears.

He shakes his head. "I already spoke to the captain. They don't want to put you or anyone else on the force at risk. There are already so many questions about what happened at the hotel."

I nod. "All right. Thank you for letting me stay." My cell phone vibrates. Apparently I had a missed call during my run. "Do you mind if I make a call?" I ask.

He lets out a low laugh. "Of course not. Make your call and make yourself at home."

"Thanks," I say as I walk toward the back of the house so I

can have some privacy. Behind me, the collars of the dogs jingle as they follow Cameron into the kitchen.

I close the door in the bedroom before looking at the phone again. I click on Jansen's contact, and the phone starts to ring.

"Hey, kiddo," Jansen says as soon as he answers the phone. "Look, some news is about to break tonight and I think I should be the one to tell you..."

My stomach knots as he speaks. "Tell me what?" I interject. I know the news is going to be bad. I can already tell from his tone. Somehow, I feel like I'm thirteen again, like he's about to break the news to me about my parents.

"I didn't tell you the whole truth about your parents and their show. I didn't think the news would ever come out, and I didn't want it to paint your parents in a negative light for you," he explains. Though he's trying to soften the blow, I don't believe a word of it. I know what's coming before he says the words. "There were some things that happened on the show. The producers swapped some DNA results to add some viewer interest to the show. There were false allegations of cheating, fraud, and much more on the show. Lives were ruined—a few anyway. A woman lost her children, a man murdered his wife after false DNA told him that his kids weren't his. Some of that is about to come out in the media. A friend of mine at the time gave me a heads-up, so I'm getting out of town for a while," he explains.

My throat goes dry. Lives ruined. People died. Though he's trying to shove blame onto the producers, I can't help but wonder how much my parents knew.

"Look, I've got to go," he finally says before the line goes dead. And I'm left wondering, left reeling, not knowing what's real, and how much of my parents' legacy is bloody and sordid.

17

The thing about blood is, once you've had it between your fingers, coating your palms, the viscous fluid clinging to your every pore, you never forget it. That warmth, the feeling, is imprinted on you, like traces are left on your soul for luminol to find. And though I don't need to look down to know it's there, I do. My eyes scan over the bubbles of red between my fingers, the stains on my skin. My heart pounds as I take it all in. It can't be. I can't have done it again.

It takes too long for me to process where I am. The subway tile, the sleek gray counters, the black shaker cabinets. The kitchen. Cameron's kitchen. The world tips and I reach out for the counter, hoping to right myself. Anxiety tightens around my chest, threatening to suffocate me. This can't be happening. Cameron can't be dead too. Because then, where would that leave me? How could I say I wasn't a killer?

One of the dogs nuzzles against my leg, dragging me from my panic. He looks up at me, eyes pleading, as if he senses my inner turmoil. I reach out reflexively to pet his head but stop when I find my flesh pale and unmarked.

Insane. I'm going insane. Hallucinations are never a good sign. Sure, they can happen because of trauma, or stress, or medication—but they should not be happening to me.

"Oh, you're already up?" Cameron asks from behind me, startling me.

My heart pounds as I try to settle myself. Maybe all this stress is making me imagine things. I need to get a grip. "Good morning," I say, trying to keep a handle on my emotions, so they don't come through in my tone. "Yeah, I couldn't sleep anymore." I don't remember getting up or walking into the kitchen. How long have I been awake?

He walks over and kisses me gently on the cheek. "Want some breakfast?"

"Sure," I say, though I don't think I can actually stomach food.

"Did you make any coffee yet?" He points toward the coffee pot.

I shake my head. "No, I haven't had a chance yet."

"I'll make some. Could you grab the cups for me?" He points toward some cabinets at the end of the kitchen as he walks to the pot.

I walk over and grab the cups, setting them out on the counter near the pot as he grabs a filter. As the pot gurgles, he drags out pans and begins making breakfast. Though I want to help, I stand on the outskirts of the kitchen, paralyzed. I can't shake the fear, even though I'd love to. My heartbeat is still kicked up a notch, my nerves refusing to settle.

"How'd you sleep?" he asks as he flips a pancake.

"Better than Tuesday night," I say as I sigh. But honestly, I've always slept fine at Cameron's side. Sometimes, sleeping next to Patrick felt good—for the first few years anyway. Now that I look back with new eyes, I can see when he started to pull away. Toward the end every day felt, no matter how close we were, like there was always something wedged between us. When did it become so bad that I rewrote our story entirely?

"They found something yesterday on Patrick's computer," Cameron says in a way that threatens to turn my guts to water. I've been waiting for the other shoe to drop because it has to. All the questions about Patrick aren't answered yet, and I know what's to come won't be good. I open my mouth to ask what he means, but it feels like my words have turned to ash on my tongue.

"Apparently your mortgage is in default. They're actually in the final stages of foreclosure and it looks like Patrick took out credit cards in your name. He ran up thousands of dollars on them."

Anger rises swiftly inside me, threatening to boil over. I should have handled the finances myself. I knew that from the get-go. But Patrick wanted to do it. He said it would take stress off of me if he looked after everything. He said I did enough. He worked in finance after all. I would have never trusted anyone else with it, but he lulled me into acquiescing, then I let it slide for so long.

"He what?" The mortgage doesn't surprise me. But taking out credit cards in my name? Lucas's words echo in my mind. Identity theft. How many people did he pretend to be? As my mind churns and I picture our house, I try to imagine where it all went. That money had to go somewhere. It didn't just disappear. Based on what I've heard, he has to have over half a million dollars. That's a good head start if he needs one. But where is that money now? How the hell did he hide it? It kills me, because Patrick never seemed like a planner, not long term anyway.

Cameron steps toward me, as if he plans to comfort me. I hold my hands up automatically, halting him. Comfort is the last thing I want right now. I need to feel every molecule of this rage.

"Look, they're going to want to question you. I wasn't supposed to say anything to you about it. But they've uncovered some pretty unsavory things about Patrick."

"Like what?" I grind out through clenched teeth.

"I'm not supposed to mention it, in case you had any knowledge and you helped him," he says as he squares his shoulders. If he wants a fight, I'll drag the info out of him.

"You better tell me," I say as I cross my arms. Cameron is focused on the stove, his back to me, but that doesn't stop me from glaring at the back of his head. "After everything else that man has put me through, don't I deserve to know?" I lay it on thick, knowing exactly the right strings to pull to get him to talk. "You know me, you're supposed to be on my side, and right now it feels like you're choosing him."

He glances over his shoulder at me, appraising me, as if he's trying to tell if I'm serious. On the stove, bacon pops in a frying pan, echoing through the kitchen. The dogs circle around Cameron's feet, as if begging him to drop the food. "You have to keep this all to yourself."

"Who exactly do you think I'm going to tell, Cameron?" I nearly spit the words, adding a little more venom to his name than I need to.

"I could lose my job."

"Your job?" I laugh. "Try losing your whole life. Then you can get back to me about the job."

"I already did once, when I lost you," he says, finally looking at me again. Pain swims in his eyes and I know that, for him, I'm the one that got away. I wish I could feel that way about him, but I don't. And I know chances are I'll never feel that way about anyone again. Once upon a time, I thought Patrick was my person, I thought he was the other half of me. But now, I realize that too was a lie. I'm too broken to let someone else into my life. Cameron deserves better, and I won't let him settle for someone as broken as me.

"Stop it," I say. I need to know what he knows about Patrick. I don't have time for his too little, too late romantic nostalgia. He needs to move on with his life. Not now, I still need him to see this all through. But after I leave, he really needs to see what life has in store for him without me in it. Maybe I'll fake my death.

"I'm sorry."

"Please just tell me." And though I don't will it to, my voice breaks.

His shoulders fall, and he turns back to the food, his head hanging. "Normally, for a missing person case like this, there wouldn't be so many resources allocated. But when Patrick went missing, his employer noticed some red flags. Things were missing, numbers weren't adding up. They think that Patrick was skimming off the top. They also think he may have stolen the identities of several employees. Even with all those things, for a regular employer it might stay on the back burner. But the company Patrick worked for, their office is just an arm of a nationwide organization that has heavy influence over this town. They've got deep pockets. They won't let this go, so we can't let this go."

My mind churns with all the information. "I know he charged up credit cards, defaulted on the mortgage, and was skimming off the top at work, but what was he doing with all that money?" If he had been buying crazy things, he definitely wasn't bringing them home. I would have noticed. He spent so much money eating at restaurants because he hated eating at home. He bought a car that was far out of our league because he claimed with the politics at work that he *needed* it. But even with that, I can't account for where all this money went. There were no signs he was using drugs or gambling—where else could that money have gone?

When he took his job, he took a pay cut compared to what

he was making off the businesses. Now I wonder if there was really a pay cut at all or if all this time, he was putting money aside and not telling me about it. I'd call and ask, but it's not like they even know that I exist.

How did he deceive me for this long? Of all things, how could I be so blind to this? I need to know what Cameron thinks, because maybe I'm too far in that I couldn't see what Patrick was really capable of.

"Did he make any large purchases that you noticed?" he asks.

"No. I would have definitely called it out if he started coming home with unexplained purchases, especially if they were expensive."

"Could he have been buying gifts for the women he was seeing?" The words feel like a punch to the gut.

"Yeah, I'm sure he could have," I manage to choke out. It's unsettling how hollowed out Patrick has made me feel. As if someone scooped out my insides and all that's left are my doubts echoing inside me. I never understood my clients who were despondent, who shut off entirely after traumatic events. Not even my parents' deaths did that to me—the pain of that was immediate, it cut me to my core. But this is something different. Now I wonder if I was kind enough, if I showed them enough empathy.

Cameron turns and reaches out to me, as if reacting to the sorrow on my face. I consider walking to him just to feel something, anything that isn't nagging loneliness. But I don't. I can't bridge that gap right now, not with him, not with anyone. He wants to help me heal wounds that I'm not ready to mend.

On the counter, Cameron's phone vibrates, and he furrows his brow. "It's the station."

"Take it," I say as I wave my hand. I don't care if he spends a few minutes on his phone.

Cameron flashes me an apologetic look and answers the call. I grab myself a plate from the dishes he's piled next to the oven. My stomach is rumbling, and I can't wait for him to be finished on the phone. Three bites into my pancakes, I can tell there's something wrong. Cameron looks away and stares at the kitchen floor as someone drones in his ear.

"Are you sure?" he asks. A low voice says something on the other end of the line, but I can't make it out.

Hope ignites inside me that they found the guy from the hotel. That they've tracked him down somehow. When he hangs up the phone, he turns to me.

"What's up?" I ask as a bad feeling brews inside me.

"The medical examiner finished with the examination of Brynlee's body." He looks down, and when he won't look up at me again, my stomach bottoms out. "She was pregnant."

I clench my fists under the table and try to swallow the bite of pancake that's stuck in my throat.

"They want you to come to the station so they can ask you a few questions," he says.

"What kind of questions?" I ask as my palms slick with sweat.

"I'm not sure. I imagine some questions about Patrick to try and figure out what happened."

"Do I have to?"

He pinches his lips together. "It's going to look very bad for you if you're not willing to talk to the guys at the station."

Frustration roars inside me. "And what part of *anything* we're doing is going to look good?" I throw the words at him harder than I mean to.

He looks down and rubs the back of his neck. I know what comes next. He'll try and talk some sense into me. But deep down he knows I'm right. "It's not like I'm bragging at the station that we're together again. We shouldn't let *anyone* know about that until this has all blown over."

Together again? We're not together. I'm taken aback. But I don't want to vocalize that. Cameron is not the secret-keeping type. He's usually as by-the-book as one can be. That's one of the many reasons why I thought we wouldn't work long term. The straight life, vanilla thing, it's not for me. I tried it, I gave it a shot—for him. College, a normal job. I considered a life outside of my family dynasty. The monotony of a cubicle, pantyhose, yearly reviews. I couldn't do it. Every day I walked through the rows of cubes, I felt more and more of myself slip away. A year. I gave it a year. But that's when I realized that this life is my destiny. I was meant to walk in my mother's and father's footsteps.

I shake my head and purse my lips. Cameron rubs my arm and I know I don't have a choice. I can't risk this looking bad for me—well, worse, really. The questions. The moment I knew Patrick was missing, I knew eventually more questions would come. I guess I thought I'd have more time. Instead of investigating and biding my time during Patrick's disappearance, I should have been preparing for the inevitable.

"When do they want to talk to me?" I ask as I swallow hard.

"As soon as you're ready. If I were you, I'd try to get it over with as soon as possible," he says as he glances at his phone. Something feels off. But Cameron has never been the type to keep secrets from me. I'm not sure he'd start now. But then again, after all this time apart, it'd be naive for me to think he hasn't changed.

I give my breakfast one last glance. There's no way I can eat it now. My stomach churns as I walk back to the bedroom. I pull my clothes on slowly, going over all the possible questions in my mind. My palms slick with sweat and my chest tightens.

"Let's go," I say to Cameron and walk out the front door. "But I need to stop at my house first to grab something."

The car idles, practically rumbling beneath me. The subtle motion is calming, but it does nothing to settle the turmoil of my thoughts. Cameron is silent beside me in the driver's seat, as if he knows it's exactly what I need from him right now. I glance at the house again, the rectangle builder home, the beige stucco. I can imagine almost every moment I spent with Patrick in there over the past five years. It guts me to think now that they were all lies.

I clench my jaw and I can see him in the foyer, his head cracked open, a pool of blood spreading across the antique wood floors. My heart skips and I freeze.

"You all right?" he asks.

I nod, though not an ounce of me feels that way. But admitting it feels like a betrayal to the strength I'm supposed to have.

"We don't have to go in," he says.

"Yes, we do. I need the details. I've got to know where that money was going. What he was doing with it. And the only way to get that is on his computer," I say. If I have to go talk to the cops about this, I need to be more informed.

Cameron's door pops open and I hear him slide out, but it takes me a few seconds to follow suit. A rare cool air hits my face. Though I've lived in Florida my whole life, the year-round heat always renders me paralyzed when winter comes around again. You'd think that I'd be used to it by now, but no.

Cameron glances back at me, then strolls toward the house. His slow gait, so unlike his usual stride, tells me that he's waiting for me to follow.

"Isn't this a crime scene?" I ask as I climb the porch steps.

"Technically, no. Until there's real evidence that Patrick committed crimes here, there's nothing we can do outside of a search. We can only render sites of a homicide inaccessible for investigation purposes. We can't hold it indefinitely."

"If you say so," I say before I fish the key from my pocket, thankful that I grabbed it from my hotel room before the police took all my stuff to hold as evidence.

A hiss of bottled air slams into me the moment I open the door. Though it's only been a few days since I've been inside, it feels much longer. Like time slowed down here. It smells off, like I left dishes in the sink—a sour stench that I can't quite place.

"There's a package here," Cameron says behind me. "Did you order something?" I turn to find him holding a box that's nearly two feet long.

"No, is it addressed to me?" I used to order a lot online, but lately I've been trying to kick the habit to support local businesses.

"No, it's for Patrick," he says after inspecting the label that's stuck to the front of the box.

"Do we open it?" I ask.

He half shrugs. "That's up to you."

Though I know I shouldn't open it, that nothing inside will be anything I want to see, I run my key along the seam of tape at the top of the box. It snaps open, the cardboard flaps popping up. As I glance inside, nausea hits me and my stomach clenches. Baby stuff. The box is *filled* with baby stuff. So, he knew. Pain scissors its way through me, shredding my insides. Part of me wants to break down, to cry, to scream. But I don't. I shove it all down, refusing to fall apart over this—over him.

I drop the box on the porch and kick it away from me. Cameron peers in and shakes his head.

"Sorry, Adele," he says.

"Don't worry about it. Just stay here. I'm going to grab what I need," I say before shutting the door behind me. I slink through the house, grab my cigarettes and Patrick's laptop then head back outside. I'd signed off on giving the Orlando Police Department remote access to Patrick's files. And right now, I'm really glad I didn't give them the machine.

When I walk out of the house a cool breeze whistles

through the rows of identical houses lining the street. The trees above us shade the lawn and a spiderweb of light dances through the branches. A dark green sedan crawls down the street and rolls to a stop in front of my house. I stop and watch the car as I wrack my brain. Do I know anyone that owns a car like that? No. Definitely not.

The door pops open and a woman climbs out. From the moment I see her frosted halo of hair, I know her. Her skin is overly tanned in a way that makes you think she probably feels like a leather handbag. She's got a beak of a nose, pointed and straight. Her face always has a sour look, like she's smelled something bad. Though it looks like she's unhappy, it's hard to know for sure since her face always looks like that.

"Who's that?" Cameron asks from behind me. I didn't realize that he followed me.

"A previous client," I say, my voice low enough that I know she won't hear the displeasure hanging on my words.

I step toward the stairs leading down from the porch. Though I don't know what Colleen is here for, I know I need to head her off. I plaster the best smile on my face I can muster.

"Hi, Colleen," I say as I approach.

Wind sweeps past us, making her navy blue silk blouse flutter. She puckers her lips so tightly, they turn white.

"Don't *Hi, Colleen* me," she snaps as she stops walking and places a hand firmly on her bony hip.

I tilt my head and appraise her.

"I've seen the news. That man, Malcom, killed himself after a session with you. I guess I should count myself lucky that my husband just threw me to the curb after you talked to him—at least he's not dead because of you. But now I wonder, what did you say to him? I've heard from a lot of women in this town that their husbands left after a session with you. Are you in the business of breaking up marriages?"

I try not to laugh at the accusation. Colleen's husband came to see me because she was sleeping with his best friend. He suspected both of their children were actually not his at all. From what I understand, a paternity test confirmed as much and he left. But the accusations that I'm breaking up marriages —that's just ridiculous.

"Colleen, I do my best as a counselor, just like everyone in my profession does, to provide the best insight and guidance that I can given the circumstances that are presented to me. I never tell anyone what to do about their marriage, whether that be separation, divorce, or staying together. That's not my job. All I do is listen and try to help people sort through their emotions."

Cameron stalks up beside me and takes a step toward the woman, like he's going to interject on my behalf. I don't want or need him to do that. I've handled everything by myself for years, I can handle this. Automatically my hand moves out to stop him.

Her nose curls. "You're a bad fucking liar. You should be in jail. You'll get what's coming to you. I know what you've been up to. Did you sleep with our husbands too? Is that how you lured them away?"

"That's enough," Cameron says as he grabs my arm a little harder than necessary. "Let's go," he says. And some part of me wants to argue. But I don't. I let him lead me to the car and I feel the death glare of the woman all the way back to the car.

It's a quick drive to the police station, to a squat building by the river. My stomach knots as we drive up. We both climb out of the car and I know I can't make it inside without smoking. I dig a pack of cigarettes out of my bag. As I clutch the cigarette between my lips, I light it, taking a slow drag. Smoke fills my mouth and I inhale it, savoring the flavor. I don't smoke often, but I keep a pack for occasions like this. Some stresses can only be stomached with a cigarette.

"Thank you for not lecturing me," I say as I put my cigarette out and flick it into the ashtray outside.

Cameron smiles and looks down. "I know you and I know the second I lecture you about doing anything you'll go out of your way to do it more."

Though I smile, I refuse to acknowledge that he's right.

18

I follow Cameron and he holds the door open for me. It kills me that I don't know what to expect. I cross my arms as I walk to keep my hands from shaking. Cameron doesn't seem to notice or sense my anxiety, thankfully.

"Just through here," he says as he waves me through double doors, past a room packed to the gills with desks, and finally into an interrogation room. Suddenly, I feel like I'm on the wrong side of an episode of *Law & Order*. I swallow hard, though it does no good.

"Do you need anything?" he asks when I take a seat in one of the cold metal chairs.

My mind screams, *Lawyer*. But I can't ask for that. Not yet. Asking for a lawyer makes you look guilty, and I can't afford to have any more attention on me than I already do. If this situation changes just a little, this could be *bad* for me. And it will be even worse for my career. "A bottle of water?" I ask. My throat is dangerously dry, though I'm not sure a drink will actually do any good. At least it'll keep my hands busy.

"Sure, I'll be right back," he says, and the door snaps shut behind him.

The cold metal chair sends a chill snaking up my spine as I look at myself in the one-way mirror. My brow furrows as I look at myself. Do I look guilty? What are they going to see when they look at me? A criminal? A sad wife?

The door cracks open and though I expect for Cam to come back through the door, a man in a bad tweed jacket and mustard-color pants waltzes through the door. My stomach bottoms out and I'm not sure if it's dread or disappointment. The man has a thick folder tucked beneath his arm. His dirty-blonde hair is thinning on top of his head, and he's got a scraggily moustache clinging to his thin lips. This guy looks like he's been working at the station for at least fifty years, like someone pulled him straight out of the seventies. He barely glances at me until he sits down at the table across from me. The folder slaps to the table so hard I nearly jump.

"I'm Detective McCarthy," he says as he pops a toothpick into his mouth and starts to gnaw on it. "Adele Johansen?"

I nod. I'm not sure why he's bothering to ask my name. He clearly knows who I am.

"And you're married to Patrick Johansen, correct?" he asks as he fishes a pen from his jacket and presses the tip to his tongue. I want to cringe. Why do people even do that?

"Yes," I confirm.

His eyes sharpen on me. I've seen the look before, when a predator starts the hunt, the moment it spots its prey. "How long have you two been married?"

"Seven years. We were together for two years before that," I explain. It stings when I say it. How do you rationalize losing that many years of your life? I gave him almost a decade.

He nods and scribbles on a piece of paper. "How is your marriage?"

My brows crinkle and I consider the best way to answer that. I lace my fingers together on top of the table. Though I don't want to be honest, I don't feel like I have a choice. At this point I know that they've found out about Brynlee, our finances, all of his lies. The shame tells me to lie, to not admit to anyone how I failed, how my life is crumbling around me. But I know I can't do that. "Complicated."

For a moment, I think the detective is going to smile. But his face hardens, and the twinge of a smirk vanishes.

"What kind of problems do you two have? Arguments? Money problems? Cheating?" The way he asks the questions, I can tell he's a man that already has the answers. There's too much confidence in his tone.

While he asks, I weigh my options. I have to be careful about how I answer these questions. Though I know I'm likely not a suspect in anything right now, some wrong answers could easily change that. "Two out of three, we didn't argue much. But since he disappeared, I've found out about money problems and cheating that I wasn't previously aware of," I explain.

He nods and makes a note. "Did anything in your relationship change before his disappearance?"

"Not really. But I found out when he disappeared that he never told his work that I existed. As far as everyone there knew, he wasn't married," I say, and I feel the edges of my wound fray. I go on to explain that he took the vacation time but kept pretending to go to work each day.

"So, you never went to this job?"

I shake my head as internally I debate how to answer his question. Should I have visited Patrick's work? Is that something that good wives do? He never seemed like he wanted me to show up there. I wasn't certain what building he worked in or where his office was. And most days I had clients to meet with, so it's not like I had tons of time to run to his office. "I had no reason to," I finally say, feeling myself get defensive.

He levels a look at me that dares me to shrink away. "My wife drops off my lunch every day."

"Then I guess she's a better wife than I was," I say with an edge to my words. It's not as if I haven't been asking myself every day what I could have done to prevent this—calculating what was my fault and what was his. But I'm so sick of my mind trying to make this my fault, I know it's easier to blame myself. At the end of the day, Patrick did this, and no one else.

"Was?" he asks, a brow raised.

Shit. A lie rises to my mind instantly. "He had divorce papers drawn up. He had a mistress. He took off. Clearly *was* is appropriate here. When Patrick shows back up, I know what will happen. We won't be together anymore. He's made it very clear that he imagined a life without me."

He folds his arms atop the table. "Fair enough. So, you'd not categorize yourself as a good wife then?"

"I tried every day. I compromised. I thought that we were happy. I checked in with him. I did everything the books tell you to do as a wife." I shake my head, frustration seeping into my words. My heart twists, hollow and somehow echoing the thoughts that won't leave my mind: *Why wasn't I enough?* "Can we just move on?"

"Sure." He looks down at the papers in the folder in front of him. "What did Patrick do for work?"

"He worked on the financial systems for different companies. He was heavily involved in payroll, vendor management, that sort of thing." Though I didn't understand the minutia of Patrick's job, I heard enough of his high-level explanations to tell the police what he did. When I asked questions, he changed the subject or gave me answers a politician might give.

As I talk, the detective flips through pages in front of him. I wish I could see what he's reading, but the paper is too far away. "So, that's what he did for this most recent job?"

I raise a brow to that. "Yeah, of course he did."

"Well, you see, I looked into the job history that Patrick provided when he was hired, and he didn't actually work for a single one of these companies. The HR department hadn't done a great job of following up to verify the validity of the resume. But it seems he was also very skilled at listing companies and roles that were difficult to nail down."

I swallow hard as I try to wrap my mind around what he's saying. More goddamn lies. How did I fall for them all? My fists clench beneath the table, cutting crescent moons into my palms.

"I'm going to guess based on the look on your face right now, that you didn't know."

I shake my head. A shaky breath slips from my lips. "No, I had no idea."

Detective McCarthy looks up, but the look he flashes me tells me that he's heard this before. "Did you suspect that he was being unfaithful before he disappeared?"

I sigh. I wish that I had suspected something, noticed something. "No, I didn't. And honestly, I hate myself that I didn't notice. In my line of work, it doesn't speak highly of my skills." If I can't recognize that my husband is lying to me daily, who's to say I can recognize anything of note in my clients?

"That must be tough," he says, and I nod. "But I don't think it's indicative of your abilities for your work. We only see the best in those we love."

I'm not sure what to say, so I press my lips together.

"Did it make you angry?" he asks, looking up from the folder. Though I know this guy has been doing this for years, his eyes are still hungry. He's desperate for me to give him the answers he seeks.

"Yeah, it did. I think it'd make anyone angry." My words don't hold even a hint of the rage that still coils within me. For a moment I wonder if it's fizzled, if maybe I've moved on. But beneath the lies, I feel it simmering there, just beneath the surface.

He jots something down and looks back at me. "I think anyone would be in that situation. But how mad were you exactly?"

"I'm not really sure why it's relevant. I found out after Patrick disappeared." It's very clear that I didn't know about the cheating, that I had no real reason to be angry with him. That, at least, I know will protect me. If I had known that Patrick was cheating before his disappearance, that would look very bad for me.

"So you didn't ever suspect anything before? You didn't pick fights with Patrick about the possibility of cheating?"

"No."

"I see," he says, and I can tell he doesn't believe me in the way his eyebrows raise, the way he grips his pen harder. "Did you know he was planning to file for divorce?"

"Not until I saw the papers a couple days ago, no."

"So, you hadn't found them before this week? You didn't, say, find them a few weeks ago and it made you enraged?"

I shake my head and sigh. "No, as I said, I saw them for the first time this week."

"Are you sure about that?"

Rage rises inside me at the pointed questions. But I know what he's trying to do. He wants to provoke me. He wants me to slip up. I am much better at this game than he is though.

"I'm sorry, but how exactly is this going to help you find Patrick?" I ask.

He folds his hands on top of the folder and straightens in the chair. "I'm trying to put the pieces together, Adele. Because right now, things aren't adding up. We thought at first, maybe your husband had left for a mistress. That happens sometimes. But we tracked her down and she's dead. Murdered. Someone tried to make it look like a suicide," he says, and he stares at me, through me, waiting for some kind of reaction.

I give him nothing, because there's nothing to give. I might have seen her right before she died. But I didn't kill her.

"There's no hint that Patrick was there that night. Or that he was involved at all. And it seems a bit odd for someone to leave their wife for a dead mistress. Usually, a mistress is killed if the husband is trying to hide something. Which leads me to the baby. Why didn't you and Patrick have children?"

I don't believe what he's saying. If they don't think that Patrick was involved, then why did they put me in the hotel? But I don't say that aloud. My lips twist. "Neither of us wanted children."

The detective grins. "That's not what Patrick's old friends say. They say he wanted them, but you didn't. You made decisions for the both of you."

What friends exactly? I want to snap. Instead, I grind my teeth. I should have just lied to Patrick and told him I couldn't have children. Not wanting children in this world is a crime. Not being able to have them though, that's a tragedy. Not everyone is fit to be a mother—and after what happened to my parents, I don't want to bring a child into this world.

"I'm not sure what you're getting at," I say. I want him to spell it out more. "Who even told you that?" Patrick didn't have *old friends*. There wasn't anyone that he confided in. He must be trying to bait me. He had a thousand acquaintances, but no one he really trusted.

"All of this evidence here, all these things I've found out, it makes me wonder if Patrick didn't disappear at all. And if he didn't meet a similar fate to his girlfriend."

I smile slowly, then stop myself. "I want a lawyer," I say, because I know exactly where this line of questioning is going.

"Are you sure? I had a few questions about Linda too."

I say it slower this time, just so there's no mistaking it. "Lawyer."

He nods, slaps the folder closed and stands up. The second he's out the door, I scroll through the contacts on my cell phone. The reception in here isn't great, goddamn concrete buildings, but it should be enough to talk to her for a minute.

"Hey, Ella, it's Adele," I say as soon as the call connects.

"Hey, girl!" she says, and in the background, I can hear the roar of the city, the click of heels against the pavement, seagulls cawing. "How are you doing?"

"I've been better. I'm actually calling because I need a lawyer."

"Where are you?" she asks.

"The Orlando Police Department, downtown." My voice makes me sound vulnerable, on edge.

"I'll be there in twenty," she says with a confidence that unknots my gut just a little.

"I owe you."

"No, I still owe you. Remember? You introduced me to Jenene," she says, and I can hear the smile in her voice.

"Aw, that's right. I guess I'll be able to hang that over your head forever," I say and let out a dry laugh.

Ella and I finish our conversation, and once I'm off the phone with her, I update Tara on everything that's happening. Cameron cracks the door a few minutes after I get off the phone with Ella. He offers me a sheepish smile and holds out a bottle of water for me.

"Were you standing behind there?" I ask, motioning toward the one-way mirror.

He nods.

"And you couldn't have stepped in and maybe said something on my behalf?" The anger is bitter inside me. I swear it pushes out of me and fills the room like a cloud. I try to narrow down my emotions. But I can't tell if I'm mad at him because I was hoping I'd conned him well enough already, or if I genuinely care that he wouldn't intervene on my behalf. This isn't good.

"There's no way I could have stepped in. You know that," he says, his voice barely a whisper. I cross my arms and ignore him until he huffs and leaves the room.

About twenty minutes later, Ella strides into the room.

She's got on a blazer with a matching black pencil skirt. Her dark hair is straightened and falls across her back and there's not a single strand of her straight mane out of place. She always looks impeccable, clothes perfectly styled, like she just walked off a runway. She says it's because it helps her in court, but I know that it's not true. There wasn't a day of her life before she passed the bar that she looked any different.

"Ella Diaz," she says to the cop who's escorted her to my interrogation room. "I need a moment alone with my client." Through the crack in the door, I can see the cop nod and make a note on a small notepad before shutting the door behind Ella.

"All right, sweetheart," she says as she slides out the chair beside me and plops her bag on it. "I've looked at what they've got, everything is completely circumstantial. And the most important part, they don't have a body. Not for Patrick anyway. They've got nothing to hold you on or charge you with. So, you're free to go. Do not answer any more questions about him unless I'm present, understood?"

I nod and the chains of tension around me loosen slightly. "I can't believe they're trying to pin this on me," I say as I rise from the table and follow her out of the station. As soon as we emerge, the Florida heat and humidity hits us like a wall. Small white clouds dot the horizon, and I pray that some rain will give us some relief from the heat.

"I can," she says with a laugh. "Your spouse is more likely to kill you than any other person on the planet."

I knew that much, actually. But it's still a bitter pill. They don't even have any proof that Patrick is dead. Cameron jogs out of the station after us, just as we reach the parking lot. His cheeks are tinged with red as he approaches, as if the heat has already gotten to him.

"I'll take you back to my place," he says.

I cross my arms. "I'm not going back to your place. I'm going to stay with Tara." Thankfully, when I texted Tara on the way down, she responded immediately, explaining she still has the house to herself, so we wouldn't end up being tormented by her mother-in-law.

Cameron presses his lips together. "Come on. Can't we at least talk about this? I can keep you safe. She can't." He takes my hand and looks down at me. "Look, you know that your parents' death wasn't an accident. It was a stalker. I think the person who killed your parents might be in town. Maybe that's who attacked you at the hotel."

I shake my head. I don't believe him. This feels like a desperate attempt to keep me at his place. "We'll talk later. I need to cool off," I say, my voice so steady, so even, it surprises me. I'm so disappointed that he let me walk into that room. He should have warned me. He should have done something to intervene.

He nods, though it's obvious he's not happy about it.

"Do you need a ride somewhere?" Ella asks.

"Thanks, but I'm all set. Thank you so much for coming down." I know she didn't have to, despite how much she thinks she owes me.

Ella offers me a quick hug, then slides into her black Escalade. Cameron gives me one last look before he turns and walks into the station. The streets of downtown Orlando aren't bustling. That's not to say there aren't people—there are—but walking down the streets, I don't have to worry about being smushed shoulder to shoulder with thousands of others. I walk in the shadow of the shops lining Church Street and a breeze slips through the street, rustling my hair. Tara isn't far away and though I know she'd probably come get me if I asked, walking will be therapeutic. The sun glitters on the buildings above me. I love seeing the city from here. It feels different, bigger. Somehow the enormity of it helps put my problems in perspective. Seeing it from the highway, it dwarfs the buildings. It all seems unreal.

The midmorning sun kisses the back of my neck and sweat slicks on my skin. By the time I reach Tara's office building, I feel like I've run a marathon. This is probably the point where I should swear up and down that I'll exercise more—but I won't. Because who am I kidding? I don't have the time or motivation for that. I text Tara from the lobby and a few minutes later she lets me know she's on her way down.

She offers me a halfhearted smile when she pops her head out of the elevator. Tara bobs along in her slacks and loose-fitting silk top. If I'd have stayed in school, I'd probably be in a cubicle next to her upstairs. But being in a cube all day, every day would inevitably lead me to being on suicide watch.

"How you doing, Delly?" she asks as she cocks her head and appraises me. Sometimes when she looks at me like this, I feel like I she can peer into my soul. I can't BS her. So instead, I say nothing.

She straightens, slings her purse over her shoulder and waves toward the door. "Come on, let's go. I'm taking you home," she says.

"Aren't you going to need to go back up to work?"

She waves her hand with dismissal. "Half day, babe." She beams at me.

"Are you sure?" I don't want to put her job in jeopardy because I'm having a crisis.

"I have like fifty vacation days saved up. No one is going to care if I take a half day." Though Tara and her husband own B&Bs to make side income, she also works for a tourism company downtown. She says that staying on the cutting edge of hospitality helps her stay competitive at work. But I think it's because she gets too bored if she doesn't have enough work on her plate.

"Why don't you... I don't know... take a vacation?" I ask as I follow her out the double doors. The second the heat hits me, my chest tightens. Humidity piles on top of me like bricks. Each step adds another to the pile. I swear it was cool just an hour ago. The weather in Florida during the winter is a fickle beast. Sometimes the cold fronts are gone before you can blink.

"Because then Peter would have to take a few days off and chances are his mother would want to come along as well. So, I'd rather just save them until after the funeral."

Tara slides into her SUV and I get into her passenger seat. If I thought the heat on the street was bad, the heat in the car is like sitting ten feet from the sun. She starts the car and the AC churns, blowing hot air around.

"So, spill. What happened?" she asks as she buckles her seat belt.

I give her a rundown of my morning and the questioning. It takes a long time to fill her in, all the while she weaves through the streets dodging potholes and tourists as they scamper along the streets. By the time I'm done talking, I feel like I've been wrung out and all my emotions are pooled at my feet.

"And after all that, Cameron didn't stick up for me, he didn't say a word for me. He didn't even warn me what I was walking into." The anger comes rising back and my fingernails dig into my palms.

Tara purses her lips and stares straight ahead as she drives. Her dark hair is half in her face, and I swear it's because she doesn't want to glance at me. There's something about her posture that's off.

"What?" I know she's got a mouthful trapped behind those lips.

"You're not going to like it," she says in a singsong voice.

I know I'm going to hear it either way. So, I'd rather rip off the Band-Aid. "Just tell me."

She sighs and throws on her blinker before turning. "He was just doing his job. And it seems to me, from where I'm sitting, that maybe you're just looking for a reason to push him away again."

I shake my head and look away. I have every right to be angry. He could have said something. He could have warned me that I might want to get a lawyer, that they were growing suspicious of me. There's something he could have done to give me a heads-up. Based on that interview, it seems like they're pretty far into an investigation and they think that *I* killed Patrick.

"I have every right to be angry." I nearly growl the words at her.

She nods and looks at me as we stop at a light. "You do. But you're still being a child."

Expecting Cameron to give me a heads-up after everything that we've been through together—I don't think that's too much to ask. And needing some time away to sit with my feelings because I'm so let down by him, I think that's valid.

"Do you want to stop by your house and pick up some of your things?" she asks.

I curse myself for leaving my things at Cameron's, after he brought them over from the hotel for me. That's not to say I don't have any other clothes, I do, but they're the B squad. A bad feeling brews inside me when we pull in front of my house. It was our house, and there's no *us* anymore. There will never be an *us* again. When we bought it, I had so many hopes, dreams for the future. I saw us growing old together. Who knew old was thirty-six?

Dread clings to me as I stare out the window at the house. I glance up and down the street looking for a car out of place, anyone walking. Will another angry client ambush me?

"Will you come in with me?" I ask, hoping my unease doesn't reach my words. I could explain to her what's happened with Lucas and my angry clients, but I really don't want to get into it. I just want my friend to help because I asked, not because I threw a dumpster of emotional bullshit her way. The last thing I want to admit aloud is how far I feel like I've fallen, how out of control this all is right now. Part of me is terrified that Brenda is going to show up, or some other client who now thinks I destroyed their life.

Tara hops out without skipping a beat. With my keys still in Cameron's car with the laptop, I have to resort to the hide-a-key. Though I search the side flowerbed for the fake rock I know houses the key, I don't see it.

"What are you doing?" Tara asks as she peers at me around the side of the house, her hand on her hip.

"Looking for the key. It was over here."

"What's it look like?" she asks, and I explain what we're looking for.

In the backyard, beneath the primary bedroom window, we find the key. A lump is heavy in my throat as I unlock the door. The box of baby stuff is still kicked to the side, slightly farther than where I left it. It's not lost on me that clearly someone has been using the key, that they've been in my house. Why didn't I think to tell Cameron about the key when I first saw the vase? It completely slipped my mind. I search the living room, as if I might see some lingering imprint, some evidence that someone was here though I hadn't noticed anything earlier when I picked up Patrick's laptop. The flower and the note should be enough to prove that, but I feel like something else is missing.

I peek into the guest bedroom, office, and kitchen as I pass them, but there's no hint anyone has been here. There are no more vases, notes. And though I told the police they *could* come in if they wanted, no one has asked to enter the premises. Grabbing one of Patrick's many gym bags, I throw several changes of clothes inside. I'm not sure how long I'll stay with Tara, but I'd rather have too much than too little; otherwise, I'm going to have to resort to my trust fund so I can buy new clothes—that's the last thing I want to do right now. Though the trust fund has always been there, I've never used it. Some part of me wanted to prove that I could do everything on my own, that I didn't need my parents to save me.

"You ready?" Tara asks as she peeks around the doorframe, and I nearly jump out of my skin.

I nod. "Yeah, let's go."

Outside, I finally let out the breath I was holding. I slide into Tara's car and look back at the house one last time. I'd rather burn it down than face the memories bottled inside—and maybe that'd be for the best. It's a memorial to the biggest compromise I made, and inside, there's nothing of me. It's a museum to the person that Patrick wanted me to be. Tara's house is across town from mine. If anyone told me back when Tara and I met that eventually she'd live in a suburban neighborhood in a two-story house that looks like it was pieced together on an assembly line, I would have said they were crazy. Back in the day, Tara swore up and down that she'd never be one of *those* people. She loved punk rock and wanted to live an antiestablishment life. Now, she drives a Toyota and works for a travel company. In her shadow, I can see the same girl with blue hair she used to be. I know that girl is still in there somewhere. The difference is, now she knows how to choose her battles. Back then, everything was a battle. Everyone was the enemy. I guess that's what growing up is, knowing when to abandon your sword.

She pulls up into her driveway. The taupe house towers above us, a monument of stucco, terracotta tile, and accents to try and make the boxy house look exotic, Mediterranean. Living in Florida though, I know there's nothing remotely exotic about it. But it still feels out of place in Orlando. Still though, even though this is a builder house, the same type that I lived in for so long—the inside feels like Tara. She definitely put her own stamp on it, while my place was a living, breathing, Pottery Barn diorama.

"You want some wine?" she asks as she holds the front door open and waves me inside.

"Actually, no. Thank you." Drinking is dangerous, one of the worst things you can do as a shrink—if I accidentally say what I really think, that could easily ruin a friendship. Usually I'll nurse a glass of wine to fit in, to clear my head, but too much —it never ends well.

She purses her lips, like she's chewing the inside of her cheek. Small lines feather out from either side of her mouth. Obviously, she wanted to use me as an excuse. Social drinking is enablement, and I hate that she needs me to give her permission.

"Don't let me stop you," I say to try and make her feel better. But it does no good. She looks like she's sucked on a lemon.

"You're no fun."

I shrug. I'd rather be no fun than impaired right now. If there are more questions coming my way, which I'm sure there are, I need to have my wits about me.

"Can I talk you into pizza? Maybe we can watch some TV?" she asks. I nod, though I know I'm not going to be the best sidekick for a pizza and movie night. But it will make her feel better and eventually that will make me feel better. She orders the pizza and I collapse onto the fluffy couch in her living room. The soft blue walls nearly glow as the light angles in through the large window in the living room. A fluffy white carpet that looks like someone skinned five hundred long-haired cats to make it sits at my feet. I can never keep myself from weaving my toes into the soft fibers. To this day, I'm not sure how she's managed to keep it white for so long. If this rug was in my house, it'd have fifty coffee stains on it.

"Where's your mother-in-law again?" I ask. In the past few years that she's lived with them, she's barely left.

"She went up north to see Elena. I swear, the second she

realized she'd be alone with me for two months, she booked tickets." Tara laughs. "Not that I mind. Hopefully she likes it enough to stay there."

I laugh because I know that's not going to happen. Peter is the favorite. She won't be gone long.

"Maybe she'll make it a habit of just leaving anytime he does," I offer.

"Oh, come on, she's got to know you need to be alone if you're going to give her a grand-baby," I say with a grin.

She rolls her eyes. "She wants a grandkid all right. By any means that doesn't involve my DNA. I can't tell you how many times she's suggested that we adopt. I wonder how many times she's propositioned people to see if they wanted to offload their brood."

"Why doesn't she think you should have any?" I ask.

"I'm too old. She said I have rotten eggs."

I wanted to tell her they were like Cadbury eggs. They never go bad.

I choke I laugh so hard. "You can't be serious. You're not even forty."

"She thinks anyone over twenty-nine is too old for having children."

I roll my eyes at that. "If Janet Jackson can have a baby at fifty, you can have one at thirty-seven."

She shrugs. "I've learned to live with it. She's got more venom than a rattlesnake."

The doorbell chimes and she hops off the couch. In a few minutes, she strolls back with pizza. We spend the rest of the afternoon watching TV and eating pizza. Though she brings up Cameron no less than seven times, I'm able to mostly avoid the topic.

At ten, we both call it quits and she feels the need to walk me to the guest bedroom, though I know exactly where it is.

"Sorry if it smells like old people, monster-in-law stink might seep over from next door."

I laugh at that. "I'll keep that in mind. Thank you."

She waves her hand as she walks down the hall. "Good night."

"Night," I call back as I close my door.

19

The house is cold when I awake, the blanket of night still holding firm, though the watery light on the horizon tells me that dawn isn't far off. There's no real reason I should be awake this early. I never have clients before ten in the morning; I guess ending a marriage is an afternoon endeavor. But somehow, I know from the adrenaline already burning its way through my system that there's no chance I'll be able to go back to sleep. The pale purple walls of Tara's guest room glow in the low light. At home, I always wake to the dull roar of traffic, construction, a symphony of the waking world. Without the sirens, children screaming, dogs barking, it feels like we're underground—hidden away.

I drag myself from bed, unsure if Tara's already left for work or not. I wonder when this ordeal with Patrick will blow over so I can get back to my life. My thoughts skid to a halt. My life. What will my life be like after all this? I don't know that I'll still be able to do counseling. I may have to start over, to rebuild. I slide from the bed, my feet hitting the plush carpet of the bedroom floor. I'm struck by déjà vu, like I already got out of bed and made this walk.

My feet stick to the cold tile as I pad toward the kitchen. The whole house is always so clean and sterile I can't tell if she's been in here or not. Tara is Type A to the core. Her house must be in perfect order at all times. I glance at the clock. It's already eight, but her car is still parked outside.

When I can't sleep, I need to do something with my hands, to be active. Breakfast. I could make Tara breakfast as a thank-you for letting me stay here. Tara is a health nut, so I know she'd appreciate an omelet.

I shake off the feeling, convincing myself that it's just sleep still clouding my mind. The tile floor bites into my bare feet when I reach the kitchen. Though I've never cooked in Tara's kitchen, I've watched her at it enough times that I can find everything I need. But before I can cook anything, I scour the fridge for my options. I'm able to scrounge up tomato, bacon, spinach, eggs, and cheese. Omelets it is.

I set to chopping the tomato and spinach first and sauté it in a skillet. Once it's ready, I throw the bacon into a pan and make the omelets. The air is thick with the scent of bacon by the time I'm done. I'm honestly surprised that Tara didn't wake up while I was cooking. She's always been an unusually light sleeper. I grab a cup of coffee for her and pad down the hall.

"Tara?" I call. But she doesn't answer.

Maybe she's still asleep.

A long narrow hallway leads to her bedroom. The doors to her room are closed, so I knock gently, and listen for her on the other side. After a few seconds, when she doesn't yell at me, I try again, this time louder. Nothing.

"Tara, wake up," I say as I bang on the door. Still, nothing. My stomach tightens as a bad feeling grows within me.

I put my hand on the knob, but it won't budge. It's locked. That's weird. Why would she lock the door while I'm here? I sigh as I yank with both hands and rattle it. The handle pops and I'm able to open it. It's a trick that worked on my parents' bedroom door when I was a kid.

My hand searches the wall and when I finally find the switch, I flick it on. Tara is under the covers. All I can see is bits of her hair streaming out on the bed.

"Come on, get up," I say as I kick the bed. But she doesn't move. She doesn't even flinch. My heart hammers. Every swift beat is telling me that something is wrong. I throw the covers off her with shaking hands. I suck in a breath so sharp my lungs ache and I double over. She stares straight up, her vacant eyes locked on the ceiling. Purple and blue rings her neck and spots her arms. There's blood everywhere, seeping through her white duvet. My mind churns over the details for too long, because it can't be real. I must be dreaming, imagining things.

I want to scream. To cry. To wake her up. Because it can't be. It can't. But I'm frozen, grief wrapped around me like steel chains binding me to the floor. Questions flood my mind, holding the grief at bay. Who could have done this? When? Why?

She can't really be dead. It's not possible. Tara's been in my life for twenty years. I can't lose her.

"Tara," I croak when I finally find my voice. It cracks, shatters, and I break along with it. My hand grips hers. Her fingers are cold, stiff in my hand.

I stumble backward, and though I'm unsteady on my feet, I feel like I'm falling. This isn't possible. It can't be real. There's no way she's really gone. My hands shake as I try to force myself to breathe.

What do I do?

My body moves automatically, and I sprint across the house. I pass her living room, the kitchen—still smelling of breakfast— then climb the stairs. At the landing at the top of the stairs, I turn left, then run down another hall to the room over her garage. My heart pounds. The door is wide open, light streaming in.

Panic wraps its hands around my throat. I slow, creeping toward the door. But I know what I'll find. I know what's waiting for me. The room is stark. Tara had always used it for storage. Right up until I asked her for help a couple weeks ago. I peek in, my eyes roving over the white walls, the beige carpet, the metal-framed bed in the center of the room. Ropes lie on the floor in a heap. And though I'm expecting it, though I knew what I'd find the moment I got up here, my mind still reels.

Patrick is gone.

20

Getting rid of all of the evidence that your best friend helped you kidnap your cheating asshole of a husband and subsequently hold him hostage until it was the right moment to kill him isn't as difficult as you'd think. I had to put the food I made on the stove on warm, so it wouldn't be cold when the police showed up. Timelines are so incredibly important when the police arrive and start asking questions. After the food was handled, I stripped the room, wiped down fingerprints, and tried to discern how exactly Patrick got free.

The ropes were on the floor, not cut or broken. It looked like someone untied him.

And now, as I stand with trembling hands, I know now more than ever I'm going to make Patrick pay. I decided weeks ago to put my plan into motion, when I really found out about the extent of his cheating, his squandering of our money, how far into the hole he'd gotten us. It was all just too much.

I do one more sweep through the house, ensuring that everything is ready, then head back to Tara's room. Once I'm sure it is, I pull my phone from my pajamas pocket. My hands move on their own, swiping through the screen until the phone rings. I hold it to my ear.

"Hello?" Cameron asks groggily. What is he doing still sleeping at this hour?

"She's dead," I say automatically. The words tumble out and once they do, the tears flow fresh. My eyes burn and my throat tightens with grief. This, at least, isn't a lie. Waves of sorrow lash me, and it takes everything I have not to sink to the floor and dissolve.

"What?" he asks, his voice rising with surprise.

"Tara, she's dead." I force the words out between sobs.

"How?" he asks.

"It looks like she was stabbed to death, but there's also purple on her neck, like she was choked," I say, and I turn away. I can't bear to look at her again. Not like this.

"Did you call the police?"

"You are the police," I say pointedly.

"Hang up and call 911 right now. Where are you? I'll be there soon," he says.

I give him the address and hang up the phone. It takes me a long time to gather the strength to call 911. When I walk the operator through what I woke up to, I break down all over again. The woman doesn't let me hang up until the sirens blare outside.

The walk down the hall through the house to let the paramedics in is the longest walk of my life. I let them in and feel as though all the energy I had left is siphoned off into the ether with Tara. The paramedics head into the bedroom and I hang by the door. It's not surprising when they confirm her death, but it doesn't sting any less.

Police file in, a crime scene investigation team, a coroner, all the while, my mind is cast adrift. As they move around her, I shift around the scene, like a piece of furniture being moved out of the way. My mind wars between anger and grief. It's a toxic mix that makes me feel nauseous. I wish my body would choose one, but instead I'm left hollowed out, wanting to scream and cry until my throat is raw. Cameron laces his arm into mine and drags me away from the bustling bodies.

"Sorry, I got held up. How are you doing?" he asks as he pulls me away.

I lean into him, allowing the familiar scent to carry me away. Nothing can unwind me like the smell of him, the feel of him against me. But even this does little to comfort me.

"This can't be real. Tell me this isn't real," I beg as I bury my face in his chest. There's only one person in this world that would kill Tara. I've got no question in my mind that Patrick did this. But why would he leave me alive? Is it because he didn't know I was in the house? Did he want to torture me more? Or did someone else do this to get back at me?

Cameron strokes my hair. But it does nothing to lessen the grief weighing on my heart. "It's going to be okay."

Cameron urges me down the hall toward the kitchen, away from the police officers. His eyes are on the room, and for a minute, I think he's going to make us move to another room entirely.

"Do you think Patrick could do this?" he asks, his voice low.

I'm not sure I even know what Patrick is capable of anymore. He never had a problem with Tara before, not before she held him hostage for me anyway. But I don't want to let the police believe that he did this. Because I'm going to hunt him down and kill him myself. "I don't think so. They weren't close. But they didn't hate each other either," I explain.

He squares his shoulders and furrows his brows. "It just doesn't make sense. Why would he kill his girlfriend, send someone to attack the police officer at the hotel, then kill your best friend?"

I know what he's asking, what he's insinuating. Because he

thinks I should have been the one to kill Brynlee. But it would make no sense for me to kill Linda and Tara.

"So, what are you going to do?" I ask, trying to wipe the tears that keep collecting on my cheeks. If I hadn't gotten her involved in all this, would she still be alive?

"Keep looking, that's all I can do," he says. "We have zero leads on Patrick. No sightings. No hits on the credit cards. No one from his office has seen him. It's like he's completely disappeared. No tips. Nothing on social media. The media is still carrying the story. If he was around, someone would have seen something by now."

"If he was around here, doing all this, shouldn't someone have seen him?" I ask, careful not to phrase it like I'm defending him.

"Most likely." He glances down the hall. "They're going to have to ask you questions about what happened. Or I can take your statement. It's totally up to you."

I know that Cameron must be breaking procedure here. There's no way that he should be allowed to take my statement. But I also have no desire to be questioned by any of the guys at his station again. "I'd rather you do it," I say. And I suck in a deep, shuddering breath. "I'm sorry for yesterday."

He nods. "Me too. I'm glad you finally learned to apologize." If I wasn't so upset, I'd slug him in the arm. "Sorry, bad time. I was just trying to cheer you up."

I nod. It's no harm done. Cameron has always tried to make me laugh to lighten the mood. That's how he is. If he doesn't know how to handle something, humor is his go-to defense mechanism. He pulls his notepad out and leads me to the dining table. Though he's a good three feet away from me, I can feel his energy. It strokes mine and numbs the threads of grief tightening around me. Eventually, I know his presence will unwind them completely, it always does.

"I wonder if Brenda could have something to do with all

this," I say, then explain to him the encounter I had with her at the hotel.

He takes down a few notes to follow up on her, then I pass along the contact info I have for her in Emma's original email.

After he's got the details on Brenda, Cameron goes over what feels like a thousand questions about the afternoon I spent with Tara, the evening, and anything else that could have happened after. But once we were both in bed, there's nothing to tell. Nothing woke me up or gave me even the slightest hint of what was happening across the house. That's the worst part, knowing she was so close when she died. If I had heard something, anything, I could have helped her.

I swallow my anguish and hold myself together after all the questions are answered. A thought crashes to the bottom of my mind and nearly knocks me over. Her husband doesn't know. I have to tell him.

"Shit," I mumble. "Her husband."

Cameron reaches over and squeezes my hand. "Where is he? You can't tell him over the phone."

"He's in Europe on a business trip."

He looks down. "I think we'll have to call the consulate for that, and they'll deliver the news. Promise me that you won't call him."

A lump is heavy in my throat. But I agree all the same. What else can I do?

"The investigators might have more questions for you later about this, okay?" he asks, and laces his fingers together. He tenses, like he's bracing for impact. "At this point, I'm not sure how much more involvement they're going to let me have with the case because of our history."

That makes my stomach churn. But there's nothing I can do about it. I knew this would happen, but I hoped I'd have a little longer.

"Are you still in touch with your lawyer?"

"Yeah. She said if I need anything else, she'll come down."

"Good. If they ask you more questions, make sure she's there."

"I will."

I'm suddenly feeling like I've lost control of everything, and my life is falling apart around me. There's nothing I can do to stop it, nothing I can do to fix it. This isn't how this was supposed to go. I had this all planed out. I need to have a handle on everything, to figure out where this went wrong.

There's concern swimming in Cameron's eyes when I look up at him. And I want to see everything I saw ten years ago. But I feel nothing. At some point though, should I bury my past and realize if he wants me, if he thinks he can really be happy with me, I should let him? Would it protect me? Would it really be so bad to settle for a guy that worships me? I tried love, and where did that get me?

"Can I crash at your place?" I ask, swallowing every ounce of pride I have because I have to go somewhere. After what happened at my hotel room, there's no way I'm staying in another hotel. And right now, he feels like the only option. My house isn't safe, and I don't really have any desire to be alone.

His lips twist into a smile. His ego must have just grown tenfold. Though I'd tell him I'm just desperate if he asks, it's only because lies are far more comfortable than the truth. I know I need him. I know I want him, but I'll bury that truth where no one else will ever find it. Not even him. Having someone know how much you need them is the ultimate power. How could I ever trust anyone with that?

"You can *always* stay at my place. I've got everything moved over from the hotel." He offers me a scant smile.

"So, you knew I'd come back then?"

"Knew? No. Hoped? Yes," he says as he opens his hand for mine. I've never been the handholding or the affectionate type, he knows that. In fact, in college, during his short stint in psychology, he tried to psychoanalyze me because of it. Abandonment and lack of parental affection is how he diagnosed me. Maybe he's right. I've always wanted to build a wall of granite between me and my emotions, then another between me and everyone else. People are a complication. How ironic it is that I built my life on psychology?

I watch the police and investigators still swarming the house. It hits me that this is my fault. If I hadn't come here, if I hadn't asked her to help me with Patrick, if I hadn't stayed here, she wouldn't be dead. She'd be at work, dreading the inevitable return of her mother-in-law.

"Do you want to grab anything before we go?" he asks as he rubs my shoulders gently.

"My bag is in the guestroom," I say and head down the hall to grab it. I don't want to lead them elsewhere in the house. I don't think they'll have any reason to go up to the spare room we kept Patrick in, but I hope if they do, I cleaned it up well enough.

On the nightstand, next to where my phone sat all night, there's another flower. But this one is dead. My stomach churns as I move closer, my eyes straining to read the note left next to it. The second I make the words out, every hair on my arms and neck stands on end.

He's next – ♡

Cameron walks up behind me and starts to say something. But I point toward the flower. He stops dead in his tracks, then urges me toward the door.

"That wasn't there this morning when I woke up," I say as I nearly jog down the hall. My limbs are heavy, stiff. It takes a lot more effort to move them than it should. Now I'm torn. If there was someone else in the house, did they free Patrick? Did this intruder kill Tara? There's no way Patrick could have left me the first flower; he was here the entire time.

Cameron flicks on his comms, speaking to the rest of the police in the house. "Suspect may still be on the premises. Proceed with caution."

Something tells me whoever did this isn't waiting around for the cops. A shiver crawls up my spine as I consider that the man who did this was in the house with me all night. Why is he doing this? Why is he after the people around me?

Grief blankets me, muting the world around me. I move through it all, but I may as well be wading through water. The police buzz through the first floor of the house, collecting evidence, taking pictures, but I may as well be cast alone in the night. They talk to me, but the words don't stick, they don't even register in my mind.

At some point, Cameron ushers me outside and the cool air pulls me from the haze. Outside, the roar of the wind, voices, sirens, assaults me. News vans line the street, huddled beneath the sweeping live oaks, their branches heavy with Spanish moss. Tripods spring up behind vans with their doors thrown open, revealing lit-up switchboards and glowing monitors inside.

My mouth goes dry as I take it all in. Panic tells me to run inside, to shield myself from this. I know it's too late. I can't flee. Their heads all turn like vultures scenting blood in the air. They've seen me and they'll connect the dots. They all start to turn at once, and I know there's no escaping it.

Denise McCaffery stands out among the journalists—maybe because she's the only one I know personally. As we walk out of the house, she jogs toward me.

"You knew about your parents' history, didn't you? Then you helped cover up their crimes so you could profit off their empire of tragedy." She hurls the accusations at me, like she's so sure of herself. "We've uncovered two murder-suicides that were connected to your parents' show after false allegations were made on the air. Lives were ruined. And you knew, you profited off that.

"Your parents ruined my life too," she shouts after me. "My father murdered my mother after they appeared on that show. Do you know what that was like for me?" Her voice breaks as she rages at me.

I shake my head. "I was thirteen years old. I had no idea. If these things happened, those are tragedies and I do not condone my parents' actions." The words fall out of my mouth automatically, though I know I shouldn't let them. My mind screams for me to say *no comment*, but I can't form those words. I have to defend myself.

"A man named Harold Craig Monroe has been posting videos online that your parents deserved what happened to them. Based on his age and location—there's a lot of speculation that he may have been the man who killed your parents."

Cameron grabs my arm and tugs me away.

"We have to get out of here," I say to Cameron, my voice too low to cut over the growing roar around us. I can hear their words, their accusations. No judge, no jury. Jose Baez couldn't even save me from this. I am as guilty as it gets.

Fear tethers me to the ground and I know I must look like a deer in headlights, my eyes red, still swollen from tears. Cameron's hand tightens around my bicep and he drags me stiff-legged across the lawn to his patrol car. This is going to replay on the news all day, all night. I know it. The words shouted at me echo in my head again and again. But they can't be true.

Everything shifts as we move, like the motion has set them off, made them truly aware of our presence. All at once a torrent opens up, as if a dam held them back and suddenly they were released. My chest tightens as adrenaline hits my blood. I have to get out of here, we have to get out of here. My mind keeps going over what Denise said—her father murdering her mother, the alleged attacker of my parents. Could he be responsible for this? Could he be leaving these notes?

A man in a red blazer and khakis runs toward us, his blonde hair gelled in place. "Adele, does your missing husband have anything to do with the death of Tara Olson?" His voice is high, nasal almost.

"Don't answer any questions," Cameron grunts as he drags me the rest of the way to the car.

"Is she being arrested for the murder of Tara Olson?" a man in a poorly fitting suit asks as he approaches, shoving his mic in Cameron's face. "Or the murders of her husband's mistresses Brynlee Travis and Ashlee Madison?"

My mind skips over the information. Ashlee is dead? I thought only Brynlee had died. If they're both dead... how long will it be before they draw conclusions about that?

"No comment," Cameron says as he swipes the mic out of his face.

When we finally climb inside the patrol car, I still feel them pushing against me.

"Are you okay?" Cameron asks as he turns the car on and throws it into reverse.

"No, I'm not," I say as we start to move. Anxiety presses in on me from all sides. The crowd behinds us parts and we pull out. But I don't feel any better by the time we reach the end of the street.

———

Hours later, nestled into Cameron's couch, with his dogs curled up next to me, I barely feel better. The moment the adrenaline left my bloodstream, I wanted to deflate. And here I've sat since, the raw void of Tara's missing presence a much sharper wound than Patrick's ever was—maybe because it's the wound I didn't expect. We started planning Patrick's disappearance a month ago, when I found out he was trying to steal my identity to access my trust fund. That was the final straw, not the cheating, not the failed businesses, not all the lies. I flip through the channels, dreading the news but knowing on a base level that I need to watch it.

A car commercial cuts away, revealing a female anchor. She's young, pretty, the kind of girl that could get Patrick's attention just by existing. Her green eyes are piercing as she stares into the camera.

"I'm Heather Hues and you're watching the news at noon on Channel Eleven. At the bottom of the last hour we mentioned a developing story that has many in our community concerned. Over the past week we've featured multiple people that all claimed to have had their marriages ruined by counselor Adele Sutton-Johansen. Though we've made multiple attempts to contact Mrs. Sutton-Johansen, we've been unable to reach her for comment. These women claim that Adele lured their husbands away, broke up their marriages, and likely had affairs with their spouses."

Rage flares inside me. Those liars. No one reached out to me for comment. Not that I would have given one.

"Should you really be watching this?" Cameron asks as he strolls back into the living room.

"Yes," I say as I turn the volume up. "I need to know what they're saying about me. We can't ignore this."

He waves his hand, as if to give me silent permission to continue. I feel sick as I watch, nausea climbing my throat. Is this what addiction feels like? There's a need that borders on a sickness urging me to watch.

"So far, here's what we know," she continues. "Adele Sutton-Johansen's husband disappeared a little over a week ago. Though we reached out to Orlando PD for details, they've said that they're unable to comment on an ongoing investigation, but they do not currently have reason to believe that foul play is suspected, despite the other deaths that we think could easily be connected to Mrs. Sutton-Johansen."

Beside her, a large picture of Patrick sits on the screen. I recognize the picture as his profile image from Facebook. He's grinning like an idiot. The tile in the background tells me it's a picture that he took in our bathroom. I wish that everyone watching this program could see who he really is, the cheater, the liar. Why the hell am I being crucified for my job? As if I wanted any of these women's husbands. Patrick lied too. He shouldn't get away with this shit. Why aren't they covering the identities he stole? The businesses he robbed? Why am I the pariah here?

"We have information from confidential sources that two of Patrick's mistresses were found dead three days ago. Now another unfortunate death appears connected to Adele."

My stomach flips and I want to vomit. This is it. My life is burning down in front of my own eyes. Would it even be possible to recover from this?

Cameron strolls over, pushes one of his dogs off the couch and sits down next to me. Though he slings his arm over my shoulder, I feel completely alone. He can't fix this. We can't fix this. This whole damn town won't see that Patrick's a cheater, a liar. I'm the liar that couldn't keep my husband happy. I failed. That's the lot of a woman, I guess.

———

My fingernails have nearly cut through my palms by the time we make it to the station. I called Ella right before we left, and she agreed to meet us there. Though I watched the city go by as we drove, I saw none of it. It blurred together, lost beneath the torrent of thoughts screaming in my mind. We roll to a stop at the edge of the parking lot, tucked away in the back near a row of ancient oak trees. Though the day is obnoxiously bright, we've got a reprieve beneath the tree.

"How bad will this be?" I ask. My nerves nearly have me sick. The stress multiplies in my veins like a virus. I want to escape this, to leave. But it's too late for that. I should have left the day that we took Patrick. Why did I stay? Why didn't I go when I had the chance? Would Tara still be alive? Would it really have changed anything?

"I don't know, honestly, but it probably won't be great."

"Are they going to arrest me?" I'm barely able to get the words out. The second they leave my lips, my mouth goes bone dry.

"I'm not sure they have enough evidence for that. But you need to be careful about what you say. Because of how close we are, the info they're giving me now is incredibly limited," he says. Concern paints his features. He's worried for me, truly.

I pop open the door, hoping that getting out in the fresh air will help.

"Adele." A man's voice cuts across the parking lot and my heart rate rises as I whip around.

Lucas stands about thirty feet from us, his thick dark brows drawn together, his mouth a firm line. His arms are crossed over his broad chest, like he's trying to make himself look more intimidating. In his jeans and polo, it doesn't work on me.

"I saw all the stuff on the TV about you. I wanted to believe that you were different than Patrick, that you were better," he says.

I open my mouth to say something, though I'm not sure what. But Lucas raises his hand, silencing me.

"You two were perfect for one another. Two con artists. I'm going to make this easy on you. I want my money back and you've got three days to give it to me."

I flinch, though he's not wrong.

My mind races. As far as my financials show, I have nothing. And there's nothing for him to take. Though he might think I've got something squirreled away from Patrick, there's no proof. Sure, I drew out money from our account with Patrick's cards right before his *disappearance*, but Lucas would have no way of knowing about that.

"Do you really think Patrick left me with anything? He took everything we had. He maxed credit cards, took out cards in my name, and didn't even pay the mortgage. They're going to take my house," I say. And somehow, admitting that aloud makes it real—even though I hated the damn thing. The gravity of it all hits me. I've got nothing. I'll have to use that damn trust fund, the blood money. I can't rebuild without it. Once it's safe and this has all blown over, I need to take my money and run. In truth, I've known about the house for a while. I could have saved it, if I wanted. But it's become a monument to my failure and compromises. Why the hell would I want to keep it?

"He didn't need to leave you with anything. You've taken plenty from others to help keep yourself afloat. Stop trying to make yourself look innocent here. It's not as if you're above scamming a few more unhappy wives to pad your pockets."

"I suggest you stop," Cameron says. On one hand, I hate him interjecting on my behalf. I can handle this. But on the other hand, him stepping in is a good sign. That means Cameron is wound around my finger like I need. Maybe this time while I'm in the station he'll protect me.

"Three days, Adele," Lucas says before stalking off.

Ella's Escalade pulls into the parking lot moments after we arrive. Though my heart is still pounding from the encounter with Lucas, seeing her puts me at ease. She slides out of her SUV, a gray pantsuit hugging her curves. A long gold chain with three small intertwined circles on it dangles from her neck. She pulls off her large cat-eye sunglasses as she strolls over, her high-heels clicking on the pavement with every step.

"I am so, so sorry about Tara," Ella says as she grabs my

shoulders and gives them a little squeeze. She holds me there, appraising me, and it takes everything in me not to break down again. It still doesn't feel real. Tara's been in my life so long it's hard to imagine how the world can keep going on without her. My partner in crime is gone.

"Thank you," I manage.

"I called the station to ask about the questioning, just to be sure this is necessary. And in this case, I think it is. They have some remaining questions about Tara. I'll be present the entire time, and if I think they're getting off topic or you shouldn't answer a question, I'll jump in. Does that sound good?"

I nod. "Yes. I just want this over with."

"I know, sweetie."

I walk to the door of the station with Cameron and Ella following behind. Cameron won't stop asking me about Lucas, why he's hounding me, what I can do to keep him away. But I can't focus on his questions. My stress levels are so high I'm practically drowning. I just need him to shut up, to leave me alone. I throw open the door of the station, hoping that at least in an interrogation room his questions will stop.

The dull hum of the florescent lights fills the waiting room. In the corner, a woman sits at a desk in a dark green uniform. She's got dark tawny skin and long box braids. I cross the room as quickly as I can, Cameron still hot on my heels.

"I'm here to answer some questions about a case," I say before introducing myself. Ella gives me a sideways look. I guess she was supposed to handle this. Cameron tries to interject again, but I flash him a look that thankfully manages to silence him. The woman tells us to take a seat and wait until the officers are ready. I sit in an uncomfortable plastic chair and wave Cameron away, hoping he'll do some work while we're here and leave me alone. I can't stand him hovering right now. Ella sits beside me and squeezes my forearm, trying to offer support.

It seems like hours tick by before an older man in a polo

and khakis comes to the waiting room to collect me. He introduces himself as Officer Baldwin. He's a couple inches shorter than me, his dark hair cropped tight to his square head. His eyes are beady, like they're being swallowed by his meaty brow.

"Thanks for coming in," he says to me and Ella.

We walk through the station, pass the bullpen that's filled with officers, then a wall of offices. At the end of the row of offices, we turn into the interrogation room. It's stark, the walls a light gray, a metal table in the middle, with four chairs shoved around it. We finally end up in a small, stark room with only a table and chairs in it. We take a seat.

"You're having quite the run of bad luck," he says, and I'm not entirely sure how to respond. I glance to my lawyer, but she just inclines her head at me.

"I guess so," I finally manage.

"A missing husband, a friend that's passed away." His comments annoy me.

"We were under the impression that you had questions," Ella says, her voice commanding in the small space.

"Oh, we do. I can jump right in," he offers, and I wave my hand to acquiesce. "So how long have you and Tara known each other?"

"Since we were in high school. So about twenty years or so," I guess, not really wanting to do the math.

"So, it's fair to say you were pretty good friends then?" he asks, but it's not quite a question.

I keep my mouth shut, waiting for a real question.

"Did you and Mrs. Olson have a good relationship?"

I nod. "Yes, we spoke daily. She's one of the most important people in my life."

"Then it stands to reason that you would want to assist in whatever way you possibly could to find her killer?" he asks as he cocks his head.

I glance to Ella again. She nods. "Obviously," I say, letting some of the annoyance reach my words.

"Good, I'm really glad we're on the same page. Did you and Tara ever fight?"

"Rarely," I say, because it's true. Though Tara and I would occasionally say something bitchy to one another, it's been years since we actually fought.

"So, you didn't fight recently, and if we were to ask her husband about that, he'd be able to verify?"

I swallow hard and try to breathe through my frustration.

"It's okay, just answer honestly," Ella says.

The idea that they think I could kill Tara is infuriating. "I didn't do this. I know it looks bad. I get it. But I would never hurt her." My voice is far more genuine than I mean for it to be. But it's the absolute truth. I gain nothing from killing her. "I lost the best friend I've ever had," I say, tears filling my eyes. "I would do anything to bring her back. I keep picking up my phone to text her, then it slices through me again, the pain, the realization that I'll never text her again—she's gone."

"Well, who would have had motive to kill Tara? Did she have any enemies?" he asks, folding his hands atop the table.

"Patrick." His name comes out automatically. If given the chance, I know he'd have wanted her out of my life. Tara and Patrick never got along. But he absolutely grew to hate her over the years.

Interest fills his eyes at my words. "Patrick didn't like Tara?"

"They've never gotten along. It made things difficult at times," I say. I'd always wanted to be able to go on double dates, to spend time with my two favorite people in the world, but it was impossible. If I had the two of them together for an hour, they'd argue for forty-five minutes of it.

"Why didn't they get along?"

"They were too different. The only thing they had in common was me. They'd fight about politics, movies, social issues. What they thought the weather should be like. It didn't matter what was happening, they'd find something to argue about. It was exhausting trying to keep them from each other's throats."

"Do you really think that Patrick would have hurt her? Did he ever try to hurt her in the past?"

I shake my head. "No, but he'd threatened to a few times when he'd been drinking. He'd said he wanted to smack the smug look off her face."

His lips pinch together at that, and he writes a note in his folder. "And what was your response?"

"I told him that was out of line. We didn't talk for a few days. Eventually he sort of apologized. But mostly he blamed it on the booze."

"I've gotta tell you, if I said those things about my wife's best friend, regardless of drinking, she'd divorce me." He squints. "And that's after kicking me in the balls."

"Can we please stick to the questions, not your opinions?" Ella asks, her words sharp.

I shake my head, because it's all I can do. I've always given Patrick too much leeway, I've always compromised, always bent over backward for him, because that's what good wives are supposed to do. We're supposed to be amenable. A light knock at the door causes officer Baldwin to shove up from the table. As he opens the door, another officer passes him a plastic bag. Though I try to glance at what's in the bag, it's impossible for me to see. The officers exchange a few words before Baldwin takes a seat again.

"Does this look familiar to you?" he asks as he slides the bag onto the table. Inside is a short kitchen knife, the handle made of wood that's so dry I'd expect to see it on a sun-bleached deck.

I look it over, but it looks like every other kitchen knife I've seen over a thousand times. My eyes cut to Ella, and she shakes her head. There's nothing distinctive about it at all. The look on the detective's face tells me that he expects me to recognize it. I can practically feel the anticipation coming off him in waves.

Though I know Ella doesn't want me to answer, I can't stop myself. "No," I finally say. "Should I?"

"It was next to the vegetables that you were cutting this morning," he trails off as he pushes the bag a bit closer to me.

"The vegetables?" It takes longer than it should for the memory to register, as if I have to wade through grief to get to it. The omelets that I made for Tara and me. The ones that I'm sure a crime scene tech photographed from every angle before sloughing it into the trashcan. "Oh," I finally say. "At Tara's, yeah. I guess it could have been the one I used."

"But you're not sure?" he asks, his head tilting to the side.

"It's not distinctive. It could be any knife, not necessarily the one that I used. I didn't pay that much attention to the knife I grabbed. I dug around in the drawer until one seemed right."

He folds his hands atop the table again and looks at me with an intensity that makes me want to squirm in my seat. I don't though. A lifetime of conning has made me comfortable with situations like this, well, not quite comfortable, but I know how to navigate them. This detective isn't a mark I'd ever pick, but that doesn't mean he can't be manipulated. Anyone can.

"Look, we know you used the knife. It was in the kitchen where you were preparing breakfast. Your fingerprints are on it," he says, his voice low and steady, like he's expecting some reaction out of me. Denial, anger maybe. So, I give him nothing but confusion.

I don't need my lawyer's input for this. I'm confident in how I want to play this out. "If you're certain, why even ask me about it then? As I said, I rummaged around in the drawer. I'm sure my prints are on several knives in her house." My words are even, masking every ounce of annoyance that I feel.

"Because we need to know what you think happened."

What I think happened. That phrase sticks out in my mind.

That's the type of open-ended phrase that I've used in sessions —*what you think happened*—because the real events are already known. "If that was the knife I used, why would that matter exactly?"

"Well—" He leans back in his chair. "We found traces of Tara's blood on the knife."

My mind reels. They're going to try to pin this on me. They want the easiest outcome, and I'm the easiest person. I wrack my brain for everything I know about convictions. My heart pounds wildly as I consider it. If they had something, *really* had something, they would have arrested me, wouldn't they? Of course there was blood on a knife in Tara's house. That's completely circumstantial. She could have cut herself on that knife a thousand times.

Ella clears her throat. "Detective, have you never cut yourself while cooking? Actually, scratch that, a man like yourself is probably only acquainted with things like Hamburger Helper. Has your wife ever cut herself while cooking?"

"Of course she has," the detective says, his cheeks starting to turn red.

"Exactly. Of course she has. It stands to reason that *anyone* who has cooked in their own home and cut vegetables has probably cut themselves at some point. It would be absolutely unrealistic to believe that a little blood on a knife in a person's home is evidence of murder. Most kitchen knives have wooden handles, which could absorb blood. If cleaned by hand, it would be easy to miss."

"Well, we believe that was the knife used to kill her," he sputters.

"You *believe* sounds like there's some doubt there. Doubt doesn't look so good in a court room, Detective. So I'd suggest that you solidify your evidence before you question my client again," she says and then rises from her seat. "Adele, it's time to go."

"One last question," he says, and I hesitate. "You had a client named Brenda Parish, right?"

I look to Ella and don't respond until she nods. "I did."

"Her husband recently killed himself."

"Yes, unfortunately I heard that. He didn't say anything to me in our session that would indicate he was suicidal," I explain, trying to get ahead of his question. I then tell him about the interaction at the hotel.

He makes note of that. "Brenda was found dead last night. Would you happen to know anything about that?"

I look to Ella, who motions toward the door. I press my lips together and refuse to answer his question. Part of me is relieved that she's dead, that I won't have to deal with her threats anymore—but I hate that her death feels like a weight has been lifted off of me.

It's clear where this is going, the accusations that will come. The chair screeches across the concrete floor as I slide it out and stand. Though Detective Baldwin doesn't look pleased, we both know that he can't keep me here. I came here to answer his questions as a gesture of goodwill. Too much has happened to me for me to ignore the questions they'll have. That knife though, her blood, that changes things.

I can't run from this. So, it's time to fight.

21

A twenty-minute conversation outside the police station with Ella is all it took to settle my nerves. She confirmed that Detective Baldwin can't hold me for questioning or bring me back in without her approval or presence. All they can do now is arrest me. Not that the idea of being arrested is at all calming, but we both doubt they have enough evidence for that.

After we've grabbed my stuff from Tara's, Cameron throws my bag into the back seat of the squad car and I slide into the front seat. My mind still races over Patrick's disappearance—well, this time his *real* disappearance. I need to find him.

"Are you going to be all right?" he asks as he squeezes my knee and starts the car.

"Maybe after I'm as far away from here as possible." Though I'm not sure I'm ever going to be able to sleep again after all this. At the very least, I know Patrick would never be able to sneak into Cameron's house in the middle of the night with the dogs there.

As we drive, my phone rings. An unknown number flashes on my screen. My fingers buzz as I debate picking up the call. The call clicks over to voicemail before I can decide for myself.

He slows to a stop in front of the small sea foam-green house, and I jump out of the car and click on the voicemail message. The call is filled with static again, making it difficult to hear. I catch a few words that are rough, a man's voice—a threatening tone. But I can't pick out the words, the caller. It could be Lucas, a stalker, an upset client. I don't know.

"Do you want to go anywhere tonight? Maybe do something to take your mind off all this?" Cameron offers me, distracting me from my phone.

I shake my head as I climb the few steps up his porch. "No, I want to stay in. I just need some time," I say. I've only had to deal with something this jarring once before, when I lost my parents. But that was different, I was younger, a teenager. Though I loved my parents, hormones served me well and made me think I was better off.

I follow Cameron into the house, trying to dissect how I feel about everything, what I've lost, what I may still lose, and his dogs nearly knock me over as they fight one another to greet me. I pet them both and make my way to the couch, the dogs at my heels as I walk. The second my ass meets the cushion, both dogs jump up beside me.

"Come on guys, you know you're not allowed on the sofa," Cameron says as he tries to wave them off. But they don't budge. Not even an inch. "Fine. Shows how loyal you mutts are."

They whine in response, as if they understood.

"Don't worry, I've got your back," I say as I scratch both of their heads.

I'm not a stranger to sleepless nights, so climbing out of bed at 2 a.m. feels like one of the most natural things in the world. Hiding my movements is essential, so when I see that Cameron is dead asleep, I'm grateful. Moonlight pools on the floor as I walk down the hall, Cameron's dogs trailing after me. It's important that it looks like I never left this house, there would be too many questions. So my phone is staying here. Location tracking —the roving eye of Big Brother—would sink me.

I slip out of Cameron's house, one of his keys in my pocket, the dogs silent behind me. I give them each a treat and urge them to go back to bed. Night cloaks me the moment I step off his porch and into the cool air. Lights dot the sky above me as I sneak through the backyard and weave my way to the street. Tonight, I need to start my hunt.

It's time that I kill Patrick. I just have to find him first.

22

As I sneak back into the house, my heart still pounding, I walk to Cameron's bedroom thankful that my entrance didn't wake the dogs. I sneak down the hall, morning light pouring in through the windows. Though the sun just came up, warmth is already blooming outside. I've had it with the seesaw temperature swings in Florida. I wish it'd just pick a direction already.

When I walk into the bedroom, Cameron is snoring softly. I pulled it off. He won't even know that I was gone. A sick smile curves my lips as I near the bed. My phone vibrates on the nightstand the moment my ass hits the mattress. I dash out of the room, back into the hall, and step outside, not wanting the call to wake Cameron.

"Hello, Emma," I say, taking great effort to not let my voice sound as strained as I feel. I keep my voice low as I sneak back out of the bedroom.

"Where the hell are you?" she snaps.

I look back at the building behind me. "Currently? A friend's house."

"Oh? How great that must be for you," she snaps. Anger

rises inside me. She's always been self-absorbed, but this is a bit much—even for her.

I need to have a conversation with Emma about our future. I need to see if I can extricate myself from her grip without her dismantling my entire life. There are two options ahead of me. I can let my life here burn and move on, or I can try to salvage a life here, whatever that looks like. Part of me is so tired of running. I'm not sure I have it in me to start over *again*.

"Let's have dinner tonight. We'll talk about it," I say to try and appease her. I know Cameron isn't going to be thrilled about it, but I can't put her off forever.

"Fine, where?"

"Collage. Meet me there at five," I say.

"Why so early?"

"Because we have things to discuss that we don't want others to overhear," I say.

She sighs. "Fine. See you then." She ends the call.

Footsteps behind me make me turn and I find Cameron a few feet away. He offers me a half smile, but it doesn't reach his eyes.

"What's wrong?" I ask.

He wraps his arms around my shoulders and pulls me into his side. He must have woken up while I was on the phone. The touch, leaning against him, it's enough to lift the weight on my chest. He's got his phone in his hand. I'm surprised that he's awake so early. Cameron has always been the type to sleep until noon.

"Nothing, just bullshit at the station."

"Anything I need to worry about?" I ask, because I've got a bad feeling he overheard something about me.

He shakes his head, but his fingers twitch against my shoulders. He's lying. I don't call him out on it though, because it won't do me any good. Instead, I press my lips together.

"What are you doing up already?" he asks as he signals for me to follow him to the kitchen.

"Had a call and I didn't want to wake you up. Your dogs also wanted to go out, so I took them," I say, just in case he noticed that I was gone earlier.

He nods. "Sorry about that, sometimes they like to wake me up early. I guess you're a good distraction so I can sleep in." Cameron digs right in to making a pot of coffee, and God, I love him for it. After a couple minutes, he hands me a steaming mug and I test it with a slow sip.

Part of me wants to hide the call from Emma, but on the other hand, I know I can't hide being gone for a couple hours in the afternoon. So, I've got to bite the bullet. "Tonight, I've got to have dinner with Emma."

"Great, she can come over here and I can cook for you both," he says with a smile. I've told him all about Emma. I'm not sure why the hell he'd want her over here.

I sigh. "No, I need to meet her at a restaurant. There are some things I need to discuss with her."

He frowns. "And you can't discuss them at my house why exactly?"

"I'd rather meet her in public. She has a tendency to lash out and overreact. In public, she at least tones it down a bit."

"What's so bad that you think she'll react that way?"

"I'm getting out of the business, at least for a while. I can't work right now anyway. And it's been starting to grate on me." When I think about how she'll react, it makes me sick to my stomach. The freakout at the hotel is just the tip of the iceberg. I know it can get so much worse. I always knew she had a hair trigger, and I should have imagined how this would play out when I started working with her. But I always thought that after a while she'd calm down, that with time she'd mellow.

His eyes go wide. He knows how much my work meant to me, how careful I was with my reputation. "What are you going to do for money then?" he asks, and there's concern behind his eyes.

"I don't know yet." I'm not paying for that house anymore or any of Patrick's other crap. So, my cost of living will plummet. If all I have to worry about is myself, I could get by working at a coffee shop, especially with the money I have hidden away. If worst comes to worst, I have the trust fund, but I still don't want to resort to that.

"All right, the whole time you're in there, I'll be outside. I need to make sure you stay safe."

"Thank you," I say, though I'm not entirely sure it's necessary.

I press my thumbnail into my palm as he makes breakfast. He walks over and squeezes my shoulder as he places a plate in front of me. I offer him a slight smile of thanks, then my attention snaps to the window. I stare out at his backyard, the lawn, the weeping willow in the back. I know I should say something, but I'm a ball of anxiety. Dread threads through me as I consider what's going to happen at the restaurant. Emma is a fickle creature, one I need to stage-manage. She knows enough of my secrets to be dangerous, but not enough to sink me. There was a fine line I walked with her.

———

Cameron pulls up in front of the strip mall the restaurant is set into and parks. From this side of the street, he'll be able to see into the restaurant, but if we're at the back, there's no way he can watch us. Not that there will be anything to see anyway. I wish he'd go home, let me do this on my own, but after everything that's happened, I know he won't.

My stomach is in knots, and even though the AC is on full blast, it feels like it's a thousand degrees in the car. My chest tightens. Though I look down, I can feel his eyes are on me. I don't have to look at him to know he's expecting something, waiting for me to say something or do something. But I can't focus on what he wants or needs. So instead I look at the window.

"I'll be parked here. If you need anything, just text me," he says as he squeezes me.

"Thank you," I say as I pop the door open and hop out of the car. Once the road is clear, I jog across to the restaurant. The air inside is thick with the smell of fried chicken. It's enough to make my mouth water. I scan the red fake-leather booths and let out a sigh of relief when I don't see Emma.

"How many, sugar?" a woman with thick blonde hair asks as she rests her hand on her hip.

"Two. Can I have a booth in the back, please?" I ask. That's the farthest I can get Emma away from everyone else in the restaurant. She'll probably cause a scene and that seems the best place for it.

I follow the waitress to the back of the room. She waves a menu toward a table at the back corner. "How's this?"

"Perfect," I say as she slides two menus on the table.

"You want a drink while you wait?"

"Iced tea, please," I say as I offer her the best smile I can manage.

She offers a curt nod and disappears. The front door chimes several times, and each time, my stomach jumps. Though I scan the restaurant over and over, each time it's not her. Finally, when Emma comes through the door, I strangle the paper napkin in my hands. Her eyes meet mine, and she stalks straight for me. She throws her large purse onto the booth and slides in. For a moment, she touches the table, then pulls her hands away like it's sticky. It's not. There's nothing wrong with the table.

"Of all the places," she says as she wrinkles her nose. It's not the first time she's been here. Though each time she's got a brand-new reaction of disgust.

"Do you want to eat?" I ask, ignoring her statement.

She shrugs. "I could eat, I guess."

The waitress strolls back over with my iced tea and drops off a water for Emma. She watches the waitress like a shark would watch prey as the woman puts it down.

"Do you want to order?" the waitress asks.

"I'll take the club sandwich," I say as I hand the menu over. Not that I really needed to look at it. I always get the same thing here. "With fries."

She looks to Emma, and Emma waves her hand, as if she can't be bothered with food.

"Coming right up," the woman says dryly.

Once the waitress has disappeared into the kitchen, I lace my fingers together on top of the table. This is going to be painful, might as well start ripping the Band-Aid off now.

"Look, with everything that's going on, I'm not going to be able to do sessions for a while, not even by phone. We're out of the business until further notice. I can't even go home right now," I explain, trying to soften the blow as much as possible.

She lets out a dry laugh.

"So, since I can't be home right now, and no one seems to want to meet for virtual sessions, I'm not going to be able meet with clients," I continue.

"Why can't you just do them at Starbucks or something?" she asks, and I swear she must have lost her edge in the past few weeks. Meeting a psychologist in a coffee shop? That screams *scam*. Who would even go along with that? Who wants to spill their secrets over the hiss of a coffee machine while a guy two feet away hammers on a laptop working on a screenplay?

"You know that's not going to work," I say. "Is there anyone even still interested? Why are you fighting this so hard?" I know that Emma can read the writing on the wall. She's been pissed about the lack of sessions, and it's not like anyone was banging down either of our doors for one.

"Not yet, but I'm working on it. I've been calling *everyone*."

I shake my head. "There you go. See?"

Her fist clenches on top of the table and her skin flushes red. "And what the fuck am I supposed to do?" She growls the words at me so loud, several patrons turn to look at us. I want to shrink in my seat, to turn away from the stares. But I don't. I can't show that it bothers me. She'll feed off it. And the tantrum will grow. She's a fire and my discomfort is oxygen.

"You have plenty of other talents for earning cash," I say. I'm sure Emma could start seeing her own clients if she wanted to. "I'm happy to give you a good reference if you want to look for other jobs."

"Nothing else is going to pull in the same kind of cash," she growls as she taps her fingers on the table. I paid her well, but not *that* well. I'm sure she can find something similar, she's just being dramatic. "No one else had famous parents that guaranteed this kind of income."

"You knew this couldn't go on forever," I say. "You always wanted to strike out on your own anyway. Now you can." Emma used to talk endlessly about starting her own practice. But somewhere along the way it seems she lost the drive to strike out on her own.

The look in her eyes sharpens and she leans into the table, her face only a foot away from mine. "So, this isn't a hiatus. You're out for good. Aren't you?" she snaps.

"Honestly, I don't know yet. But what I do know is that I'm sick of it. So at the very least, I need a long break. After being accused of breaking up marriages because I want to steal husbands, and letting my client kill himself—that's just left a bad taste in my mouth." It's not like I could start this up here again, anyway. I'd have to move, rebrand myself. If I want to carry on a life here, it's going to have to be much different. Everything would change.

"How fucking nice for you." She spits the words at me,

nearly yelling. The eyes are on us again. Even the people in the kitchen are peering at us.

I shake my head. "I'm sorry, Em, I wish I had better news for you. But they've burned my reputation to the ground. The calls have dried up. No one wants to see me anymore. This is like trying to get blood from a stone." If there was something to be done here, I would have done it already. How could she not know that? I didn't want to give this all up. I had a pretty good gig going on. Now that's all gone.

She looks at me through her eyelashes. And something flashes behind her eyes. Her lips curve into a slight smirk. She looks like the Joker. Not the nineties animated one—the Heath Ledger, face-scars Joker.

"Don't worry, Adele. I'll make sure they find him for you," she says, a threat barely veiled behind her words. "I think I have a pretty good idea of where he is."

I have no idea what she means, and the look on her face isn't giving me any hints. I swallow hard as she slides out of the booth and snatches her purse.

"There are a few other things I think the police would be interested in hearing about. Not just Patrick," she says as she smiles.

"Well, make sure you don't leave anything out," I say dryly, daring her. What's she going to tell them? That we did research on clients to help with my sessions? I did nothing illegal.

"Don't worry, I will," she says as she storms out.

The waitress comes over just as the front door chimes. She drops the food off but looks toward the door like she isn't sure what to say.

"Can I get a to-go box and the check please?" I ask. My appetite left with that bitch. But at the very least, Cameron can eat my sandwich. My mind reels as I consider everything that Emma said. How can she be so sure that Patrick will be found? How would she even know where he is? It has to be a bluff.

Cameron opens the front door and strolls to my booth as I'm packing the food up.

"Everything all right?" he asks as he helps me throw fries into the box.

"It went about as well as I expected it to."

He squeezes my shoulder and offers me a smile. "You want to talk about it?"

I shake my head. "No, there's something else I need to talk to you about in the car though."

After I pay the check and we get back to the car, Cameron turns to me expectantly. "What's going on?"

The lie is ready on my tongue. I just wish I didn't know to tell it. I hate lying to Cameron. But if I have to, I will. He starts the car and rolls down the street.

"I've afraid that Emma is framing me and that she did something to Patrick," I say.

His brow furrows and he waves his hand in the air for me to continue.

"She hinted that she knows where Patrick is and that she's going to tell the police. She's pissed I'm not working with her anymore. So, I have a feeling that's the direction this is really going in."

"Do you think she would have done anything to him?" he asks, with far more concern in his voice than I'd expect.

"Honestly, she's capable of anything," I say, my voice low, careful. "I wonder now if there was something going on between them. I saw calls when I was looking at Patrick's phone logs. If she found out about Brynlee... Ashlee... She's always had emotions that were out of check."

He presses his lips together like he always does when he's thinking. "Has she acted any different lately?"

"The past few weeks she's been moody, on edge. But I didn't think anything of it. She gets like that occasionally," I say as I shrug.

"When we get home, I'm going to call the station and talk to the detective about this."

"Just don't tell him the information came from me. He doesn't trust me at all. There's no way he'd take it seriously," I say as I lace my fingers together in my lap.

He nods. "He's that way with everyone. The key is making him think that things are his idea. Then he'll listen."

"That's good that you know him well enough," I say and my stomach churns. After all these years, I can't believe it still makes me sick when I lie to him; that's why I usually don't bother. It's like he's my kryptonite. We pull up to his house and we both hop out of the car. Cameron calls the station and I walk to his kitchen for a bottle of water. I crack it open and try not to listen to his conversation. I catch snippets though and, based on what he's saying, it doesn't seem like Emma has made it there yet. She may not. But I plan to call her bluff. I walk to the living room and plop onto the couch. Cameron joins me a few minutes later.

"How'd it go?" I ask, my nerves gnawing at me.

He shrugs. "As well as it could be. He listened at least. So, he's going to look into her. Apparently, they've looked a little, but this should be the push they need to look more."

"That's good news," I say, trying to force myself to feel a little hopeful. It does no good.

He takes a step in front of me, forcing me to look at him directly. My eyes meet his, and I chew on my bottom lip. When I look in his eyes, I see us ten years ago. It feels like we could still be the people we were back then.

"Let's take your mind off all this shit," he says as he smirks at me.

"And how exactly do you plan to do that?" I ask, grinning back at him.

He rests his hands on my hips and pulls me into him.

23

I bolt upright in bed, my heart racing. A whisper of a nightmare haunts the back of my mind. Though I try to focus, to remember even a moment of my dream, it slips through my fingers like smoke. Beside me, Cameron snores. Though I'm thankful that he's here, it does nothing to calm my nerves. My head is full of static as I look around the room. Something feels off, wrong, but I can't place what it is.

Gray light filters into the room from the streetlights. I look at my phone, finding it's a breath away from 3 a.m. My throat tightens and I slip from bed. There's no way I'll be able to sleep without getting a drink. I pad down the hall, careful not to wake Cameron. The second I step into the hall, my guts tighten with anxiety. I can't even take three steps in Cameron's house without nearly tripping over one of his dogs, but they're nowhere to be found.

In the hall, I whisper their names. Nothing. The pit in my stomach opens up. Suddenly, I feel like one of those idiots in a horror movie. Now all I need is to run up the stairs away from a killer. My fingers fumble against the dark walls of the kitchen. I flick the lights on and close my eyes against the blinding brightness. I blink until my eyes adjust. There's something on the floor. It takes a moment for me to see properly. I suck in a breath so sharp that my lungs ache. Thor and Loki lie on the kitchen floor, hunks of raw steak scattered around them. My heart stops.

Are they dead? They can't be dead.

I fall to my knees beside them, and at the sight of the slow rise and fall of their chests, I breathe a sigh of relief. Adrenaline is acid in my veins. Feet scuff on the floor behind me. I turn with tears in my eyes, hoping to see Cameron. Instead, a man in a mask looms over me. His blue eyes are focused on me, and I recognize them immediately. The man from the hotel. I kick backward, propelling myself against the tile floor until the knobs of a cabinet bite into my shoulder blades. My mouth pops open, and I have every intention of screaming. But it's like all the oxygen has gone out of the room. No matter how hard I try to scream, nothing comes out.

"What the fuck are you doing here, Adele?" he asks as he cocks his head, his eyes wide. The voice. I know that voice. My mind whirs as I try to place it.

"How do you know my name?" I force the question out.

"I know everything about you," he says with a smile so cold, it chills my bones. "Just like I knew everything about your parents—before I rid the world of them, of their taint. And here you are, spreading the same venom and lies that they did."

I weigh the options quickly in my mind, how I should play this. I want to attack him, to hurt him myself—I'm sure I could take him. But that won't suit my needs, that won't help me here. So, instead, I take in a deep breath and scream so loud my lungs ache. The pounding of Cameron's footsteps down the hall makes my pulse quicken. What will this psycho do to him? Cameron bursts into the kitchen and the guy darts out the back door. Cameron looks between me, still on the floor, frozen against the cabinets, and the back door, still rattling on its hinges. His eyes hold the question he won't ask.

"I'm fine, go," I say as I grip my chest.

Cameron runs out the back door, his gun drawn. Shock still tethers me to the floor. There's no way I could force myself up, even if I wanted to. It's obvious that this guy is the stalker who killed my parents—but who is he really? Did the media attention around Patrick's disappearance draw him out? I wonder if I could pin Patrick's disappearance on him.

If Cameron doesn't catch him, I'm getting out of here. I won't let Cameron put himself at risk for me. The longer he's gone, the more worried I become.

I hear his voice outside, coming toward the house again. Panic taints his voice, and I can tell that he's on the phone with someone from the station. When he opens the door, his brows are furrowed, his mouth drawn. In one fluid movement, he pulls me off the floor and into his chest.

"Are you okay?" he asks into my hair.

I am okay, maybe in shock. But I can't be okay after this—I have to show that I'm shaken, that this affected me. The tears come swiftly as I draw on my sadness from Tara's death, and I try desperately to breathe as the waves crash into me. Cameron strokes my hair and whispers to me that it will be all right.

"We need to get your dogs to the vet," I say as I pull away and wipe my tears on my shirt.

"I already called a vet that's coming here. A few patrol cars are on their way as well. We're going to find him," he promises.

"We can't stay here. He's just going to come back," I say as I cross my arms tight across my chest.

"We're not going to run from this," he says, his voice calm, strong. Cameron is so steady, I know he could weather any storm. Me though? I feel like I'll be swept away entirely by the next breeze.

"We don't know what else he's capable of." I tell him what the guy said to me about my parents. "Please, please take this seriously," I say, and my voice cracks. This must be the man who's been breaking into my house, leaving the notes. Who else could have done that? Did he hurt Tara? Free Patrick?

"I am taking this seriously, Adele," he says, as if my words have wounded him. It's been a while since I've heard him sound so offended. "If this is the guy who hurt your parents, we'll find him. Don't worry. I won't let him hurt you."

"Please come with me to stay somewhere else outside town. Just for long enough that he won't be able to find us," I beg. Cameron knows how much I hate begging.

He looks down and I know what he's thinking. All of our time together taught me to read him like a book. His expressions, his movements, they're a language only I can speak and understand. Slowly, he rubs his chin, and I know he's going to give in. The battle is already won, the white flag halfway up.

"Fine, but we can't be more than twenty minutes outside the city. I've got to be able to get to the station if they need me," he says.

It's not far, but hopefully it'll be far enough. I'd be more than happy to lock myself away in a seedy motel if it meant I wouldn't have to worry about any harm coming to Cameron.

"Deal." I have to force myself not to smile.

There's a knock at the front door and I nearly jump out of my skin. Cameron gets the door, and I stay behind in the kitchen with the dogs. I still feel terrible for them. A man in a black button-up and jeans walks in and kneels next to the dogs. He drops a duffel bag on the ground and pulls on latex gloves before examining one of the scattered pieces of meat.

"Sleeping pills," he says as he pulls a small pill out.

"Will they be all right?" I ask. I can't stomach the idea that Cameron's dogs were caught in the middle of this.

The vet nods. "I'm going to give them something to counter the pills. They should be back to their normal selves in a few hours, albeit groggy."

A ten-pound weight lifts from my chest. So now it only feels like there's a thousand pounds weighing on me. Cameron and the vet carry the dogs into the primary bathroom and the vet gets to work on them. While they're busy with the dogs, I search for pet-friendly hotels that we can stay at.

It takes half an hour for the vet to finish with the dogs. Then Cameron has to talk to the cops about what happened. By the time they're finished, the sun is edging on the horizon and my eyes burn with exhaustion.

24

"Local counselor and daughter of famed counseling duo of the nineties—the Suttons—Adele Sutton-Johansen was seen being questioned at the Orlando Police Department yesterday. Though we asked Adele and the police if she's been arrested or if she's cooperating with the murder investigations into her estranged husband, Patrick Johansen, or her best friend Tara Olson, neither were willing to comment. So far it does not appear that she's been arrested, according to court records. However, according to reports from our sources inside Orlando PD, it appears that Adele is a suspect in both investigations," a news anchor clips into the camera before sweeping her long golden hair over one shoulder.

"This is becoming an addiction," Cameron says from the doorway. He's asked me to stop watching the news at least fifty times. I have to admit, watching it is becoming an unhealthy fixation, but I can't help it.

"I need to know what's being said," I argue, sounding far more defensive than necessary.

"We have breaking news that wife of Malcom Parish, who killed himself recently after an alleged counseling session with

Adele Sutton-Johansen, has been found dead. Brenda Parish was found dead at her home, and so far, police confirm that foul play is suspected. They're asking the public that if you know anything about Brenda's death, please reach out to Crimeline at—"

My phone buzzes in my hand, and I shut off the TV and glance down at the screen as Emma's name flashes on the screen. I push off the couch and accept the call. My mind is still reeling, trying to digest Brenda's death.

"Emma," I say as soon as the call connects.

"Can we grab dinner?" she asks. Obviously, she hasn't changed. Emma has never been one for small talk, which I prefer.

"When?" I ask, glancing back at the TV. Our last talk didn't go so well, and I'm wondering if meeting her is a good idea at all. It's not like she's going to have good news for me. But I can't deny that I'm curious to see what she wants.

"In a couple hours at that fish place by the lake. You know the one."

I nod, though she can't see me. "Yeah, I'll see you there at six." I imagine that Emma wants to discuss going our separate ways. She'll want money from me, she always does. And with the news already clamping onto my story like a hungry croc, it might behoove me to stay in her good graces. Clips of Emma doing a tell-all on the news would be a nail in my coffin.

"See you then," she says.

———

Anxiety prickles in the pit of my stomach as time ticks closer to six. Though Cameron offered to come with me, his constant presence is starting to make me feel suffocated and uneasy. He's promised to look into Brenda's death while I'm gone, to see if there might be any lingering connections to me that will look bad. The last thing I need is another murder connected to me.

The restaurant is nearly empty when I stroll in, my purse clutched tightly at my side. It takes me a minute to find Emma tucked away in the back. She's sitting at the end of a row of empty booths, like she planned this all out with the server. This place is rarely empty. The décor is red and brown, and it's like the colors manage to absorb all the light in the entire place.

Emma glances up and her eyes meet mine. A slight smirk curves her full lips in a feline way. "Adele," she says in her slow, deep voice. There's a look in her eyes that gives me pause. It's not quite a warning, but I can tell she's up to something.

I slide into the booth seat across from her. The top of the table has two menus strewn across it, shadows of glass rings, and a glass of wine for Emma. By the look in her eyes and the stains on her teeth, I can tell she's had at least two.

"I would have ordered you a drink, but you're so hard to pin down sometimes." Her words hold a trace of venom, but that's as per usual these days.

"It's fine. I'll grab something when the waitress comes over," I say.

A whisper of a smile tugs at the right corner of her lips. Seconds after I'm seated at the table, a young waitress clad in black saunters over and takes my drink order. We make small talk until the waitress returns with my tea. Once she walks away, Emma props her arm on the table and leans forward, a predatory gleam in her eyes.

"I'm glad you were able to come," she says without an ounce of sincerity. If there was any more sarcasm on her words, it might actually drip onto the table.

"What is it that you need, Emma?"

"It's so nice to hear you ask that. I'm always at *your* beck and call, and you never think about what I might need." She preens as she talks.

I want to roll my eyes. It's not as if Emma isn't well paid for what she does. I give her forty percent of every appointment. She pulls in one hundred grand a year, easy. With her designer clothes and purses, it's clear she isn't exactly struggling.

"Either get to the point or I'm going to leave," I warn her. I'm not going to sit here while she runs her mouth. It's no secret that she's unhappy, she has been for a while. But I know well enough that her problems aren't ones that I can fix. And believe me, if there were ones I could fix, I probably would. Her constant misery grates on me. She's not one to suffer in silence.

"How are things going, Adele?" she asks, picking up her wine and swirling it slowly.

"I'm guessing if you're asking that, you probably already have a good idea of the answer," I say, annoyance reaching my words. There's no way that she's missed everything on the news lately. I know some of it has focused on her.

"Yeah, I do. It looks like you're pretty well finished based on what I've been seeing on TV. You're never going to work in this town again, anyway. Unless you want to dress up as Cinderella and work in the parks." She takes a sip of her wine, then smiles with teeth that look almost bloody from the stain of wine on them.

"Glad you've been able to work that all out. That's pretty much what I said the last time we met. Did you finally come to terms with it? Are you here looking for severance or just to rub my nose in my failures?" Anger needles me, urging me to raise my voice or snap at her. But I force myself to keep my tone even.

"Why can't I be here for both?" She tilts her pointed chin up with the question.

"I've got nothing to offer you, Emma," I say because it's true. If I'm going to recover from this, I'm going to need absolutely every penny that I've got hidden away.

"We both know that's not true," Emma says as she sets her wineglass down on the table.

I raise a brow at that. "Patrick cleaned out what we had. The house is about to foreclose, and he charged up all the credit cards."

"As if you weren't smart enough to keep something on the side? You might have loved Patrick at one point, but you never fully trusted him. There was always a seed in the back of your mind that told you not to fully give yourself over," she says, and I'm surprised that she suspected that about me. I'd always tried to teach her to read people, to understand more than the info that someone was giving her. But she never seemed particularly skilled with it. I guess she learned. I'm not going to admit that she's right though.

"I don't know what you're talking about. Patrick would have known if I was skimming. He was too tightfisted about the finances. He needed to know everything going in or out," I say.

She half rolls her eyes. "Do you think I've suddenly become an idiot? I met Patrick. I knew him. He might have wanted to know some of the numbers, but you could have easily hidden stuff from him. There's no way that you told him everything."

I ignore her comment. She's right. Of course, I could have hidden things from Patrick. I did hide things from him. But I never told her about any of that. "How much is it that you're after?"

"A hundred thousand will keep me from talking to the media. One fifty will stop me from ruining your life further." Her eyes tighten as she speaks, one of her tells that she's lying.

My head cocks automatically. "Ruining my life further? What does that mean exactly?" I feel like a dog with my hackles raised, waiting for someone to strike. I think I know what she's hinting at, but I need her to say it. "Have you been sneaking into my house, leaving me notes?"

"Did you really think this was all divine intervention?

Karma finally catching up with you?" A wicked expression crumples her features, making her jawbone more prominent. But there's still something off about it.

She can't really mean that. That she was responsible for everything. This is all too far beyond her. She might be pissed that I cost her some cash, but she's not a murderer. That, I'd be willing to bet my own life on.

"You're going to have to be more specific," I say, trying to keep my cool and failing.

She looks down her straight nose at me, her eyes gleaming. "How specific do you need me to be?" Her words make her sound like she's speaking down to a child. I want to punch her.

"Cut the shit, Emma," I say, my temper rising. Emma loves to play games, and they always irritate me, but they seem to be the only thing that keeps her entertained.

"Tara, the leaks to the media, none of those were accidents. I'm the one who put Denise on your trail in the first place after I saw her sob story posted online about her father killing her mother. I noticed it was all connected to a talk show I recognized. So, I sent her your information. There's more. And if you don't give me what I want, I'll go to the media and sink you completely. It's only a matter of time before you end up in jail, but I'll make sure to speed up the timeline."

"You killed Tara?" I hiss, suppressing every instinct I have to jump over the table to see what damage I can do with the butter knife on the table.

She leans back, not like she's scared and trying to get away from me, but like she's a cat batting her prey, getting great joy out of seeing the struggle.

"With my own hands? No, come on, you know me well enough to know that I'd outsource something like that."

"You hired someone to kill my best friend?"

The gleam in her eye confirms it. Though she says nothing

aloud. "Bring me the money by the end of the week, Adele. Or you might just end up like Patrick."

"What the hell is wrong with you?" I spit. I knew she was capable of some questionable things, but *this*? No.

"You sent the police to my door. *You* got my face splashed all over the goddamn news. I have to leave and start over because of you. You ruined my life, everything I had here. I lost my job, I lost my future. And now, I'm going to do the same to you."

The threat falls flat. I don't really think she can do much worse to me now. My career here is already over, no matter what I do. My options are limited.

"Tick tock, Adele. Tick tock," she says as she slides out of the booth.

Emma is lucky that I can't murder her in front of a restaurant full of people. But oh, how I want to. I can imagine myself wrapping my hands around her slender neck and squeezing until the blood vessels in her eyes burst. Or grabbing a steak knife off of one of the tables and stabbing her in the spine with it. There are so many ways I could kill her.

25

After a restless night of sleep, I'm still unsettled from the conversation I had with Emma yesterday. Cameron has been fussing over breakfast for close to an hour, while I've been forcing myself to stay away from the TV. It's become too toxic for me to watch how it's all unraveling, the things that are being said about me. In the back of my mind, I've been plotting, thinking about how this will all end for me. There has to be a way for me to recover from this—not to do sessions again, but so I don't have to completely start over. If there's a way, I know I'll figure it out.

In my pocket, my phone buzzes. Again. Without looking, I know it's Emma. She's been calling since I woke up. Every time she's called, I've smashed the button on the side, silencing her in a way I've always wished was possible in person. She's threatened me, tried to dismantle my life, and has spilled some of my secrets to the media. And now, she's after my money and wants to frame me for Patrick's disappearance. The bitch can kiss my ass. With my reputation where it currently is, it's not like she can make it much worse.

As the phone buzzes again, I silence her. Relishing in the

rage I imagine she's feeling across town. It's the least I can do since she's trying to ruin my life.

"Who's on the phone?" Cameron asks from behind me. I turn to face him. He's got a basket filled with biscuits in his hands.

"Just Emma."

"Are you going to answer?" he asks, eyeing me. I'm sure the conversation from last night is running through his mind.

I shake my head. "No. I've realized it's probably for the best if I don't."

He nods. "I suspect you're right." He motions toward the bread. "Are you hungry?"

I force myself to smile, to try and weasel myself into this new normal as if it's nothing, as if I've always belonged here—because that's all I can do to cope right now, to try and figure out a path forward. Cameron signals for me to follow him to the table. As usual, there's too much food. I wish he'd stop being so wasteful, but this is just who he is. I'm not sure I could change him at this point, even if I wanted it.

"What is all this?" I ask, looking over several dishes that aren't familiar.

"French toast casserole, frittata, spinach omelet, turkey sausage, and monkey bread," he says as he places the biscuits on the table.

"Interesting mashup you've got here," I say as I take a seat at the table, which is set up in a breakfast nook inside Cameron's kitchen.

"I wasn't sure what you wanted, so I made some options," he says as he waves to the casserole. He's never going to stop wanting to feed me. This is just what we do. What he's always going to do. Cameron needs to save me. Maybe that's why he became a cop. He couldn't save me, so other people became his goal.

We fill our bellies as the sun burns on the horizon. During

breakfast, Emma calls me four more times. Each time, I hit the button on the side and Cameron looks increasingly worried.

"Do you want to try to get a restraining order or something?" he asks as he reaches over to squeeze my hand.

That's an idea, but I don't think it would do any good. It wouldn't hurt to put something in progress though.

"What does that process look like? How do we start it?" I ask as I consider the possible ramifications. This will set her off.

"I can get the paperwork started tonight. Someone from the station will have to call to let her know that it's been filed. A judge would then set a date. Most likely, they'd give you a thirty-day order, unless Emma violates that order or causes a scene in the courthouse." He explains it with such ease it's like he's reading it from a textbook.

The more I think about it, the more I realize that I need to do this. It may also help me rein in her behavior.

"Let's do it," I say as I squeeze his hand back. "It'd make me feel much better."

I walk through the paperwork with Cameron. He helps me complete it and sends it over to the station. Once it's in process, the knot in my gut eases slightly.

"When will Emma be notified?" I ask him.

"It's a little late in the day, but I put a rush on it. So, tomorrow. It'll likely be a few days before you get a court date. According to Cliff, they're backed up right now," he explains.

"But she'll be notified when?" I ask.

"Tomorrow, first thing."

I have one night to get myself ready. After tomorrow, everything is going to change.

26

My night and day blurred together in a stream of anxiety. Though I wanted to ask Cameron every five minutes for updates on the restraining order, I held back, and only asked once an hour. At noon, we got confirmation that Emma was notified. Since then, the silence has been deafening and uncomfortable. I expected rage, the phone calls to increase—something. Instead, I didn't get so much as a whisper or a whimper in return. I guess some fires die with smoke and some die with no warning at all.

In bed, next to Cameron, after such a long and stressful day, I should feel relief. I should be able to unclench my jaw, but I can't. As he breathes deeply, lost to sleep next to me, I stew. Something's got to give.

For so long with Patrick, I blamed him for my unhappiness. He was part of it. Now I wonder though, am I too far gone for happiness? Maybe it's something I just don't have in me anymore. Joy isn't like riding a bike.

A cool breeze wheezes outside, rustling the trees outside the window. With the glow of the full moon, and the shadows of the branches cast on the wall, it's like the night is putting on a puppet show. I watch the movement, hoping that it'll ease me toward the sleep I'm so desperate to find. The shapes shift with the wind, making a web of shadow on the wall. As I watch, something in the center blooms, taking center stage. I suck in a sharp breath, as the figure of a person—their torso and head—blacks out part of the wall.

My heart seizes as I bolt up in bed. Part of me wants to reach for Cameron, to wake him up too. The rational bit of me takes hold as I blink frantically. In a moment, the shape all but disappears, leaving nothing but the web on the wall. Maybe I imagined it. I shouldn't wake him up, then I risk looking like a paranoid crazy person. I slip from bed, pausing for a minute to make sure that Cameron is still asleep. Once I'm sure he is, I creep to the window, scouring the darkness.

The willow tree that stands sentinel in the middle of the yard sways in the wind. Sweat clings to my palms as I grip the windowsill. My pulse is so loud in my ears it drowns out everything else, the night, and almost my thoughts.

There's no one out there. You're being stupid, I tell myself over and over again. Did I really see something? Or was it the first ember of a dream crackling in my mind?

The questions force me down the hall because I have to know. I have to be sure. No one knows where I am, so I should be safe. Goddammit, I'd feel so much safer if the dogs were here, not that I'd ever tell Cameron that and risk damaging his male ego.

Moonlight from the spare bedrooms casts squares of light down the central hall. I curse myself for not grabbing my cell phone, but then again, I'm probably investigating nothing. In the kitchen, I glance out the window, getting a different view of the backyard, but still there's nothing.

Stop being stupid and just go back to bed.

I sigh and glance into the fridge, looking for a midnight snack. A crack from the back of the house makes me jump and whip around. Did Cameron drop something? No. He was completely asleep. I slam the fridge and run down the hall.

"What the fuck?" Cameron yells from the bedroom. Adrenaline burns in my veins as fear seizes me.

"Stay there, don't fucking move," a female voice calls out. It takes me a few seconds to register the voice. Emma. How the hell did she get in here?

I burst in through the bedroom door, unsure of what exactly I'm going to do, but I have to do something. Emma stands in the middle of the room, dressed in all black. She looks very much like a shadow. Her hair is pulled back into a tight ponytail. She's got her arms extended as she points a gun at Cameron. Cameron sits in the middle of his king-sized bed, looking disheveled but nonplussed, as if this isn't the first time an armed intruder has woken him up in the middle of the night.

"Emma, put the gun down," I pant as I grip the doorframe. Though I didn't run far, the panic has me out of breath.

Cameron's attention shifts to me as Emma swivels the gun and aims it at my chest. "The first one of you that moves gets a chest filled with lead," she growls. Even in the darkness, I can see the sharp edges of her face, how feral she looks.

"What do you want, Emma?" I ask as I hold my hands up. I expected this. Though I don't know how she found me—someone probably gave her Cameron's name, and then thanks to all the tricks I taught her for readings, she found his house. That's my guess anyway.

"As if you don't know what I want. You burned your life to the ground, took me with you, made the police question me, and now you're trying to get a restraining order put on me? Jesus Christ, Adele. You deserve a bullet to the skull, just so I can even out this karmic imbalance a little." She moves her head exaggeratedly as she talks, as if she's so frustrated with me. Her body is begging her to move forward, to shoot me. Her hands tremble as she holds the gun, and I'm unsure if it's because she's so hyped up or because her arms are getting tired.

"You owe me money. I know you've got shit squirreled away. You're going to get me that money or I'm going to shoot you both," she growls before grinding her teeth together so hard it makes *my* teeth ache.

I prepared for this. Of course, she'd try to come after me for money. After the bullshit with Lucas, I knew she'd be next. Though my heart threatens to beat its way out of my chest and my head swims, I will myself to be calm.

"If I had money, don't you think I would have taken off the moment everything started to fall apart?" I ask. I didn't because I couldn't leave Tara. We had a plan. Patrick had to be taken out, but it needed to be at the right time.

Her eyes narrow as if she hadn't considered this before now. "So, you mean to tell me that you've got nothing stashed away?"

I glance at Cameron, then back to her, trying to give nothing away to either of them. "I've got nothing, Emma," I say, holding my palms up to her. "Why else do you think I'm here? If I had money, I'd have run and rebuilt my life somewhere else."

"Bullshit," she rages as she turns the gun back on Cameron. "Give me the money or, I swear to God, I'll shoot him."

Cameron's eyes meet mine and I know he wants to tell me something. Probably not to intervene, but I can't stand here and do nothing. Emma has to be stopped and she played into the role I set up for her beautifully.

27

I lunge for Emma, my hands outstretched for the gun. A shot cuts through the night. The symphony of rage and terror fills the room and my mind spins. It's so overwhelming that my mind breaks everything down. The data comes in like snap-shots, not video. First, the shot illuminating the room. Emma screaming with triumph as the bullet hurls toward Cameron. Two bullets hitting the headboard, before a third lands. Cameron groaning as the bullet cuts through his body. Where, I can't tell from my position. Her body shifting toward me as she tries to aim the gun at me.

An eternity, or what feels like it, passes before my body hits hers. My shoulder cries as it connects with her rib cage. Her arm slams into my jaw. Pain echoes through my head, my teeth. I have to take her down, to get the gun away from her before she hurts one of us. We fall together toward the floor and I groan as my hip connects with the wood floor. It takes me a moment to gather my bearings. My arm flies toward her face but connects with her forearm as she tries to block me. As my arm connects with hers, she grunts, and the gun goes flying.

"Just give it up, Adele," she groans as she struggles beneath me.

"Not a chance," I snap back.

Emma's fist soars toward me. I'm too stunned to move as it makes contact with my eye, slides forward, then skids over my nose. I suck in a sharp breath as an ache awakens in my sinuses and radiates through my skull. Tears pour uncontrollably from my eyes. In all the years of counseling, I've never gotten into a physical fight—I haven't even had one start in my office—and damn does it show. Cameron moans on the bed, clearly injured, and I know what I have to do. I climb on top of Emma as she tries to kick me. She's smaller than me but, trying to wrestle her to the floor to keep her away from the gun, I'm aware of how much stronger she is than she looks.

Cameron struggles on the bed, like he's trying to get up. I'm desperate to know how badly he was injured, but I have to stop Emma first. She wrenches out of my grip and slides out from under me. My gaze cuts to where she's going. The gun. The gleam of the metal catches my eye beneath the dresser. Emma crawls toward it. I won't let her get to it. My heart feels like it's slamming against my ribs as I force myself up. I dive onto Emma's back, grip her ponytail in my hand, and she collapses beneath me. But the moment I think she's down and I release her hair, she rolls onto her side and tries to buck me off.

With the view of her back, the only thing I can focus on is her ponytail. My hand curls around it, and I yank her head toward me before slamming it to the floor. She moans, and I have to force myself not to smile. I bare my teeth as I knee her in the back, so her stomach is flush with the floor again. She tries to pull away, the hair slipping from my grip a little, but I hold tight and slam her face again. A crunch warns me that I might have broken her nose. One more slam, and she's unconscious beneath me.

I sit on her back, my hand white-knuckled as I grip her hair.

As Cameron's footsteps sound on the floor behind me, I'm painfully aware of how crazy I must look, panting, with an unconscious woman beneath me. He loops his arms around me, pulls me from the floor, and deposits me on the bed. In a couple seconds, he's got Emma in cuffs, and with a kick of the gun to the other side of the room, I know she's been completely disarmed.

"How bad are you hurt?" I ask, wanting to check myself, but I can't force my body to move.

"Bitch got me in the shoulder. I'll live. Are you okay?" he asks as he looks me over.

I nod, though I'm not sure he can see me in the darkness. I look to the body, still immobile on the floor. Checkmate, Emma.

The moment I met up with Emma and she admitted to trying to ruin my life, I knew that I had to do something. That's the kind of shit no one is allowed to get away with. Luckily for me, Emma was everything I needed her to be. She was so easy to stage-manage, to manipulate. If she'd paid attention, if she'd followed any advice I'd ever given her, she wouldn't have fallen for it. But in my life, I've learned a few things.

Some of us are born to change the world, and some of us are born to let the world change us.

28

There are voices in the other room when I wake up. A low murmuring. The far-off voices. At first, I think it's a dream or that I'm back in the hospital with Cameron, his shoulder being patched up. Morning light filters around the curtains and bathes the room in an amber glow. Though I strain my ears to make out what Cameron is saying, I can't understand a single word. Is someone back here talking to him about Emma? About what happened last night?

We were at the hospital for hours answering questions, getting him looked at. The nurses really wanted Cameron to stay the night, but he was so insistent that we come back to his place and I just wanted him to be comfortable. It's bad enough that he's going to be stuck in a sling for a couple weeks, the least he can do is be home if he wants.

I slip from bed and find Cameron in the living room with two officers. They're all huddled together. A pit opens up inside me; a bad feeling grows there. I'm frozen to the ugly carpet, while they stare at me, silent.

Cameron edges toward me, the way you'd approach a dog you thought might be dangerous. He's never looked at me like this. I wrap my arms around his chest as he urges me toward the sofa.

"Take a seat," he says as he waves me toward it.

The two other men take turns glancing at each other, then me. I want to go back to the bedroom and stay there until the other officers are gone. I feel distinctly out of place. Like I shouldn't have come out. Maybe I shouldn't have let them see me. I sit down and tuck my hands beneath my legs to keep from fidgeting.

Cameron sits next to me, perching on the edge of the sofa, but the other officers don't move. They stand statue-still a few feet away.

"Adele, they have some news about Patrick," Cameron says in a careful, even voice. He says it in the way I imagine you'd talk to an egg you were coaxing not to break.

A lump forms in my throat. I want to ask, but I can't get any words out. All I can do is wait. I know the words he'll say. But I'm so anxious for them to be out. For the world to know. Each second builds pressure against my chest, until it feels like I'm being pressed backward into the sofa. Can they feel this? Do they know I'm feeling this?

"Patrick is dead," he explains.

I cover my mouth with my hands like a good wife would. "What happened?" I manage to force out. I remember what Cameron said about keeping up appearances. It takes me a minute, but I force the tears to come. It must be convincing enough, because both officers shift on their feet and clear their throats.

"They're not sure yet. The medical examiner should have an idea in a few days," he says. "It looked like there was a struggle, another man was found dead nearby. We think he may have been stalking you."

I nod and pretend to struggle to get the next question out through my grief. So, the stalker is gone too, then. "Where was he?" I ask, as I try to scan my brain for the other questions I should ask. I wish it was just Cam and me here. The last thing I want right now is having to ensure that I'm grieving the appropriate amount.

"Not far. They found him in a housing development that fell through a few years back," he says.

Florida is one big hunting ground for housing developers. It always seems like there's a new neighborhood popping up out of an old orange grove. But sometimes, they don't get off the ground. Throughout the state there's a handful of foreclosed neighborhoods, skeletal remains of the promise of a booming economy scattered all over the state.

I put my head in my hands to shield my face, as much as it is to steady myself. I knew they'd find him eventually, but I thought I'd feel better when they did. Instead, I feel wrung out, like I've been hit by a truck. I want to ride out this storm in bed instead of facing it, which is so damn unlike me. Normally I face everything head on. The only thing I've ever shied away from was the police. And here I am, in a room of cops.

One of the comms strapped to a belt of one of the officers sparks to life. I'm so startled, I nearly jump.

"We need to take this. Do you have this under control?" one of them asks Cameron.

He nods. "We'll be fine. Thank you."

They both offer me their condolences before disappearing out the front door, taking my anxiety with them.

"How are you really?" he asks as soon as he shuts the door behind them.

I shake my head. "I honestly don't know. I wasn't really expecting to find out that he was dead. I figured I'd find out at the end of all of this that he was with Emma or that stalker." The lie is sharp on my tongue, but I don't flinch against it. The timing of them finding him so soon after the incident with Emma is just... perfect.

He nods. "Are you going to be okay?"

"Yeah, I just need to get used to the idea. How did they find him?"

"Emma told them he was there."

I swallow hard again. "How did she know he was there?" I let my words tremble on my tongue as they come out, and the last word is thicker than it needs to be, like I'm on the verge of tears.

"She claims she saw you going into that neighborhood the night before he disappeared."

"But I was home all night," I argue weakly.

He nods. "We know. The location tracking on your phone shows you were at home. And no one else has come forward saying that they saw you leave. There's no evidence that you left and nothing to corroborate her story. Also, after the attack last night, it's unlikely we'd give much stock to anything she says. We think it's clear that she killed both men. She likely killed Tara as well and tried to pin it all on you."

I press my lips together and take out my anxiety by chewing the inside of my already raw cheek. Looking at this a week ago, I should have known this was coming. But it's one thing to think about it objectively before it happens. Now though, it feels different, not quite like how I thought it would. No weight has been lifted. I don't feel like I won, like I normally do.

"What should I do?" I ask, because I feel like I have to do something.

He pulls me into his chest, hugging me close. It unwinds me a little, but it does nothing to stifle the flow of adrenaline in my blood stream. "There's nothing you can do now. It's out of your hands. Let us do our jobs, we'll see if we can connect the dots to Emma."

The second the cops really start sniffing around Emma, they'll find the trail I left for them. She won't be getting out of jail anytime soon. Attacking an officer is a serious charge. She looks good for this murder though, and the easier it is to close a case, the more likely the police are to go for it.

"Where did you go last night?" Cameron asks into my hair.

My breath catches. He noticed I was gone? Shit.

"I just got up to go to the bathroom and took a walk," I say.

"Don't lie to me, Adele. I looked for you. You weren't here," he says as he takes a step back. His eyes darken as he looks at me. "I'll lie for you, if you need me to. Patrick was a shitty husband and didn't deserve you. I'd do whatever I had to, to protect you. But you have to tell me. You need to lay it all out."

Tears fall down my cheeks and I chew my bottom lip. Do I tell him what I tried to do? What I wanted to do... This is a leap I'm not sure I can make.

29

Things can change in a second. In the space of a breath. One moment, reality exists in a specific frame, and in the next, everything has shifted, shattered, turned to ash. When Cameron told me they found Patrick's body, I wasn't surprised. How could I be? From the moment he *disappeared*, I knew this could only end two ways. But I certainly had one end in mind. The thing about trying to kill your husband is, you can't do it right away. He had every reason to leave, to flee, and those were just the reasons I knew about. I uncovered so many more after the night I knocked him out and whisked him away to Tara's house.

It should feel like one chapter ended and another began. But it doesn't. Something has forever changed inside me, something that longed to be free of him. There's that other half though, the small almost silent voice that wanted him to change —that wanted him to want me, for me to be good enough to make him stay. That part of me ached to know that I was enough. That part that will forever need that validation but can never have it. I want to burn that sliver of me to ash. I should be free. I shouldn't question it. But maybe I'm not meant to be free.

The interrogation room at the Orlando Police Department

is becoming like a second home to me. Settled into the cold, metal chair, I am gripped with numbness. I just want to feel something. But I guess I don't deserve that. Not after all that I've done. Ella sits at my side, her short hair swishing each time she moves her head. Her pantsuit is a violent shade of teal, and I can't get over how much I love it.

Detective McCarthy slides through the door, a thick folder in one hand, a donut and coffee in the other. He glances at me and his mustache twitches in response. So much of his lips are covered I'm not sure if it's a weak smile or a sneer. I'm surprised it's him, and not Baldwin. But I guess Baldwin has Tara's case and McCarthy has my husband's.

"Adele, I'm so sorry for your loss," he says.

I'm actually aware of the fact that I should cry. I should look sad, put some effort into looking like one of those puppies locked in a cage on the Animal Planet commercials, but I don't. I can't force myself to do anything. I'm a prisoner to my inability to feel. I knew this day was coming, I planned for this day—but yet, I'm lost. I hate to admit that I wanted it to play out differently. Some part of me hoped that along the way I'd find the real Patrick again. With his death, the chapter is closed for good. There will be no closure, only questions, accusations, my mind screaming over and over again that I wasn't enough.

"Thank you," I manage after too long of a pause, once Ella nudges me. I need to rein my emotions, to control myself so I can craft the narrative that I need here. But I'm not sure that I can manage it. "It's all still a shock."

He nods in a way that I assume means to be sympathetic. "Are you aware of the circumstances in which we found Patrick?"

I shake my head, because I should have no idea.

"About thirty miles west there's an abandoned housing development. They built three model houses out there about ten years ago, but then the builder went under. Those houses have been decaying there ever since," he explains. I remember those houses well. What he fails to mention is that the developer ended up going under because they were using materials that were incredibly dangerous that led to the deaths of several small children. The lawsuits did them in.

"I'm familiar," I say.

"Someone called in a tip about a car that had been parked out there for a while. It hadn't been taken seriously, because it was assumed that they were just squatters or those damn urban-exploring YouTuber kids that we have to keep kicking out of abandoned places." He shakes his head. "But it ended up being Patrick's car and he was in it, a single bullet fired into his temple.

I swallow hard. "So, it was a suicide?" I ask.

"The medical examiner hasn't made the official declaration yet. But there are a few signs that it might be ruled a homicide. The body of Gerald Hastings was found nearby, so he could have been the culprit. But I have a few questions that could help determine if our thoughts on this are correct."

"Okay," I say, trying to sound like I'm far more willing to help than I feel.

"Was Patrick left- or right-handed?"

"Right," I say. Always the opposite of me in every respect.

"And did he have access to firearms?"

I glance to Ella before I answer, then shake my head. "Not that I'm aware of. But I'm not really sure what he'd been up to at this point."

"We've checked the database to see if he had a concealed-carry permit or anything indicating he'd purchased a firearm. However, that doesn't tell us anything about personal transactions. He could have easily purchased a weapon from a gun show or from an individual," he explains, as if he's said these same words a thousand times. "Did he have any friends with weapons?"

I shrug. "I don't really have any idea. I never had any reason to ask and he never spoke about it. The only friend he really had was Lucas Daniels. But their friendship fell apart shortly before Patrick disappeared."

"Oh?" he asks as he makes a note of my words in the file in front of him.

I take a deep breath before I give him the run-through of the breakdown of the relationship and my recent interactions with Lucas. He raises a brow at that.

"How much did you know about this?"

"All I knew was about the failure of the business. That's why he ended up getting the new job. I didn't know about how he screwed him over, any of the money he owed, or the alleged identity theft," I explain.

"How was your marriage?" he asks, before folding his hands atop the folder on the table. Though we've already covered this, I know he's asking again for a reason.

Ella clears her throat. "Is that line of questioning really necessary? You've already asked about her marriage."

I glance down at the table and weigh how to answer.

"It is," the detective says. "I want to make sure we got the whole story."

"It's fine." I glance at Ella, hoping to put her at ease. I know what I'm doing here. I know how to play this. "Complicated," I say. I'm so tired, like my emotions have been wrung out. I have to tell the truth. He can definitely look into how things were between me and Patrick. The mistress and not telling his work that I exist, that paints a picture.

"I appreciate your honesty."

"Things had been strained between us for a while. But so much came to my attention after Patrick disappeared. I didn't know about the job, the money, our mortgage, the mistress, the divorce. I wish I had known. But we'd been growing apart for so long that we basically lived in separate worlds."

"I hear that more than you'd think." He looks down at his notes. "So, you didn't know about the mistress?"

"I didn't know anything about it until after he disappeared," I explain.

"All right then. Is there anyone else that you think had a reason to harm Patrick?"

I shake my head. "No, not that I'm aware of. But Patrick kept me out of so much of his life, who really knows?" My eyes burn, real emotion filling them for the first time. "He fooled me. I truly thought he was a good man. That he loved me. Maybe one day early on he did, but now that the fog has lifted, all I can see is how stupid I was."

He reaches across the table and squeezes my hand. "That's what love does to us."

I offer him a sad smile, wiping tears away. Maybe for him, maybe for everyone else. But never again for me.

He pulls a photo of a man, with a square jaw and blue eyes, from the folder in front of him. The eyes capture me immediately, and the full view of his face.

"Do you know this man?" he asks.

I shake my head.

"This is Gerald Hastings. The dead man who was found near your husband. The stalker we believe may have killed your parents. You've never seen him before?"

"I don't think so. Not that I recall. Is this the man who attacked me in the hotel and drugged Cameron's dogs?"

He nods. "We think so."

"I wish I could help you, but I don't know him."

He nods, as if I've given him exactly what he wanted.

"Did Emma admit to leaving messages in my house or breaking in when I wasn't home?" I ask.

He shakes his head. "No, we didn't find any evidence of that."

"Didn't Cameron bring in the notes and the vase for fingerprinting?" I ask. Cameron took them, and I distinctly remember him mentioning he'd run prints on them.

For a moment, the detective flips through the folder in front of him. "I don't see any note of that, there's nothing like that on the evidence log."

"Why did Gerald kill Linda?" I ask, as the pieces click into place in my mind. He was in the hotel room wearing the mask. He murdered her.

"From the evidence, we believe she came into the room while he was looking for you. She likely startled Gerald and he killed her," the detective says before locking his jaw, the muscles in it twitching as he clenches. "But we'll never know for certain."

I want to dig deeper, to ask him more questions about that, but his eyes drift to the door. Our meeting is over.

"Thank you for coming in today, Adele. If we need anything else, I'll reach out to Ella. I'm so sorry you had to go through all this."

I sniffle and wipe the tip of my nose softly, though no more tears will come. The look on his face tells me that my job here is done. Good.

30

No one ever tells you how loud fire is. Or how hard it is to set a fire that can't be traced. Luckily, builder homes have lots of problems—and more importantly are made of materials that burn easily. As long as you don't set fire with an accelerant, it's incredibly hard to trace arson. The tragic misfortune will mean my insurance pays off the house, so I don't end up with a fore-closure. Though my real purpose was to destroy any remaining evidence of what Tara and I did.

The living room is quiet as I hold my breath, watching the court case intently. The thing about murder trials is that they take forever. And they draw more attention than I'd ever imag-ine. Emma looks so different sitting behind the defendant table in the courtroom. Her blonde hair has dulled; everything about her seems to have dimmed somehow. Maybe that's what jail does to you. It's the least she deserves. For a long time, I never thought she'd be capable of killing. Not until she attacked Cameron and me. That action, that bullet tearing through Cameron's flesh, it told me exactly who Emma is. During the course of the trial, and from Cameron's intel, I found out that Gerald murdered Tara and Patrick's mistress to try to make me look guilty of killing them both. Funny thing is, it just made it easier for them to look guilty of killing Patrick. Though I'm still not sure which one of them did it. I guess it doesn't matter. With some of the incendiary texts she'd sent me when she was mad at Patrick, I couldn't have planned it better myself. If you ask me, the evidence is all circumstantial, but they really need to solve the case. There's too much media attention on it. And Emma made herself look *really* bad when she shot a cop.

The courtroom on the TV erupts into murmurs as a back door opens and the jury files out. My stomach clenches as I watch all twelve take their seats.

"It looks like the jury may have returned with their verdict," a news anchor says, speaking over the footage.

A woman, likely in her fifties and clad in a navy-blue pantsuit, stands up. She and the judge share a short exchange before she passes a paper to the clerk.

"You've reached a verdict?" the judge asks.

She nods. "We have, Your Honor."

"How do you find the defendant on the first count of first-degree murder?"

"Guilty," she says.

My stomach leaps. The first count was for Tara. I'll never get her back, but knowing that Emma will rot for her murder, that helps ease the pain.

"And on the second count of first-degree murder?" the judge asks.

"Guilty," she says.

I wasn't so sure they'd be able to convict for the mistress. The evidence there wasn't so cut and dry. But I guess that didn't matter to the jury.

"And the third count, second-degree murder?"

I lean forward, clasping my hands together as I rest them on my knees. I'm not the praying type, but I can't deny that at this moment, I really wish I were.

"Guilty," she says before looking at Emma. The camera pans and though Emma is trying to hold herself together, her cheeks are tinged with red, her eyes glassy. The only count they escape is Linda's murder. They didn't have enough evidence for that.

Checkmate, Emma.

I run my hand over my belly, the baby within stirring. She might be my biggest lie, the child that will solidify things with Cameron, not that I need it. But this child will keep him from questioning me, from looking too close. I will keep her safe, just as she kept me safe.

My last lie. My child. My salvation.

31

It's been two months since Emma was convicted, two months of looking over my shoulder, wondering if it's all really over, if I really won. I wanted to kill Patrick. I tried to kill him, his mistresses, but someone robbed me of that. Did I really win if I'm constantly looking over my shoulder wondering if I'm next? Will I really be free? This isn't quite what I expected.

My hands rub over my belly again, like they do a hundred times a day. Anytime my anxiety peaks, I wait for the baby to kick me, to remind me that I'm not alone in all this. Cameron is beside me in the car, but there's a wall between us, a wall of lies that I built. I can't tell him everything I've done, everything I probably will do. He turns to me and smiles, as if he can sense my unease. I try to return it, but I'm sure that it comes off as a sneer.

"Are you excited?" Cameron asks as we roll to a stop at a traffic light. "You've been so quiet today."

My gaze meets his and I do my best to muster a smile. Before I got pregnant, I considered the best path forward. I knew Cameron could save me, shelter me. He was my key to making it through all this. I agreed. I played my part, I won. Some part of me should be happy about this.

"So excited. I'm just nervous. It's our first time really seeing the baby since it looked like a blob," I say, trying to explain the emotional distance that's been growing between us. I should have tethered myself to someone I had no history with. Someone that couldn't possibly make me feel guilty. Someone who deserved a person like me.

He reaches over and squeezes my hand. "In four months, the baby will be back there." He motions over his shoulder to the back of my car.

I follow his gaze, as if I can picture the car seat, diaper bag, the soft round head with downy hair. I can't. None of this feels real. Right.

Cameron pulls the car into a space in the parking lot of my ob-gyn. The appointment is a rush of questions, goo on my belly, and finally finding out we're having a little girl. I never imagined myself having a daughter. I thought I'd have a son.

"I can't believe it," Cameron says as he drives out of the doctor's parking lot and turns down the street.

"I know," I say, and it sounds too mechanical. A tear rolls down my cheek because this all feels so wrong. I'm torn as to whether the hormones are to blame or if something really is wrong.

"Do you feel up for a walk?" Cameron asks as he rolls the car into a park a few minutes from the doctor's office.

Tall oak trees heavy with Spanish moss rise high above several small picnic areas. Trails weave around the pavilions, disappearing into the thickening wood behind them.

"Sure," I say, hoping nature will brighten my mood. It's been a long time since I've been for a walk or been out in nature. In fact, since I moved in with Cameron, I've barely had a moment to myself. Even when he's at work, I swear there are eyes on me.

Cameron climbs out of the car and I follow suit. The humid air envelops me the moment my feet hit the ground. This time of year kills me. It's like summer is slowly trying to kill us all. Cameron walks toward one of the trails, waiting for me to catch up. When I finally do, he weaves his fingers into mine and holds my hand a little too tight.

The low rustling of leaves and lizards echoes through the forest around us as we carve a path through the foliage. A dirt trail cleaves a part in the trees and eventually opens to a wooden walkway over a stream. Birdsongs rise around us, audible over the hollow thuds of our feet on the wood. The wooden walkway ends with a small gazebo lined in benches. Cameron's grip on my hand loosens and I suck in a deep breath, trying to calm myself. Normally, nature makes me feel better, it soothes my soul. But not today. My daughter does a flip in my womb and kicks me hard in the side.

"Thanks," I grumble as I push back on my belly against what I guess is a foot.

Cameron walks in front of me, tracing the length of the walkway. He glances at the trees for a long time, like he's bird-watching. I can't help but appraise him, the square of his shoulders rising and falling as he breathes. He turns, his eyes narrowed on me. He closes the distance between us, and I tense.

"Adele," Cameron says as he takes my hand in his again. He lowers himself to one knee, and I have a flashback to my first proposal on the beach when Patrick asked me to marry him. *Run.* My mind screams at me. As if it's trying to convince me not to make the same mistakes again.

"I love you more than life itself," he says as he pulls a small velvet box from his pocket. "From the moment I met you, I couldn't get you out of my mind. You let me love you for a long time, and it was the greatest honor of my life. I thought we'd be together forever." He lets out a little laugh. My heart pounds as

I try to digest this. How I feel about it. What the *real* Adele wants. As if that version of me still exists.

"I was stupid, and I lost you. I tried to move on. I dated other women, some for months, some for years. But they never felt right. I always found myself comparing them to you, how it was to be with you. And now, I know that we came back into each other's lives for a reason," he says, as he opens the box. Inside, a simple band with a huge diamond stands in the center, swallowed by velvet. How the hell did he afford this? It has to be at least a twenty-thousand-dollar ring.

"Do you like it?" he asks as he pulls it right out and slips it on my finger.

"It's huge," is all I can manage.

"It's a three-carat diamond," he says with a slim smile. "I want to show you how much you mean to me. As the love of my life, the mother of my child. Will you do me the honor of being my wife?"

Some part of me, the largest part, wants to say no. It's a primal reaction, one I can't quite make sense of. It's so jarring, my jaw locks and I yank my hand away. The ring feels like a chain dragging me down. I don't want this. Not again.

"Adele?" he asks as he stands back up, his eyes scouring my face.

You have to say yes. You have to. I tell myself over and over. "Of course," I manage in a voice so small it doesn't sound like my own.

He grabs me, wrapping his arms around me until I squirm. "Sorry, the baby is making me hot," I say as I fan my face.

"Let's get you back to the car," he says as he ushers me toward the path.

Once we're back in the car, the AC is such a sweet relief. Cameron drives toward the house and I try to avoid looking at the ring. Over us, the sky darkens as an afternoon storm rolls in, and it feels like the sky is echoing my mood.

"Adele, do you know how I knew we were meant for each other?" he asks as two fat drops of rain pelt the windshield.

"How?" I ask, though I'm bone-tired and sick of romantic sentiments. I just want to go home and go to bed. I am done with this day.

"We've killed for each other," he says without looking at me. His arms are stick-straight as he grips the wheel, his knuckles white.

My eyes sharpen on him, the words swirling in my mind as my heart races. I must have heard him wrong. Automatically, my hand cups my belly. "What did you say?" I ask, my voice kicking up in pitch.

A low laugh slips from him. "We've killed for each other. How many other couples can say that? That's how I knew we were meant to be together."

My mind reels, and my right hand grips the door handle. Who does he think that I killed?

"You don't have to say anything. I know what you did and why you did it. And you know what, I love you anyway." His head turns and his eyes meet mine. "You killed Linda just so you could come back to me."

The monster, the darkness in me, is reflected there. In the eyes I've known for nearly twenty years. He can't be saying what I think he is. No. This has to be some kind of trick. The notes. They were from him. That's why they weren't listed as part of the evidence. *He* was in my house. He was watching me.

"Cameron, who did you kill?" I ask.

"No, Adele. That's not the right question. You should ask who I wouldn't kill. Who wouldn't I kill for you?"

I swallow hard as I meet his eyes. "Did you kill Patrick? And his mistresses?"

He nods sharply. "I had to, Adele. It was the only way. Every day that he should have appreciated you, he was with those women. He was going to sink you, destroy you. By killing him and those women, I set you free."

My mouth goes bone dry as my pulse kicks up a notch. I can't ask him the question that forms in my mind. This man, the father of my child, he's a killer. He killed *for* me. Because of me.

"Tara was an accident. And I am so, so sorry I took her from you. But looking back, it was for the best. Because now, you're all mine. Forever."

A LETTER FROM DEA

Dear reader,

I want to say a huge thank-you for choosing to read *The Marriage Counselor*. If you did enjoy it, and want to keep up to date with all my latest releases, just sign up at the following link. Your email address will never be shared and you can unsubscribe at any time.

www.bookouture.com/dea-poirier

I hope you loved *The Marriage Counselor*. I poured so much of my heart into this book. I'm grateful that you picked up a copy. If you enjoyed the read, if you could write a review, it would really help. I'd love to hear what you think, and it makes such a difference helping new readers to discover one of my books for the first time.

I love hearing from my readers—you can get in touch on my Facebook page, through Twitter, Instagram, Goodreads, or my website.

Thanks,

Dea Poirier

KEEP IN TOUCH WITH DEA

dhpoirier.com

 facebook.com/dhpoirier
twitter.com/DeaPoirierBooks
instagram.com/deapoirier

ACKNOWLEDGEMENTS

I am so thankful for my incredible editor, Laura Deacon, and the amazing support team at Bookouture (thank you all so much for everything that you do).

To my critique partner, and the best friend I could ever ask for, Elesha Halbert-Teskey, as always, I appreciate you. You're the best <3.

To my readers, thank you so much for joining me for another book—one that's a little different from my usual style. Your support, kind words, and reviews are wonderful. Thank you for helping spread the word about my books and helping me find new readers!

To my family, thank you for everything. *Kiss noise.*

Made in the USA
Coppell, TX
23 May 2023

17192515R00146